BEN MIRE

# Demons in Cotton

*First published by DBJ Creative Press 2021*



*First edition*

*ISBN: 978-91-987008-0-0*

*This book was professionally typeset on Reedsy.*
*Find out more at reedsy.com*

*To Sofie,*
*The anchor for my stormy mind*

# Demons in Cotton

# Prologue

I breathe in.

A first breath. The first breath I ever take among Life's beautiful creatures.

Finally! The bursts in my chest become too much to contain, and I jump high into the air screaming my first breath out into the world. This is the moment I have been waiting for since my consciousness first saw the Light.

I have become a being made to live, laugh, cry, and die.

I have become a warrior.

I breathe in.

The excitement spreads through every limb of my new body. I hold my second breath for as long as I can and listen to the short pulses flowing the breath through my veins. I love it! My lungs burn and everything around me fades into a blur. I let go and fill them again. I want them to burn again. I want my body to scream in desperation. I want the world to fade just to relive my first moments again, and again, and again.

I want it all before it is too late.

I breathe out.

I wipe the sticky sap off my face with a new breath locked in my chest. I must see the world before all is taken from me. My eyes follow the trail of sap my body created when I fell. I laugh, it is the first time I see, then I laugh again. I have never laughed before. The Light pains my eyes, but I do not blink.

The pain passes and the sight fills me with awe. A tree-trunk rising as massive as a wall, only interrupted by the hole I was birthed from. Tree branches stretch to the infinite sky and wave. Winds of Light dance among the branches. They sing the most beautiful song. I laugh again. They hear me too. I spread my glimmering wings and lift to join their celebratory song. Together, we celebrate my survival. Together, we sing for my success, just as we sing for the day they stand in a body birthed from Life. They are my siblings, my brothers, and my sisters. They are all waiting to become my fellow warriors. They are waiting to save Life.

And for Life, we are willing to give up the Light.

We are willing to give up who we are.

I am pulled down.

*Our creation is broken.*

Everything becomes Light as the voice whispers in my ear. The creature circles me. Then it disappears in a burning light dissolving all shadows into nothingness. My cherished breath turns to ice as Darkness creeps up on me between the roots guarding our cherished fortress. The demon felt my presence the moment I was chosen. Arms wander up my body. They pull me down below the protective roots. Teeth bite into my wings. And my wings give in. Pain crushes me as hands tear me apart. I scream. Darkness licks my back dry.

*Where Darkness dwells, Light cannot fly.*

The dark arms claw at my body, then their disgusting fingers dig into my mind. I fight the urge to resist their tainting touch. I must accept these shadows to become one with the world I want to save.

*Where Life goes, Darkness follows.*

The fingers dig deeper. They find all that is me and all that is Light. Their touch destroys it all. They search through all my memories only leaving what can be tainted. Greed, hate, desire, fear, it leaves it all. Darkness continues deeper down my core. I give up the last of me with a silent prayer.

"Please guide me through the shadows and show me the path to enlightenment. Show me how to fight for those too weak and those doomed to live within Darkness. Show me how to make Life a better place."

I breathe in. I breathe out.

"Let me once again sing by the tree, and dance in the wind." It is the last memory the Darkness touches. It leaves the memory to rot among the ruins of what once was. The vague memory of a better life to taunt me for as long as I live. We knew Darkness would leave it. Our war depends on it. Darkness loves that our war depends on it.

*Save what Life gave us. Save what Darkness tainted.*

The creature wheezes in my head. A voice growing more foreign with every word. Even after I have forgotten all else, its voice will haunt me. It will become nothing more than a stranger's voice hidden in a memory of dancers whirling around tree branches. It will remind me of what is important, even when my heart turns dark.

I hope it will remind me.

For the sake of Life.

Darkness shows its ugly face. A fanged smile and charring eyes. It laughs. It longs for meeting me. Another Light for it to quench. The glowing smile fades as darkness shuts its disgusting mouth. Only two glimmering sparks burn fiercely in the distance.

Then in a blink. Nothing is anymore. All becomes Darkness.

Only a stranger wheezes from afar.

*You have become one with Life and Darkness. You are no longer worthy of our Light.*

A wheezing voice greets me as I awake. It is the first I ever hear. Before its whisper, all was nothing. Before its whisper, I was nothing.

With its words, the world explodes in a flood of sparks, and within the sparks, winds whirl around shadows in a shining dance. The winds sing with astounding beauty. Then my mind goes blank, and I am left to dwell in loneliness.

*You will love. You will fight.*

My mind fights to focus on something, anything, but it is fruitless. All is emptiness. My breaths move through my mouth faster and faster, but the emptiness crossing my lips leaves no sensation at all.

*You will die.*

The voice, again, and layered under it the song of beauty repeating the wheezing words in a haunting choir. The voices thunder in my ears but no matter in which direction I look the source remains hidden.

"Who are you?" I scream.

Do I even have a voice?

Am I even real?

I am only answered with silence accompanied by darkness in a sad duet for the hopeless and lonely.

For those like me.

For those who do not exist.

For those without memories.

For those without history.

For those who are nothing.

I force myself to scream again.

"Who are you?"

*The life of your Love will be your reward, and your death.*

I look up, or down.

"What do you mean?" My screams fall down the emptiness unnoticed. Not even an echo answers me.

*Go forth, my knight. Save your Love from the Darkness tainted onto our creation of beauty. Save Life. Follow the warrior's heart planted in your being. Be the knight of Light the world needs.*

"Please," I whisper. "I don't understand."

I am sure now. I am certain of it. I am falling to my death.

This is my end.

*Go forth and lead the path to Light, Gabriel warrior of the snake.*

The demon's words wheeze as hot knives through my last moments of falling through the emptiness and accompanying it is the familiar song taking the command to a new horrifying level.

# The Girl & The Bear

# Chapter 1

I hit the ground.

There should be pain, but there is only cold stretching along my back. I lay completely still as my thoughts try to patch together a mess of inconclusive fragments. Light and dark, screams and silence, hope and disbelief, all blends on an uneven canvas. My mind continues to wander until I catch a glimpse of the single fragment of importance.

I am not dead.

The clarity in my realization bursts me out of my comatose state. I am alive! I grab my arms, my chest, my legs. Any and every part of me my hands can reach, I pinch.

I have a body. I can touch. Slowly, I push my hands together and tie them closely around each other, and I feel everything, every little wrinkle and every little dent in my rugged skin.

I am alive. I repeat the words louder and louder until they are too big to be confined within my thoughts and burst out through my mouth.

"I am alive!"

It is so unreal.

I slap my face. My cheek turns warm from the sudden strike. It is real. It is not just in my mind.

Everything is real.

I am real.

"Hey!" I shout.

My words immediately bounce back at me and fill the room with the sound of my voice.

It sounds terrible.

But I have a voice.

Laughter. I laugh. Loudly as if I am going insane. Maybe I am. Maybe all this is just me being trapped in my own craziness. But then, what an idiot I must be. With a mind so empty the echo can go on for days, I surely must be the dumbest of them all.

I laugh for so long my stomach hurts. I laugh until only wheezes pass between my lips. Tears run down my chin. The stomachache, the wetness, and the salt taste drive me to more laughter. Weak, wheezing laughter.

This must be madness. It is the only truth making any sense.

I mean Gabriel, warrior of the snake. Such a title can only be one born out of madness. It is the only reason that brings all the pieces together.

But then again, would madness make any sense?

"Where am I?" My laughter turns into cries of fright and panic. "Please." I curl into a ball and lay on the cold floor, waiting for anything to make sense.

I cry. I cry until my eyes are unable to force out more tears.

The room becomes visible from one moment to the next. My first instinct is to curl my arms harder around my head and hide behind my own shadows. I scream, certain of the end finally coming for me. But the end never comes, and my scream fades off only to bounce between the walls in a one-voice-choir.

My second instinct is to look up into the light. I catch a glimpse of the two beams illuminating the room before I return to the safety behind my arm and the shadows. The light is so bright it burns. My eyes slowly adjust, and I let myself look again. This time I look to my right. I cast a shadow, not just the shadow behind my arm but a wonderful shadow spreading across the dark floor. I move my arm in a wave, a tiny wave nothing more.

It is all I dare.

The shadow instantly waves back at me. The uneasy lump in in my chest erupts in a tickle from the depth of my stomach. I laugh. I wave again, bigger and bolder this time, and the shadow copies my movement without waiting. I wave both my hands and giggle when the shadow does the same. My movements become bigger and more complex with each time. I walk, I run, I jump, I attack. My shadow duplicates it all with flawless perfection. I corner the shadow on the wall and laugh.

"I got you now," I say. "What are you going to do about it?"

The shadow answers with a discomforting silence.

I let my fingertips touch the shadow's fingers one by one. The sparkling explosion reverts to the cold lump in my chest it once was.

It was just a dumb game, I tell myself, just a pointless, dumb game. But I know all too well I can't look the shadow in the eyes again because of what it forces me to realize. It is just a shadow. It will always be just a shadow. No matter what I would have wanted it to be.

I force myself to look away from the shadow and focus on the curved walls in my room. I dare myself to look up into the light beams once more. My room is two globes stacked on top of each other. The walls are dusk grey. Four tunnels leave the lower globe where I am, they are way too small for me to fit through, though. There is only one way to go, up to the light beams and all terrifying and exciting awaiting me behind the light. Whatever it is, it is way more terrifying than exciting.

I continue examining the two tunnels in the bottom, hoping my first impression was wrong. Maybe they are soft and can be stretched for me to fit through. I guide my hands over their edges but stop myself at the sight of my arms.

For the first time, I see myself.

And I instantly regret it.

I am a terrifying sight. My rugged and scaled skin glimmers in the new light. Each scale is a jaded knife imbued with blood fixed onto my skin. I feel them now, each scale stabbing against my touch. I touch my face with my clawed hands. Sharp fangs signals death to all who face me. Two small holes create a nose between my fangs and my narrow eyes. I have a killer's face. The long claws on my fingers get caught between the scales. I look at my body. The light shatters against my shining armor and spreads onto the walls. I stand in the beams and watch myself illuminate the room. The reflections wander across the walls as I move. Green and red on dusk.

This is not insanity. This is hell. And I am the warrior guarding it. I am the monstrous serpent at the bottom of the pit.

Gabriel, warrior of the snake. The words make sense now. I am the snake. I am the wingless dragon dressed in blood and jade

# Chapter 2

*Follow the light.*

The chorus of heaven lingers behind each whispered word. Every note reaches me with its beauty. My body remembers a flowing dance, and I wish I was among the dancers unaware of who they are. Up in the top globe, the light turns brighter as the whisper fades back into the shadows, and with it, the song and the memories of a dance leave me.

The whisperer wants me to climb up to the two light beams and bathe my face in the sharp rays. The light grows brighter until I can no longer look directly at it. Even glancing in its direction burns my eyes.

I don't need to climb up there, I tell myself terrified of what the fate awaiting a fanged monster of the snake might be. I can stay here in this prison forever and pretend the light never came through the windows. It is as easy as closing my eyes and everything will be dark again. If I close them for long enough, I will even forget what the light looks like.

I might even forget my hideous scales.

In reaction to my hesitation, the light bursts into flaring rays, and the floor turns into glowing coal.

*Love is your destiny*

The word destiny echoes through the walls of my prison.

"What destiny?" I scream, pushing myself against the wall to avoid the coal slowly burning me alive.

"Why are you hurting me?"

Silence is how the whisperer answers me. Silence and flares.

I look up. My eyes dry out immediately. I close them and cover my face just to feel the burn crawl through my scales. Soon, I will also burn, along with the room trapping me.

My scales curl under the flares. The scales let go of my flesh and the fibers of tissue underneath bubble from the heat.

"Why?" I cry.

*Love.*

The bubbles burst on my skin one after the other in painful fireworks. The water underneath vaporizes in an instant.

I scream.

"I will do it." The heat continues to rise. "Don't you hear me? I, Gabriel of the snake, give up! I accept my destiny. Just, please, let me be."

As if destiny was the magic word, the room turns cold, and the light fades.

*Love is your destiny.*

"Love is my destiny," I repeat, hoping it will please my cruel ruler. Anything to not endure the torture one more time. The singers echo the words behind the whisper. Love. Love. Love. Their heavenly voices turn haunting. Seeing my muscles rebuild themselves and my scales curl back into place makes the experience even worse.

Small dents show themselves along the curved wall. They go all the way up to the two beams in a path created only for me to climb. The floor heats up under my feet. In the fading light, the faint choir chants Love. It could all be my imagination, but I doubt it.

Why? I let myself think before throwing myself at the dents. My claws scratch against the wall. I panic as I lose my grip and my feet touch the floor. I jump again as fast as my brain can command my legs to move.

I look down, the floor looks as dark as it was when there was no light on its surface. It just so happens that this darkness can burst into flames at any given moment.

For love and for destiny.

I climb knowing love will not be what awaits me. The rays will ignite again as I reach the top and burn my face of my bones. Then my body will regrow, and I and the whisperer can continue this cycle of torture forever. That must be the destiny awaiting the horrifying monster of the snake.

My claws grab onto the dents with surprising ease. I look down. The floor has turned red from the heat now emitting from it.

Love. Love. Love. The voices I just moments ago wished to join celebrate me choosing life in glorious happiness.

The light turns bleaker as I get closer. I swing myself over a bulge between two dents. I continue up as fast as I can, scared that it too will burst into flames. When I finally reach the windows, I dare to look down at the red floor again. Red flames arise. This whispering devil knows exactly how to motivate his beloved pets. I quickly grab hold of the right window with my hideous clawed hand.

I lift myself and let the bleak light gaze on my face. There is absolutely nothing at the other side of the window the whisperer was so eager for me to look through, only a pale white light.

"I am here!" I scream and look back down.

There is nothing but the cold dark floor there now.

"What do you want me to do now?" I fail to hold my voice steady as I break into tears. I shake so hard I'm afraid to lose my grip, but even though my hands want to vibrate my bones out of my skin, they never leave their place. My claws and the dents are too well molded after each other.

I want to tell myself to breathe slowly, that I am not afraid. I am only trapped between a cold dark floor threatening to burst into flames at any sign of hesitation and a pale white light described to be my destiny. Either one is a path to certain death. That said I am too terrified to even breathe.

"What do you want of me?" I stutter. "What do you want me to do?"

In front of me the light shifts from pale to sharp in a sudden blink.

Or was it my eyes lying to me to comply with all other insanities this prison built for me?

The light sharpens again. I wipe the tears off my face, seduced by what meets me in the sudden flashes. A new world takes shape. White shelves. Tiled floors, altering between black and white. Pieces slowly fade into place. A lamp hangs from the ceiling. It is in the shape of a flower with six leaves in six different colors. Blue, yellow, red, green, pink, and orange, then it starts over again.

It is beautiful. Just, so beautiful.

Toys grow from the shelves in front of me like they were flowers just like the lamp. Teddy bears, cars, dolls, every kind of toy I did not know I knew the name of until now. Tears fall from my face, but not in fear this time. It should be fear, nothing about the world flowering in front of me is natural, but the tears are from happiness. If I was in hell just a moment ago, this on the other side of the windows must be heaven. I push my face closer to the glass and feel the cold against my skin.

No, I remind myself. Scales. I have scales.

The depressing reminder sinks back as quickly as it surfaced as something new captures my eye on the heavenly side of the window. An old man walking past the shelves on the tiled floor still fading into place under him. He whistles loudly to himself and his grey moustache dances joyfully. He climbs a chair and hangs an airplane with colorful propellers on the ceiling. He admires his work before he pushes a button, and the propellers start to rotate. Shortly after, just about at the same time as the old man has stepped down from the chair, the airplane starts moving in big circles. The airplane gives off a loud boom at the end of every other cycle. The man laughs for himself.

"Boom," he says with the airplane. "I love that part."

Then he walks away and leaves me admiring the plane. The propeller creates a colorful circle breaking the lamplight. With the view in front of me, I forget everything. I am no monster. I am the admiring crowd awaiting the next wonderful toy to grow from the shelf.

It is a stuffed lion that finally sprouts from the shelf next to me. It smiles a gorgeous fangless smile and waves a welcoming clawless wave.

It all looks so lovely.

# Chapter 3

I lose myself in the ever-changing paradise. Time passes by in steady, comfortable flow, and even though the imaginative arms on the clown-clock swing around the grinning face more times than I care to count, my body never seems to tire from hanging by the window.

Cotton cloud-shaped price tags grow from the shelves, and I notice the pink dragons hanging in threads from the ceiling. Each dragon holds a differently colored balloon with hearts or flowers printed in even brighter and happier colors. Heaven builds itself in front of me. The complete opposite to my prison. Dullness and darkness threatening to burst into flames at any sign of me longing to go back down in contrast to the fantasy world outside growing with promises of colorful explosions every second.

The voice wanted me to look at it. Is that my hell? To be imprisoned in darkness and forced to look at heaven every day.

The fear of turning to charcoal is more terrifying.

The old man comes back. He dances in a way that can only be from the pure joy of living in heaven. I want to live there too. I resist an urge to slam the window. I am certain no matter how hard I punch or claw, the glass will never break.

I reach my hands to the window and push against it. Claws against glass. Reptile scales in contrast to happiness and pink dragons breathing tones instead of flames. My reflection meets my gaze, two yellow longing eyes above deadly fangs.

I want to go through the glass so badly.

Instantly the glass caves beneath my fingers. I throw my arms away from the glass just in time to avoid falling through.

What was that? For the first time, I look at the glass and not at the world on the other side. The polished surface seems unbreakable. I touch it again one finger at the time, and lastly my whole palm, and I feel nothing. Could it be? My excitement and curiosity become unstoppable as I push harder against the transparent surface.

I want to go through.

My hands melt through the glass. It all happens so fast I never get the chance to think before the air outside tickles my hands. Even the air is more joyous than in the prison I live in. My heart races. I am elbows deep. My face rushes through the window. The fresh air hits my face in the gentlest breezes. The man continues his dance between the shelves, unaware of my presence. At this point, I don't care. It is all so wonderful. I take a deep breath and let the outside fill me.

I am part of heaven, I think. The joyful air trickles down to my lungs. I want to be all heaven and no more hell. The air stings. It hurts, and I cough, forcing the air back out again just to drag another breath into my lungs. My lungs scream in pain. My body recoils back into safety so fast I barely succeed in holding my grip. I lift myself up with shaking arms. My eyes are tearing as I hyperventilate to fill my lungs with healthy air. Every breath of toxicity leaving me tears through my throat and my lungs like claws scratching their way out. I regain control over my muscles with each breath emptying my bloodstream of the toxic gas.

What happened? My confused thoughts blurt out, even though I know. Heaven judged me as unworthy. Paradise is toxic for monsters like me.

The punishment built for me might not be such a bad one after all.

I push my hand against the window, not letting it sink through. I clench my fist and scratch my claws against the surface. Not a single mark. It's solid glass, but if I just want to get out bad enough, it will let me through. Just to let the world show me I don't belong there again, and again.

It is not a bad punishment at all.

On the outside, the man dances towards me in the toxic environment he thrives in. The man walks up to my prison. He takes it in his hands and lifts it into the light. Even though I see how hard he squeezes my house, it does not affect the walls on the inside. Everything is exactly as it always has been.

"How about you, my brave little teddy bear?" He asks in the same jolly tone he sang to himself in. "Do you think someone will find you and fall in love with your cute and cuddly fur today?"

Love. I shiver from the word. He said love. He stares right at me, almost fooling me to believe he can see right through my dark windows.

"Of course, someone will! You're too cute for anyone to ignore."

I look at him, then at my clenched fist. I open my hand and look at my claws. If he only knew how wrong he was. No one could want this.

No one.

I clench my fist again and slam it into the window. Hard. I slam it again. I slam it repeatedly until my hand goes numb from the pain and I continue to slam it even more furiously. The old man stands on the other side of the window, happily singing while he swings my prison through the air.

"Today is the day. Today is the day someone falls for you." His singing turns into a whistle while he puts me back on the shelf along with the other toys. Then he bops my prison on the nose.

"Today," he says one last time before disappearing to another part of the store.

In this world, everything is a punishment. It is what I never will have and what I never can become. A bell above the entrance door shimmers. A group of children rushes into the store. Their cheer fills every corner of the store as they see all the toys piling up in front of them.

"So, so. What are we doing today?" The old man walks up to them.

Each child stops what they are doing and looks up on the man.

"The usual, sir." One girl says. "Admiring all these wonderful toys of yours."

"Is that the case?" The man chuckles. "They are wonderful, aren't they? Just remember, be gentle and they are only for looking if you don't plan to buy them."

"No, sir. We will be as gentle as we can."

"Well, then. Why are you wasting your time?"

The children scatter throughout the shop as if his words are the go signal. No more than mere seconds later two brown eyes meet mine on the other side of the glass. A blond boy scanning through all the plushies locks on me for just a second, and it's mesmerizing. He moves on just as quickly as he got there, then the next child comes by. A girl in a pink and white-striped sweater. Her eyes are clear blue. She picks a plush cat next to me and cuddles it, then she puts it back carefully.

"On Friday, I will take you with me home," she says.

The day continues with child after child passing by my prison. Each child more fascinating than the last, each smile more contagious than the last. Some of them only walk around dreaming of what they one day could have, and some of them fulfill their dreams by buying the toy they always wanted. This place is all in all the most joyful house this world can offer.

But when the day ends, my prison is still on the shelf in the same spot as the beginning of the day, untouched. The children were too busy with all the other wonderful toys available to even consider the prison of the snake. The shop owner ends his round for the day by taking me down from the shelf again, looking sadly into the windows.

"So today wasn't the day after all," he says. "But maybe tomorrow. Yes, I think tomorrow is the day someone will notice how truly adorable you are."

He puts me back and continues to whistle the same melody he was singing this morning. Inside the prison, I look after him mopping the floors one last time before turning the lights off and leaving his store for his lovely home somewhere far outside these boundaries.

I know he is wrong. He will always be wrong. There will never come a day when someone chooses the prison of the snake.

# Chapter 4

Lanes of colorful toys turn into haunted streets in the bleak nightlight. Joyful faces become dead demons with their last smile frozen in a death promising grin. The sight should not fill me with relief, but it does. Their colorful faces no longer remind me of the hell I'm trapped in. Heaven and hell come closer to each other at night.

During these hours all toys become their own individual prisons. Each plush animal hiding a cell behind two hollow eyes; A cell with threats of flames, haunting songs, and false promises in whispers of love and destiny. Only guards patrolling the premises are missing. From the look of it, that might be the old man's role, he makes sure no child buys a toy where a living prisoner resides. If that would be true, he would be the cruelest man of all in this world.

"Today is the day someone will choose you." He lies to give us false hope.

I shake the thought away. It is impossible. The outside world is too innocent to lean in such evil ways. What is on the other side of the window is simply the idealistic life. A world solely built from love and happiness.

Love. The word once again stabs through my heart. The whisperer lies. He tried to trick me into thinking there was a meaning in all this. I nearly fell for the possibility of a happy ending, but it was nothing more than a lie.

One last glance at the outside before I return to the grey dullness of my prison's belly, I tell myself, just one while the darkness steals all the temptations away. The uncertainty of whatever flames await me still makes me uneasy about climbing back down but I'd rather face death in a fire than having to relive the realization of never getting to be part of paradise. One last glance turns into another and then another. The shadows move with the moonlight and still, I glance. The outside is after all an addictive view, even though night turns it into a ghost town.

My intoxicating view is abruptly ended from the floor darkening again, not from the night passing this time. No natural darkness flows that way. It is a dark mass slowly crawling across the floor, spreading over it mindlessly. It engulfs every tile, in a slow river pouring downhill on horizontal tiles. In the nightly silence, the sound of its flow takes the shape in crazed laughter and under it a faint chant.

"Pain." It says over and over again.

*Nightmares.*

The whisperer catches me off guard. Startled, I momentarily lose my grip on the dents, just to catch them.

Nightmares? I think. The laughter rises into a crescendo and my question is answered.

The dark mass disappears through closed windows, leaving the store untouched from its passing. I look for it, but it never returns. Just like the whisperer never returns to tell me what the nightmarish flood was.

My climb down is slow and cautious. After each step, I look down, searching for changes in the grey floor and aware of every sign of a temperature increase. The room never changes, though, but the torture only becomes worse that way.

My body should be sore from hanging on the dents all day. But every one of my muscles are as fresh and agile as before. I am a creature created to hang on dents for whole days without rest. I am built to watch the heaven outside and long for what could have been. I am built to watch dark masses poor across horizontal floors and wonder.

I punch the wall. I punch it again.

"Why?" I ask. "Why am I here? Why are you burning me? Why are you torturing me? What do you want me to do?" My anger dissipates and leaves me crying. "Please just leave me be. Whatever I did to enrage you, I will never do anything like it again. I promise I will do everything you tell me if only you tell me what I should do."

The whisperer's answer is silence. The silence of someone not listening. Someone who ignores you. Someone who wants you to suffer.

I curl up against the wall. And as I sit there with tears running down my scaled face, the room becomes darker as the light through the windows grows weaker. Only my sobbing sounds through the emptiness.

# Chapter 5

The nightly shadows are slowly pushed away in favor of the morning light. My dark walls once again turn grey. A new morning in heaven begins, and hell continues in eternal gloom.

The doorbell shimmers, and a baritone voice bounces between the walls as the mustached man enters, singing and whistling with tunes just as joyful as yesterday. His tunes would not be as happy if he knew of the son of the snake living inside one of his toys. His steps would be more cautious if he knew of the dark river crossing his floor at night.

"Today is the day someone falls for you." He sings. The light from my windows disappears as his body blocks the sunlight, he bops my prison on the nose. He cares about his toys. It is heartwarming to know he wants all his toys to get a nice home. An itch in my thoughts tells me to go up and watch him dance between the shelves. Maybe I even get to be told no one can resist me. It is tempting, but temptation has nothing against the loneliness haunting every moment of not getting chosen and every hopeful thought being crushed under the realization I never will be chosen. No child wants a teddy bear housing a monster of the snake.

*Love.*

The voice repeats its most precious word once again. Even the singers force the word louder than before. As if it would make me change my mind. Throw flames at me, I don't care. Kill me, just do it. I don't want to live anymore.

The bell chimers again as the children rush through the door.

Love, I think awaiting the whisperer to thunder the words with me. I glance at the windows and the flickering light from children passing by. Any moment now, the floor will turn red, and my scales will burn.

If I give in, I will have to suffer through the joy outside hollowing my soul with desire. Such are the laws of this prison I live in. Torture by heat, or torture by desire. My muscles tense as I sit myself down to die with dignity. The pose of a man in peace with his decision. Come and take me. Show me what your mercy truly is.

A child bursts into laughter when he finally gets the toy he always wanted.

"Spider-man!" He screams, not a teddy bear.

Come and take me, I think.

A girl begs her parents for an advance on her allowance, just this once, so she can afford the prettiest doll in the universe. They give in after much thought and consideration.

Come and take me.

A lion becomes the center of attention as a girl won't get her wish fulfilled. A teddy bear leaves the store in a bag, but not my teddy bear. It is never mine.

Show me your mercy, come and take me.

Wave after wave fills the store as every child leaving is followed by a new entering. They all find happiness. Some get to take it home some get to live with their longing dreams one more day.

Come and burn me, I think but no flames want to touch me.

"Burn me!" I scream. "Do your best! Force me up there, force me to look at heaven, force me to realize how miserable I am." Nothing happens as the ecstatic screams from the children rampage freely. "Please show me how cruel you really are." My scream fades into a whisper.

The whisperer plays a game of patience, and I can only win by waiting for its patience to run out. Faintly, the chorus sing Love once again. I brace myself for the psychological attack.

No matter how long I wait nothing happens. My own memories of the song play a game with me. It is just me sitting in an empty room listening to the voices of children finding their happiness. The itch in my thoughts has become a wound I cannot ignore. I wag back and forth in a reflection of the battle raging within my mind. Cheering children storm the shop as a new wave runs through the door. They sound so happy. My heart is so empty. My waging turns into a full swing. My teeth grind against each other, and my breathing whistles as it pushes through my closed mouth.

"Fight," I order myself, but it comes out as a weak whimper. I will fight. I must. I cannot give up. I will give up. My will falters with each whistling breath. I am not strong enough.

With a cry on my face, I surrender to the pressure from the joy outside. I give up.

"For love," I whisper and let my claws grab onto the dents.

As I climb, I listen for the whisperer to give me its approval by once again saying the word I dread to hear, but as I reach the window, not a single word has been spoken.

I am immediately treated with the same view as yesterday, and the same high when I see all the happy faces, and the same low when I realize none of their smiles are for me.

"Mr. Reston, someday I want to be like you." One child tells the shop owner.

The man gives off one of his trademark chuckles.

"That makes an old man happy to hear. Do good in school and one day your wish just might come true."

"Thank you, Mr. Reston." The child blushes and runs away to his friends by the toy trucks.

Another child tugs the shirt of a clerk beside Mr. Reston.

"Mr. Simonson, what is your favorite toy?"

"Fire trucks." The man answers without hesitation. "The sound of those sirens always makes me feel like a hero."

"No wonder you like the cars' shelf so much." Mr. Reston laughs, Mr. Simonson laughs with him.

"Yeah, that toy truck definitely is something extra, almost like the real deal."

"What's your favorite toy, Mr. Reston?" asks the curious child.

"Plush animals, I find them too cute." Mr. Reston answers. "That's why we have so many of them."

Mr. Reston looks in the direction of my prison. Then he almost unnoticeable shakes his head. He has noticed none of the children so far have even looked in my direction.

No one will ever choose me, I think and for the first time, I truly let myself realize I want to be chosen. I want nothing more. I want to be loved.

It is such a surrealistic need. Wanting to be loved for the prison you are trapped in. But I accept it as my destiny. And after the day ends, I continue to wait for the chosen one. And even though every day of rejection hurts me to the core. I continue to climb up every morning, commanded by nothing but the whisperer's silence. All I need as motivation is Mr. Reston's comforting voice telling me today is the day someone will love me. I even climb up at the sound of the clock clown's 9 AM giggle just to be closer to the door's shimmering bells when he enters the store.

And just like him, I never give up hope. I tell myself today will be the day, I will be chosen. Today is the day someone will love me.

And every night when the dark mass starts its nightly stream through the store, I climb back down broken-hearted and tell myself not to fall for it again. But I am too aware of my own weakness to believe the words myself. The hurt is never enough to drown my addiction for Love.

# Chapter 6

It is one of Mr. Reston's worse days. In addition to the decreased number of visitors, the airplane wing is broken, and he spends most of the day by the counter trying to glue it back without success. He curses for the first time since I inhabited his shop.

*Love.*

The whisperer's voice thunders in my ears. The sudden abruption to the silence that has become our new normal since the day I gave up catches me off guard. I look around without finding the source. It is when I taste the sweet wind dancing between the branches and happiness sings in my ears, I realize my imprisoner is back from his long slumber. Every nuance in the singers' voices fills me with awe, and the promise of flames hiding under their song settles in my chest in an uneasy storm.

Shortly after the choir fades back into the silence, the shimmering bell sounds and interrupts this day's slow pace. The addict in me immediately triggers from the sound. Is this the one? It asks just as it has done every time the doorbell shimmers. No, my rationality answers, it never is. Yet, I stretch my head in all directions in hope of a glimpse of the visitors. I finally see them as they enter the section closest to mine, two parents holding their daughter while scanning the shelves. Their heads move at a slow pace, his thinning blond hair and her long brown floating above fluffy ears as they focus on the toys lining up in the neat lines Mr. Reston has arranged.

"What do you think Kelly?" The mother asks. "Isn't this the most beautiful doll you have ever seen?"

She holds up a doll with a blue and white striped dress, her face briefly shows behind a dolphin. Dark make-up in abundance fills every little corner of her eyes. She sighs and the doll goes back up on the shelf.

"Come on, honey. Don't you see anything you like?"

They walk into my aisle, and I catch a glimpse of the girl hanging between her two parents. The nougat blond hair falling in waves over her shoulders and her red dress. She hides her face in her father's neck. A pair of red and white striped socks reach halfway up to her calf and purple shoes hang on her toes fighting for their place on her feet. Her knees and elbows are covered in ugly scratches. My heart sinks at the sight. She is hurt. Nothing should get to hurt a girl like her.

For the first time since their entrance into the store, Mr. Reston looks up from his airplane.

"Oh, hi there!" He says. "How may I help you?"

The father looks up from his daughter. His brown eyes are framed by what once was a thick blond hair and traces of a beard he forgot to shave this morning.

"We're looking for something for our daughter," he answers.

"I see." Mr. Reston leaves the airplane behind the counter and walks up the aisle with his happy wag. "What kind of girl do we have here? Is it possibly a lovely princess?" When little Kelly never leaves her father's neck, he switches tactics. "Or maybe a teddy bear girl?"

Kelly looks up at him with a face still red from tears. It is the most beautiful face I have ever seen.

How can anyone be so beautiful?

Mr. Reston's big smile scares her back to the safety of her father's blue shirt. My heart shrieks as if it was stabbed.

"A teddy bear girl, I see." Mr. Reston gives her one of his trademark chuckles, the one who sounds like a chicken clucking, it makes every kid smile. "I have all kinds of teddy bears. Everything from cute ones to brave warriors who can protect you from every dangerous monster you can possibly face." He gives her elbows and knees a quick glance. "And you, my little darling, look like you need a warrior."

He turns to the mother while he searches through the shelves for what he calls the bravest teddy bear warriors in the universe.

"Does she hurt herself often?" A question asked with such a calm and softness neither the father nor the daughter hears him.

"Recently, yes, very often," the mother answers, showing a line of perfectly white teeth that outshines her brown hair. "And she won't tell us how."

"I see," Mr. Reston says and leans forward to Kelly once again. "What might a pretty girl like you have for favorite color?"

The shy girl gives him no answer. "This little girl loves everything pink," her father answers in her place while he caresses her small back, "or yellow sometimes."

"Pink you say?" Mr. Reston turns to the shelf I live on. He glances at me. My heart races. Please, tell me I'm pink. Please tell me I'm everything the little girl loves most in this world. The glance remains just a glance and any trace of hope burning within me is immediately suffocated. He picks a teddy bear from the shelf above mine. It is so pink it makes me nauseous. "This is Arthur. He is the teddy bear of the round table, and do you know what? He is an honorable knight. Everything you tell him will stay with him and he will fight every dragon you ever have the misfortune to meet."

I glimpse Kelly once again as she looks up at the pink teddy bear. My heart bursts with overwhelming happiness. My happiness flares even stronger when she rejects the pink abomination and returns to the safety in her father's neck as quickly as the glance on the teddy bear lasted. Our eyes lock, just for a short moment. The whole world stops, and all my thoughts go numb. Then in the silence and stillness, two pieces fall into place with a clack in the back of my head.

"You?" The softest voice whispers in my ear. A little girl's voice, and I become complete.

"Okay, no Arthur." Mr. Reston puts Arthur back on his shelf and continues searching for another teddy bear.

"Pick me." I realize the words were not a thought. They were whispered, and I wanted to scream them. In frustration, I watch Mr. Reston pick another teddy bear from the shelf above me. A yellow one with red pants and matching suspenders. He is so yellow the sun would be jealous.

"This is Sam. The most loyal friend you will ever have. He will follow you to the end of the world, and even further. He will climb mountains with you and share every one of your heavy burdens."

Kelly looks at the teddy bear but rejects it just as quickly as the last. To my delight she does not hide her face this time and I get to take in every little pore of her pretty face.

"So." Mr. Reston is relieved to finally get through to her, "which teddy bear is your favorite?"

Kelly's eyes scan the shelves. I push my face closer to the window.

"Please, pick me," I whisper.

Her eyes lock on my prison. I hold my breath.

Mr. Reston follows her gaze and sees the teddy bear I live in. For a moment he is surprised and turns speechless. Then his whole face cracks up in one of the biggest smiles I have ever seen.

"So, you like Chester." Mr. Reston pauses as his smile becomes too big to speak any words. "He is the best teddy bear you will ever find. With him, you will never have to be afraid."

He picks me up and as I come closer to Kelly, my teddy bear reflects in her eyes. It is blue with black eyes. It is not even close to as beautiful as Kelly.

"Do you want to hold him?"

Kelly looks at Mr. Reston's big smile and then back at me. She nods and stretches her arms out towards me. As Mr. Reston gives her the teddy bear, she drags it close to her body and hugs it, and through the eyes, I can see her red and round cheeks so close only the glass eyes separate us.

I want to crawl out through the eyes of the teddy bear and grab her face, and never leave it.

This is where I belong, I think. Next to her is where I always want to be.

I push myself closer to the window tempted to go through, just this once. But I remain inside fearing what would happen if she saw me.

"I think we have a winner!" Mr. Reston laughs.

"This one has been in the store for quite some time now," he continues and turns to Kelly's parents. "And I am so happy someone finally sees just how wonderful he is. I promise you this, he will give her so much happiness

Mr. and Mrs.... Marcsinzky, right?"

"Yes," both parents answer. They are just happy their daughter's tears are gone. The teddy bear is none of their concern. The man stretches his hand towards Mr. Reston.

"Milton Marcsinzky and this is Laura and Kelly."

"Richard Reston." Mr. Reston grabs the hand and shakes it firmly. "It is always an honor when one of my toys brings such happiness to a child."

"Goodbye, Chester." Mr. Reston says as Milton pays for my prison cell. "I hope we will see each other again soon."

He waves at the teddy bear and Kelly answers the joyful goodbye by waving Chester's arm back at him.

I do not wave back at him. I do not want to see him again and if he knew about me, he would understand. Kelly looks straight into Chester's eyes as they walk across the parking lot and, seemingly, looks right at me.

"I love you, Chester," she says and hugs us.

"I love you too," I say and push my hand towards the window embracing her hug with a glass window between us.

# Chapter 7

For the first time since the day I landed inside Chester, I have the chance to experience the outside world. Every moment is a fight between my will of absorbing as much of the world as possible and my desire of catching every glimpse of Kelly I possibly can. My view wobbles between the grey asphalt and the blue sky, and everything in between. It all falls flat in comparison to Kelly's blond hair. A lone car on the parking lot rushes past my view before I once again get to see thick white lines on the asphalt, followed by the brick building that is Mr. Reston's shop upside-down, asphalt again, and Kelly's beautiful face. The small car comes back into view, and everything stops so quickly I momentarily lose my balance.

"This is mom's car," Kelly explains. The shyness I saw in the store is nowhere to be found in her smile. "Mom has named it Sedan, but dad calls her Little Banger." She lowers her voice into a whisper. "Just don't call her Little Banger when she can hear. The name upsets her."

We close in on the car until we stand in front of its headlight. Kelly gives it a pat on the hood. "Sedan I want you to meet Chester. He is a new member of our family." Chester's paw stretches towards the hood and pats it lightly with Kelly's help.

"I think Sedan likes your new teddy bear." My view changes again, and I get to see an amused mother watch her daughter introduce a teddy bear and a car to each other. "Why don't you hop in so Sedan can show Chester how beautiful she sings."

"Of course!" Kelly says and then whispers into Chester's ear. "Don't worry if Sedan coughs, she has asthma but still runs like the wind on a stormy day."

"More like a calm breeze on a sunny day," her father murmurs to himself.

Even though the complaints Kelly's father is the one driving Sedan. Sedan coughs thrice before finally starting.

"Maybe she has a cold too?" Kelly whispers before the fourth attempt succeeds.

"Buckle up!" Milton says over the sound of the engine. The engine screams before his wife punches him lightly on the shoulder.

"Stop it," she says and suddenly the engine goes silent. "Are you ready Kelly?"

"No, wait!" Kelly screams at her mother. "Chester has to be safe too."

Both parents exchange amused looks. Their hands touch as Kelly's dad stretches over to the back to help her buckle me up. His wife misses his loving touch as she picks up her phone to snap a photo of this wonderful moment.

"Smile," she says and the phone flashes.

"Now you can drive again," Kelly says proudly and hugs the teddy bear, pushing her face closer to mine once again. "You see, I don't want anything to happen to you."

In a reflex, I glance at her seat belt. I don't want anything to happen to you either, I think. Nothing in the whole world shall ever put you in danger. Not on my watch.

"Come here." She releases Chester from the hug and turns his head towards the window. "This is the road to my home. It is your home too if you want to live with us?"

Home. The word tastes heavenly. I glance at my grey walls, then at Kelly's radiant smile. What a wonderful place that must be. My home.

I follow Kelly's fascinated gaze to the outside of the window. Houses pass by at a comfortable rate. Our minds connect once again with a clack, much fainter this time. Small visions pass by and blend in with my already astonishing view.

"That house over there, that is where Kevin Hill lives. He has the biggest dog you have ever seen. You can even ride on it." The vision of little Kelly riding on a white and brown spotted dog with a small tail and the biggest cheeks hanging from its face passes by as a shadow wandering down the lawn.

It behaves just like a steed on its way to the battlefield. "And the house over there, that is where Mrs. Danderby lives. She is a teacher, but she is okay. And she has like thirteen cats or something." Now a stiff woman walking around her house with cats in her pockets appears. She takes off her glasses and polishes them with a towel, then she looks into the casseroles on the stove where a new cat looks up at her. It's Kelly's imagination passing before my eyes.

Love, I think. Is this truly it?

She continues for the whole drive. Not forgetting a single house. Simon, the sports-pro with quick feet and the world's best aim. Aresh, the hungry, who loves hamburgers more than life. Ashley, the dancer who can go all day on her toes. Dacey, a circus artist who can juggle anything.

"And in that house, lives Mrs. Dubél." The house she now points at is grey and taints a street full of light with darkness and gloom. "She is scary. Her food tastes yucky, and she makes you watch documentaries all day. All they talk about is fake moon landings and wars no one remembers anymore." Kelly's mother gives her daughter a questioning but amused look. "It is so boring! She also likes to be called grandma'."

"Kelly." Her father looks back at her through the rearview mirror. "Do you really have to talk about my mother like that?"

"But it's true!" Kelly whines, crossing her arms over her chest. "I can't help she never known how it is to be fun."

"I do not want to hear that when we visit her tomorrow." Her father takes on a much darker tone than his eyes show, but Kelly never notices the difference.

"Okay," she sighs. "But she is boring."

All I can think of is how lovely Kelly is. Even with a frown on her face, she is the cutest little thing in the world.

"This was what you meant," I say convinced of the truth in it. I look up to the car's skylight as if the whisperer lives there. "This is the love you were talking about, the destiny you were so persistent on showing me. Why didn't you just tell me? I wouldn't have protested."

As always, the answers to all my questions are met with silence.

"We are home." Kelly suddenly yells happily as if all the talk about her grandma' never happened. "Look, Chester. Up there on the left window is my room. I have the best view in all of Vesterville."

In the direction she points Chester's head, there now is a clear blue house so beautiful it could be a piece of heaven fallen down to earth. The corners and window frames are white as clouds. It is the complete opposite of her grandma's house.

"You can see all the way to the playground," continues Kelly. "And if you push your eyes together like this." She squints her eyes. "You can get a hint of the sports field. We don't like that place very much."

"You don't?" Her mother asks.

"Of course I don't." Kelly frowns like someone who has eaten a sour lemon. "It's like Mrs. Dubél's wars but in real life."

"Really? I always thought you liked fun with sports."

"I do." Her irritated tone fade into a whisper.

"So, what don't you like?"

"Nothing." Kelly looks down at her feet dangling from the car seat, and her sad look returns. A vision of ghostly faces laughing at a girl on the ground flashes across my mind like a bolt. Each hollow smile tears through my heart.

I will turn every rock or mountain in the world to find what would make her happy once again. Whatever she needs, I will do. In my own imagination, each smile turns blood red as I slit their throats out. I will kill them if I have to. The thought catches me off guard. No, I tell myself, startled by my brutality, I don't kill. I'm not a monster. I will never be one.

"Hey," her mother says and removes a hair from her daughter's face. "Why don't you show Chester his new home instead of this boring car?" Kelly looks up at her mother's apologetic smile and in a blink, the faces are gone. Her smile returns.

"Yes!" She yells without any sign of heavy thoughts which haunted her just seconds ago.

Before I know it, she pulls Chester out of the car, if she unbuckled me, I never noticed it, and runs towards the house. The view from the window shows the bumpiest view I have ever experienced with everything going quickly up and down, and at more than one time the world went upside down. I look away to control the nausea. Suddenly, she stops, and my view comes to a complete halt.

"Here is Mr. Hedgehog, he guards the house against burglars and the neighbor's dogs."

I look out through the window, trying my best to focus on whatever it is she suddenly found important enough to stop Chester's rollercoaster-like journey. It is, just like the name suggests, a hedgehog. For her a mighty hedgehog with the bravery of a thousand wolves. For me a grey statue of concrete.

"Hello, Mr. Hedgehog. Have you seen anything suspicious today?"

The grey statue looks at us with no sign of consciousness. I focus on the eyes, hoping to see a movement. Somehow, I convince myself more lizards like me have crossed her path. The only movement is the wind catching the grass beside the statue. I sigh. Mr. Hedgehog is only a product of a child's wild imagination. Just like Sedan. Just like Chester.

"Okay," Kelly continues like the statue answered her. "Well done, Mr. Hedgehog. We are so proud of having you at our service." She salutes the hedgehog, Chester does too. "Come on Chester, let's show you the house."

The rollercoaster ride continues for a few minutes. There is no point in even trying to observe the world bouncing past the window, so I look away. Whenever Kelly explains something for me, I look outside again. Even those pauses go nauseatingly fast.

"Here is my room," she says finally, opening a door to the right of the stairs.

I am faced with pink. Her bed, her chair, her desk. Everything is pink. It is like she lives in a pink fluffy cloud. Is Chester also this pink? I think before remembering how Mr. Reston looked at me when they told him her favorite colors are pink and yellow. My prison is not pink. It is blue. I look around in the dark room contrasting from all the pink on the outside. The irony, if Chester was pink, would be hilarious, though. I giggle.

"Do you like tea?" I turn back to the window which now is directed towards a small table and three small chairs. The view goes up and down when Chester nods.

"Great!" Kelly says and laughs. "We have teatime every day, and today you're our guest of honor." Then she leans closer to Chester's ear and whispers. "Just don't tell Gleason, he gets jealous." She looks cautiously at a fox at the end of the table, he certainly looks jealous of her. "He sits there all day waiting for the next teatime, just so he won't miss it."

Inside the teddy bear, I look at the pink fox who obviously has been put there by Kelly and laugh. Her worries are wasted on me. I will not tell anyone. In fact, I cannot tell anyone. I'm stuck in here forever.

"And look out there." She now shows Chester the window. "Didn't I tell you it was the best view in Vesterville?"

As she tells me, the playground rises in front of the window. There is nothing even similar to a sports field. And the playground is only good if your ideal playground contains rusted bars, a rotten roof, and dog shit at the end of a slide. I look over to her again and I am met by the dreamy look on her face. All she sees are towers and colors.

"I will take you there tomorrow when we get back from school."

I look forward to it, I look forward to every step we share on the weird playground. And I look forward to seeing her enjoy playing with Chester. Every second of experiencing her smile will make me the happiest monster in the world.

"But first it's teatime." Kelly continues and runs to the little table where Gleason has been waiting all day for his moment. During the sudden movement I catch a glimpse of her two parents standing at the door looking at their daughter and her new best friend with smiles on their faces.

# Chapter 8

She sleeps now. The girl who chose a blue teddy bear for a room full of pink, sleeps after a long day. Kelly, who chose me to love and protect her from all evil. I still can't believe it. I am the most grateful monster in the world for having her choose me. In the stillness of her breaths a calmness like nothing I ever experienced before flows over me. I will always be grateful.

They all sit on the sofa as one small family. The TV has been off for an hour, and Kelly played with Chester and a cute pink-haired doll until her head fell to her chest in the middle of Chester telling Peaches how strong and careful he is. In truth, her thoughts had been taking short breaks for the last 30 minutes. To her parents, though, it happened without any warning, she just shut her eyes and fell asleep.

The conversation between her parents quickly shifts towards talking about their workdays and what bills must be paid, topics not suitable for a child's fragile ears. Their voices fade away as I focus all my attention on the dreams spreading in Kelly's thoughts and I let them flow over me. Foxes, hedgehogs, and a teddy bear jumping around in one happy dance. They all laugh as they enter a castle with a slide and take the stairs to the top tower where they dance to the view of a village in the form of a sports field. I laugh just as Kelly does in her dreams. Her happiness spreads within me in a glimmering web.

Laura's and Milton's voices slowly become frustrated as the conversation proceeded. What began as white noise in the land of foxes and hedgehogs, and one blue teddy bear grows into an unignorable lion roar. The bills outgrow their salaries. The teddy bear can be what tips them over the edge this month. Neither of them wants to return it, their daughter's happiness means too much. The necessary compromises are what heat the discussion, his or hers. Who spends the most on the unnecessary? Laura suddenly hushes her husband, just at the tipping point between rational discussion and a discussion fueled with anger.

"Honey, it's bedtime now," Laura Marcsinzky whispers softly into Kelly's ear

"I don't want to." Kelly yawns.

"Yes, you do." She lifts Kelly up in her arms. "You have to show Chester what a good girl you are and brush your teeth."

"Chester doesn't have teeth."

She is completely right about that. He is just an empty space under a fluffy skin.

"Doesn't he?" Laura gives Kelly a confused but amused look and skillfully covers the frustration she voiced just a minute ago. "How about that? You know what? He might grow some one day and if he does, he will be just as happy to have learned all the tricks from you." Laura picks up my prison and their own impending doom. "Come on, Chester, now how long do you have to brush your teeth? Can you tell him, Kelly?"

Kelly looks at her mother, then straight through my windows, and for a moment when our eyes meet my heartbeat slows down. Everything slows down, and the moment lasts forever.

"I love you," I whisper like I have done so many times today.

Kelly does not answer me. She will never answer me, she only talks to the prison. This numb and insensitive prison of cloth created to trap a warrior of the snake.

"Two minutes, and make sure to not miss a single tooth. You don't want anyone to feel left out."

"That's right." Her mother nods her on the nose. "Come on now, let's get ready for bed."

Even though her mother does most of the teaching, Kelly successfully shows me how to brush every single tooth. It seems to be much more complicated than just rubbing a brush against your teeth. You have to really get in there, forcing the brush around every corner.

“Dirty teeth are unhappy teeth,” she says with a mouth full of foam.

“Dirty teeth are unhappy teeth,” Both I and her mother repeats.

“Can I tell Chester a bedtime story?” She then asks.

“Of course, you can. Which one do you want to read him?”

“Little red riding hood. Or Goldilocks and the three bears. Or Pinocchio.”

“You have to decide on one story.” Laura’s smile plays over her determined face.

Kelly goes into a state of complete thoughtfulness. “Goldilocks and the three bears,” She decides with a determined face.

Even though she cannot read every word, she tells the story perfectly. She even gets a little angry when her mom fills in some of the details. Angry enough for her mom to leave us alone, and when Laura finally leaves us alone, I am relieved.

Every page thereafter is heaven. I never look at them, I do not really listen to the story either. I just listen to her voice, and I dream myself away to a time where we can be together. A time where I lay beside her in the bed and listen to the story she tells me, not the teddy bear I’m held in. Then I kiss her goodnight and leave just to come back again when she sleeps so I can listen to her calm breaths.

“You see, she used their things without asking them and that made them angry. If she had just asked, maybe she could have played with baby bear and everyone would have been happy, do you understand?”

How she lectures Chester amuses me. This stupid prison deserves every bit of it. She puts the book away on the nightstand next to a copy of snow white and the seven dwarves, another story for another wonderful night. She turns the light off and curls down between the sheets. She hugs Chester closely, and, I think, I feel her body heat. It makes me warmer than I have ever been.

“Did you hear what mom and dad said downstairs?” She whispers.

I flinch. What? For a moment, I almost lose grip of the wall.

“You get used to it. They talk like that all the time.” She pauses and thugs me closer between her arms. “And I’ll never let them take you away from me. Never ever.”

I will never let them take me away from you either, I think. Never ever.

Kelly yawns. "But you can feel safe. They won't do it. Before they could, but you're luckier than that."

She falls asleep. I am not even sure if she took the time to finish the sentence. She will have to wait until sunrise before she can finish her troubling conversation with Chester.

Downstairs the conversation between her parents starts all over again. Loudly. I want to walk down to them and tell them to stop, tell them how much damage they are causing their child. But the prisoner of the snake is incapable of any action with the outside world. The prisoner of Chester the Blue Teddy Bear is only allowed to observe and listen. It is my punishment. Their argument heats up. Borderline screaming, it suddenly stops. Yes, she will try not to buy as expensive brands next month. Laura gives up to save them from the ugliness their fight was heading towards. Her sigh while telling him it is time for bed, at least for her, is audible all the way upstairs.

Laura's and Milton's voices fade, and Kelly's lovely breathing is all filling the room with its soothing calmness. She breathes in, sucking Chester's fur into her mouth, and then out, pushing it back. I savor every moment of the sound of her breathing and hope for her dreams to stay happy throughout the night.

Devilish laughter breaks through my dreaming state of mind and as on-demand, the dark mass comes crawling on the floor as I have seen every night since me landing inside Chester. It still scares me. When it interrupts its steady mindless flow across the floor to close in on Kelly's bed, it terrifies me. Her father's snoring increases in volume, but the mass takes no notice. The mass moves with a plan in contrast to all the times it passed Mr. Reston's store.

Kelly moves over and protects her face from my view. But nothing in her movement shows the calm she gave of seconds ago. She worries. I push closer to my window. My breath dies in clouds on the windows.

"What's happening?" I whisper as I follow the mass flow up the foot end of her bed. A glimpse of white glimmers through the dark, and I glimpse a creature. Its fangs shine in the moonlight. Then, they all come clear, all the small ripples of pitch-black creatures, each one with a glimmering smile.

It was never one entity I saw flooding the floor, but one horde of laughing monsters wandering across it.

Hundreds of noses rise to the air and sniff. Their target is close.

The chant so synonymous with the mass echoes throughout the room. "Pain."

One of them quickly crawls to Kelly's face under laughter of excitement. Kelly turns over again, her conscious unaware of the creature now threatening her, but her subconscious alarms her of the danger closing in. The creature raises its hands towards Kelly and as I scream at it and slam the window with all my force, it pushes its paws into her eyes.

"You coward!" I scream.

The creature stops, its paws still deeply buried into her eyes and mind. It looks straight at the horde. Then it smiles, a horrible and gritty smile colored with sharp white teeth and digs deeper. It laughs.

"Leave her be!" I scream so loudly the inside of Chester shakes. I slam the window, I slam everything.

Kelly sobs in her sleep when her dreams react to the invader. Her heavenly dreams turn from tea parties with a king to screams of pain and unanswered cries for help.

"Please, dad. Leave mom be."

*Nightmares.*

The whisperer is barely audible over my loud punches. The creature lets out a sigh of relief, whatever it has started is close to completion. It pushes its arms even deeper into her dreams. I must out. Let her world kill me, I don't care anymore.

*Save her.*

I push my hands against the window. I fall through them frictionless and land on her bed. In confusion, I look around myself, forgetting to hold my breath. I realize I doomed myself the moment the air fills my lungs. The dark creature stands above Kelly's head. I rush to kill it before the air destroys me. Nothing else is important. My thoughts already imagine its body bleeding while I devour it from the inside out. It will bleed from my hideous fangs, and I want nothing more. I push my claws deep into where a smile haunts its face.

My claws dig into warm flesh. I take one more breath.

"You don't touch her," I scream repeatedly as I rip it into pieces.

The screams from the creature only infuriate me further. The more it screams, the more I want to hurt it. For everything it caused Kelly, it must suffer thousand-fold. I breathe. I don't even stop when the feeling of claws against flesh stops. I don't stop until all my rage is gone. Long after all traces of the creature is long gone.

My claws are no longer colored by the creature's black blood. It evaporated into the air like it never even existed. I stand there panting. Letting the air cleanse my thoughts. The air should burn, I realize. I can breathe. I look at Kelly whose dreams have turned calm again. She is safe once again.

I break down and cry uncontrollably.

"What is this?" I ask myself. "What the hell is this?"

*Warrior of the snake. Protect her.*

I look up from my once bloodied hands. Only tears taint them now. The flood of darkness continues pouring upwards onto the bed. One was only the beginning. Maniacal laughter floods the room and as the dark creatures rise from the fog their words chant through it.

"Pain." Repeated over and over again. "Pain. Pain. Pain"

Their nostrils move in search of Kelly. They lock on her and charge her in one synchronized flood.

"No!" I scream and throw myself at them. All my thoughts disintegrate in images of monsters dying by my hand. Everything becomes black blood and screams.

Their chant and evil laughter interrupt in screams of pain as I tear through them. I kill every single one of them without remorse, all while constantly roaring. Their blood warms my scales. Their bones crunch between my teeth. As the last one of them finally comes face to face with me I sink my sharp, serpent teeth into its neck. The dark blood fills my mouth. It tastes sweet on my split tongue. The creature squeals under my breath as I loosen the grip.

"Never ever come near my Love," I say as I let my teeth sink deeper until its neck crack.

The creatures around me evaporate. The blackness silencing my thoughts slowly fades away and I realize the extent of what I am.

I am not a killer, I think, just as I did when Kelly showed me children laughing at her at the school ground. I cannot be a killer. I am a warrior of the snake. I am noble.

But slaughter felt so right, and their flesh tasted so good.

It all felt too perfect.

I look up at the ceiling where I imagine the whisperer living. I am a murderer. I am a monster just like the Nightmares, created to kill and hurt.

I hate myself.

But I will do it again.

Because I am a monster. A monster who enjoys taking the life of others. A monster who loves the taste of blood. And as I curl into a ball at Kelly's face, the whisperer wheezes again.

*Love*

If only the air could become toxic again and remove me from this realization.

It is my only wish.

# Chapter 9

The next coming hours are dedicated to the night, and loneliness. No more demons come crawling up the bed. No more whisperers or singers demand my attention. It is just me laying on the bed next to Kelly, sobbing the time to pass.

The light leaks through the curtains in small tendrils. It never burns which would be a fitting fate for a monster like me. No, the creators have other plans.

Chester glows as strong as the morning light. Even though I have never seen it before, I know it to be the signal for me to return to where I belong. Kelly moans from irritation and tries to hide from the relentless daylight but as the morning gets closer the light grows stronger and hiding becomes pointless.

I have not moved one bit. I do not care if she sees me and screams in horror. At least then she knows about my existence. The air becomes heavy and stings through my throat. She opens her eyes and for a moment she looks directly at me. No Chester between us, just the air we breathe. If she gets scared and crushes me between the palm of her hand and the madras, I am okay with it. Leaving this world would be such a relief. Leaving it by her hand would be my desired choice of death.

Her eyes fixate on me for what seems like an eternity and when she finally opens her mouth, I have held my breath for longer than I thought was possible.

"Chester!" She says happily.

I look up just in time to see her stretch over me and grab the teddy bear.

She never even saw me.

"I missed you, Chester. Did you miss me?"

"All night. I have missed you all night," I answer her.

"Good," she says in her imaginary conversation with the teddy bear I wish I could be part of. "Today is school, and you are joining me, so we don't have to be apart at all. We will never be apart from now on."

I look at her hugging the glowing teddy bear. I swallow the nauseating heaviness in my heart and walk up to them. Chester glows stronger by the second. I take a deep breath of the torturing gas filling the world in the daylight. I want to hurt. I want to burn from the inside out just as much as I want to survive to see her laugh. I push my hands against Chester's soft walls and feel them, my arms and then me pass through until I am once again inside.

"Let's go and see what mom and dad are doing," Kelly says and drags Chester out from the bed and runs down the stairs.

I... I fight to remain calm. I sit down on the dark floor cleansing my lungs from poison one breath at a time.

"I love you," I say. The words fall flat to the floor. I am all alone. I say the words again feeling them tremble under my tears.

"I love you."

"I love you."

"I will always love you."

# Chapter 10

"Do you have everything?" Laura Marcsinzky corrects her daughter's shirt. A unicorn puking rainbows. Laura finds it questionable. Kelly finds it above all cute and funny, but her mother´s hesitation seals the deal.

"Yes," Kelly says while she fights, and loses against, the impulses to jump up and down on the spot. "Do you think they'll like Chester just as much as I do?"

"Of course, they will like him, honey." Laura counts everything in Kelly's bag just to be sure, then she ruffles Kelly's hair. "Okay, all set. Do you really think your friends can stand waiting for you any longer? They can't wait to see this teddy bear of yours."

"His name is Chester, mom," Kelly corrects her.

"Yes, Chester the mighty. Let's prove to him how fast those running shoes truly are. Are you ready? Get. Set. Go!"

Kelly spurts out through the door towards Sedan. Chester's head bumps back and forth in the same gut-twisting trip she pushed me through yesterday. She throws Chester to the seat and fastens the seat belt around him. Even though he is nothing but a soulless teddy bear, a journey like this should break his neck in more places than I can count.

Then she hugs us, so lovingly it heals all broken necks.

"I hope they won't like you too much, Chester. Because then they might take you from me. And I can't stand losing you. So, you better keep yourself by my side, okay?"

Like I would ever leave her.

She tells Chester about all her lovely friends, which to like and who to dislike. I crawl down to the bottom, wishing for the wheezing voice to make its presence heard. Its ever-repeating words would give me something to hate, besides myself. Our companionship has never worked in such a way, though. It is based on terror and pain, and Love and Nightmares. Warrior of the snake protects her. A hint of darkness awakens on my tongue. It is only a memory. My own imagination playing games.

Blood, I think. Our companionship is based on dark blood. I hunger for the first time since I got trapped in Chester's hollow body.

Outside, Kelly continues her discussion with Chester and describes her day for him. He doesn't listen, but I do while greedily licking my teeth hoping for the imagined traces to be real.

I am an addict, I realize that now. An addict who abhors every aspect of his very being.

As the car door opens and Chester's hollow body echoes the sound of children screaming on a playground, I imagine drinking the blood. My imagined self sucks a dark creature dry of any drop hiding inside its veins before it gets the chance to escape into vapor. I imagine all the screams, horror, and pain as I eat them all alive.

This cannot be who I am, I open my eyes wide in panic, I must be something nobler than the monster my fangs and claws prove me to be.

But. The sweet, sweet taste tells me a different truth.

Outside, Kelly shows Chester to her friends. They give off jealous awes, just as Kelly hoped for. At the same time, I curl into a ball on the floor. They pretend Chester presents himself to one of the other girl's dolls. They hug. I hide my face from the outside light. Chester says hi to another toy, and I drown myself in self-hate.

A school bell drowns all the voices. Children laugh as they run to the classroom. I imagine Chester's head bumping up and down fast enough to injure him for the rest of his years, if he was a living creature that is. Dead objects feel no pain. They have no emotions that can get hurt. Chairs scrape against a concrete floor. The laughs go silent, and left is only the sound of chalk against a black board. It chills me to the core of my spine.

"Welcome back." The stiff voice of a woman in the upper years of what should be called her second youth sounds through the room. It is even more chilling than the sound of her writing on the blackboard. "Have any of you done anything fun you want to share with the others?"

Even though it is tempting, I do not follow the urge to see the monster creating such disastrous sounds. My memory of Kelly's imagination knows exactly what she looks like. A skinny woman, with glasses and a perm making her look way older than she really is. She has more cats at home than a girl like Kelly can count.

"Yes, Kelly!"

I flinch at the mention of her name.

"Mom and dad got me a new teddy bear. He is so cute and cuddly."

"Great, Kelly. Just remember; all toys must be in the backpack during class."

"Yes, Mrs. Danderby."

Mrs. Danderby asks again. One of Kelly's classmates has been to her grandparents, another has played a football game and won. 2 to 1.

"It is truly a fantastic feat," Mrs. Danderby says. Then she continues with writing on the blackboard. They start with the word of the day. The class reads it out loud, loudly sounding all the vowels and consonants. PE-OH-AR-CE-EL-A-AI-EN. Then someone screams out.

"Porcelain!" He sounds so proud.

"That's right, Porcelain. Very good, Simon. Now, everyone. Write it down. I will ask you to spell it to me at the end of the day."

She continues to explain the rules of addition until recess. If one should believe the increasing whispers between her pupils, not a second too early. Loud cheers accompany the ringing clock. A schoolyard goes from dead to overflowing with life in mere seconds. Kelly's voice joins the others in their happy and naïve conversations, and in the chaos, beauty and harmony are born. Talking turns into a play where Chester is front and center, and with his words, he saves a doll named Molly from a fearsome dragon named Bo. But the real hero, the one who saved Kelly from dark monsters digging into her dreams, I stay hidden, never allowing myself a single moment to look at the magnificent scenery. I know deep down in my core, I'm not compatible with such beauty. I am compatible with death, and I hunger for more.

The boy, Timmy, imitates the sound of fire shooting from Bo's mouth. Miraculously he has regained his powers just a few minutes after Chester saved Molly. There is no way Molly will ever survive it this time. Chester draws his sword, it catches fire.

"Why do you want to hurt us?" Kelly says with her Chester-voice. It is the darkest voice a girl like her can manage but it is still as cute as she is.

Bo shots more fire. "I have a splinter in my foot." The voice is as dark as a little boy can manage. "It hurts."

I look up. Such a foolish way of viewing the world. Soon Kelly will use Chester's surprised voice and say something like "A splinter? Why didn't you say so?" and relieve Bo the dragon from his pain. They will probably become best friends forever, just as they did at the beginning of the recess.

I await the scene to play out with involuntarily suspense, but their voices have suddenly gone silent. I hear a soft hush.

I wait, worried by the silence. Worry grows to panic. I quickly climb, swinging past the bulge on the wall so fast I nearly miss the next dent. Something has happened. As I reach the window, Kelly's cheek covers all of Chester's eyes. She hugs him with everything she got.

"What do we have here?" Says a voice drooling with resentment. Just hearing it makes me sick. "The three sissy-tears and their flimsy toys."

Laughter arises on the now silent playground. The laughter of demons in child skin.

"Let me see." Suddenly, Kelly shakes as the boy grabs Chester from her.

"No!" she cries, but she is too weak to withstand his pull. The view of her cheek changes to a boy's face. He has an evil grin all over. The blond hair falls over his small eyes under the baseball cap. I recognize him from Kelly's bad memories from yesterday.

"So, this is the great and brave Chester, smiter of dragons and savior of dolls." The view changes as he turns Chester back and forth to get a better look.

"Please, can I have him back?" Kelly's tears muffle her voice.

"Have him back? Why? He is mine now. I actually always needed one of these. I just never knew it until right now. It will fit well with all the trash in my garbage can."

My blood rushes faster through my body. I push myself closer to the window, and I scream.

"Give her Chester back!"

The fury burns and as I spit words at him, the glass gives in, and I slip through it. I see it as the sign that all is permitted, even tearing the boy into pieces of unrecognizable flesh. I throw myself towards him, showing me teeth. Preparing to seal his fate with my first bite.

I hit his hard shell. Then I fall. I fall to the ground. It was like hitting a wall. I reach out, trying to get a grip. My attempts only end in me continuing to hit the invincible concrete wall between us until I hit the mud, the same mud on which Kelly stands on her knees begging to get Chester back. My lungs burn as acidic air fills them.

"Do you think Chester likes dirt?" The boy continues.

"No," Kelly answers with nothing but a whisper. Her fear reaches down to my spine in shivers. The shock from it only fuels my fury, and I continue to hit whatever it is standing between him and me.

I do not tire, and I never will.

"No?" The boy says in surprise. "But you like dirt, then he must like dirt too. Is it so that he has never tried it?"

Kelly remains silent. She looks down at her hands sobbing.

"Then you maybe should let him try it." The boy hands her Chester and when Kelly hesitantly looks up at him, he continuous adamantly. "Feed him dirt."

She looks at Chester then at him. She shakes her head.

"Do it!" He screams and takes one step closer to her, pushing the bear in her face. I stop attacking the façade shielding the boy from me and look to Kelly. The tears in her eyes. The shame on her face. She grabs mud from the ground.

"No, Kelly," I say. For the first time, the air bothers me. My breath gets heavier. The burn spreads into my arms and legs.

"I am sorry," Kelly says and pushes the mud up in his face. She smears it around while her sobs have turned to outright crying.

"Good girl," The boy says happily. "Now it is your turn."

Kelly looks up at him and before I react, he grabs her and shoves her face into the ground.

"I want to see you eat it."

Kelly takes dirt in her hand and puts it in her mouth. She shakes so hard it smears all over her face. The disgusting taste wanders across her tongue. Her mind shows me how every little grain tastes along with the metallic taste of fear.

"Chew," he demands.

She chews. The mud grind between her teeth. A horrifying sound, and all I can do is stand still and watch it happen. Completely numb.

He leans closer to her face.

"Now swallow."

She swallows. The dirt flushes down her throat and fills her stomach.

He laughs.

She coughs. I do too.

"Good, disgusting girl," he says. "You are now as dirty on the inside as you are on the outside. Just as ugly too."

I walk up to Kelly's face in the mud. The boy pats her on the head and walks away, laughing. They are all laughing. They are all telling the boy how amazing he is. No one even looks back at Kelly. In a terrible attempt to comfort her, I try to remove one straw of hair from her face. It is in her eye, all dirty from the mud covering her face. The same wall that covers the boy covers her. I cannot touch her either. My lungs scream for me to return to safety, but I could not care less. I try to comfort her by stroking her cheek, I must try.

"I'm sorry Chester." She presses her dirty face into the teddy bear's dirty fur. "Please, don't hate me. He forced me."

Chester's stone face says the magic words he always does. Nothing. Exactly what a little girl needs.

No. It is everything a little girl never should have to withstand. I stand with my hand on the wall which separates us from each other, wishing for just one second. One second where I could tell her Chester never will hate her, neither will I.

My wish is not fulfilled. Instead, I stand like a fool slowly realizing my breath no longer holds up my body.

Why can I be out at night? I think. Why can I be out when she is asleep but not when she is awake?

Chester glows. I look at Kelly who cries into the mud and give her one more stroke with my hand she never will know tried to touch her. Then I slowly crawl back to safety within the room residing behind Chester's fur. I barely make it. The last steps take forever.

Survive for Love, I think during these vital steps. My lungs cave under the air and when I cross the barrier between outside and inside, they give in.

I must survive for Kelly.

# Chapter 11

"You see? We are safe here. They never walk this far of the playground." Kelly balances Chester between two small branches. By 'they', she means the demons on the playground.

We are far beyond the boundaries of the school. Way too far beyond them. She pushed Chester, and me, through a tunnel under the fence. Then she took us from the playground and under the road on the other side. This is not a safe place. I expect to see the real Nightmares come crawling in the shadows, just waiting for the right moment to strike. However, I know Kelly is safe from them. The wall covering the demon boy has made me sure of it. Her world and mine are not compatible during the day. I can walk outside during the night but in the day her world wants me dead. I cannot touch her or anyone, I never will. In the same manner, my world's Nightmares are harmless during the day.

"I haven't told anyone about this place, not even Timmy or Daniella," she explains. "No one can know about this place. Do you understand?"

My view changes in a nod.

"Good." Kelly sighs, as she absolutely has seen adults do. "We have everything we need here." She picks up a box hidden under a pile of leaves. "We can even hear when class starts again." She raises her head as if she waits for the school clock to ring any minute. I listen too, and yes, the children laughing on the playground sound as clear as if we were among them.

She opens the box and shows Chester the content of a young girl's most precious belongings. A postcard of two kittens playing with a ball, a school photo, two hairpins, a bottle cap, and a bottle of nail polish. To others this means nothing, but to her this means everything and consequently, it means everything to me.

"This." She points at the postcard, "I got from my aunt before she moved away. She had the cutest kittens and always gave me the best cookies. And this." She picks up the school photo of a girl just a little younger than Kelly. It is the same face, the same smile, and the same shining eyes, just a little younger. "Was me a year ago. Can you believe it?" She looks at her younger self. "I look so small. I'm much bigger and stronger now." She raises her arm and flexes it to show muscles too small to be seen. Then she laughs the most beautiful heartwarming laugh I never tire from hearing.

I laugh too, it is so contagious, and we laugh together, though only one of us knows it.

I finally feel safe here, too.

"That was fun," she continues and catches her breath. She picks up the two hairpins and fastens them to her hair. "Don't I look like the prettiest princes in all the land?"

"Yes, you do," I say. I let go of the grips with my hand and let my claws on my feet hold me up, then I bow for my queen. "My lady you are truly the fairest of them all."

She laughs again, unknowing of my compliment. Laughter of water pouring down a beautiful waterfall.

"Thank you, you are quite handsome as well."

"Thank you," I say, convincing myself the words were meant for me, her knight in shining scales.

"And this," she says, picking up the bottle cap. It has a picture of an industrial building with the name Vesterville written below. Above it says Since 1989. "This is from dad's favorite juice. He gave it to me and told me to hide it. I had to make sure no one ever finds it because it will be worth a lot of money one day. So, I put it here where it always will be safe. They don't make things like these anymore, he told me. This, mommy told me I can use when I'm old enough." She holds up the bottle of nail polish. "It will be so much fun. I will paint my nails in all different colors, and everyone will be so jealous." She looks at her nails. "It will be so pretty."

I am certain of it as much as she is. She sits herself down on a pile of leaves and looks around, seemingly in harmony with herself and everything around her. The girl who cried while cleaning out the dirt from her tongue is nowhere to be found. She cried even more when she tried, and failed, to clean Chester's mouth.

"What do you think, Chester? Isn't it perfect?" Her now dry face looks in Chester's direction, and me. I stretch myself as far as I can to look further outside of the glass window but see nothing of the view she describes as perfect. But what I see is unnecessary, her view already flows inside my head filtered through her mesmerizing imagination. Colorful shadows of trees break through my view, they wave slowly at each cloud passing by on a clear blue sky. The wind catches a leaf and guides it between the branches. It falls peacefully down to her nose before ending in the pile she sits in. Kelly takes a deep breath and lets it all out. Her sigh is the song of angels.

Maybe just once, I could let myself outside and feel the harmony. Would it really hurt that much? Wouldn't it be worth it? I lean harder against Chester's eye and push my weight against its surface.

The outside wind hits my face and the sun gazes against my scales. In the sun light, they shine with a glorious green glow. I look around in awe of what her world has to offer. She used nothing of her imagination when her eyes showed me the outside view. The birches wave in harmony, and the clouds wander by in the same slow manner. The dark creatures I thought I saw were only shadows of a paranoid mind. The wind dances between the branches. This place is the paradise in my dreams before I woke up in Chester, only the song is missing. This is more than perfect. I take a deep breath, forgetting myself and expecting the cleansing air to fill my lungs. The acid burns immediately. I cough, which results in me taking in more toxic air. I throw myself back in, filling my lungs with healthy air. It is done too quickly, and my claws lose grip of the ledges. I fall to the ground and crash into the hard floor. All the healthy air leaves my lungs. For a moment, my body forgets how to breathe all together and my struggle to recover becomes a fight to survive.

How can this world treat me like this? I think with empty breaths. How can

I be in a world where I can only live in darkness? How can I live in a world were the only living aware of my existence are Nightmares? Slowly, fresh air trickle down my lungs again and replace the toxic gas flowing through my veins. I will never get to see the world for the beauty it really is. My life is one in darkness. The school clock rings.

Why me?

"Let's go, Chester! We can't let them miss us," Kelly says and pushes us back through the tunnel to the playground and the classroom.

# Chapter 12

Three kids walk across the playground. A boy, two girls. A dragon with a splinter, a princess in distress, and a heroic teddy bear inhabited by a reptile. They suddenly disappear. Nowhere to be seen. A group led by a boy with a baseball cap proudly crosses the playground. Only laughter from the group fills the vacuum. The boy told a joke, he is a comedian and a leader. Respected and feared by all.

I watch them from the safety inside Chester. The great warrior Gabriel murderer of Nightmares hides in the bushes with three kids, a dragon, and a princess. Kelly hugs harder around Chester's neck. Her fright has me in its grip, just as all her feelings take me hostage. Every feeling of terror, joy, and boredom makes me shake, laugh and yawn. It is a blessing to share her joy and a curse to suffer her sadness. The dirt still tastes bitter in my mouth, and the gravel still grinds against my teeth.

The boy in the baseball cap suddenly stops and looks in our direction. The laughter stops in an instant, and all three children and a murderous reptile hiding in the bushes stop breathing. He picks up a handful of sand from the asphalt and blows it in our direction without ever leaving the bushes with his evil glare. If Chester really was alive, Kelly would have chocked him to death by now. The boy's face splits in two in a big smile, flashing his teeth and gums. It is as ugly as he is. I want to rip them out one by one and watch him scream with a bloodied mouth.

"Desert. Hope you like it."

Once again, the group bursts into laughter. Loud and uninhibited. They continue their stroll across the playground. The fright releases its grip on my mind. The conflict between my own anger and Kelly's feelings becomes less heated. Only my own fury controls me now.

"He let us go." Timmy releases a sigh.

Kelly giggles in relief. They act like him leaving them alone was an act of kindness. The proof of baseball cap Frank's nobility. He spared them from his justice. And the laws of our two worlds have spared him from mine. Everyone stays hidden in the bushes until they know there is no risk of crossing the groups' path. Then they laugh the laugh of survivors after facing and winning unbeatable odds. Just a second later, the whole playground comes back to life.

The three talk about how their toys are the best friends on this planet, just like they are. Chester hugs Bo the dragon, and then he kisses Molly's hand. Molly giggles. I, the reptile demon, observe from Chester's eyes.

They reach the end of the playground and the cars lining up just outside the fence. All the parents take their time to talk about whatever it is parents talk about while they wait for their kids to break out of their bubble and realize that the world is more than just playing with friends. Kelly is not among the quickest to make this realization. Baseball cap Frank already stands with a bald dad in a suit looking way to expensive. The car they stand in front of also looks like something costing far beyond the ones next to it.

"So Frank, how has the big guy's day been?" The bald guy says with a voice so authoritarian it is heard over all others. He smiles as if the world was a place free from problems or evil, as if monsters like his son not existed.

"It was okay, I guess," Frank answers. "We played football, and my team won."

That he forced a girl to eat mud from the ground never crosses his lips. I bet Frank never tells his dad about the real events during the recesses. That would be too horrible. That would kill his father's smile.

"Honey! I am here!"

Kelly suddenly stops walking. We both look in the voice's direction and see Laura standing by Sedan. As if it was planned the three sissy-tears scatter. Equally synchronized they all scream:

"Mom!"

Laura leans down and catches Kelly midair. It is a perfect catch that tells the world their life is perfect.

"How has my beautiful girl's day been?"

"So good," Kelly answers.

Kelly always lies to her parents. I realize that now. The girl crying after swallowing mud lies every day.

"Please forgive me, Chester," She repeated for the remainder of the first recess while rubbing the dirt off his nose. The nose was still stained brown when she gave up. She cried in desperation imagining Chester being disappointed in her. Each image I got to see of her thoughts painted Chester with a bigger frown on his blue face and tears in his eyes. In her imagination, he could not forgive her, but we never blamed her. Only Frank.

It was Mrs. Danderby who finally got the dirt away with a napkin.

"Chester has met so many new friends, and they played, and they had so much fun."

"So great!"

"And Mrs. Danderby taught us how to spell porcelain. Mom, do you know how to spell porcelain?"

"Can't tell you I do hon'."

"It is spelled: P-O-R-C-E-L-A-I-N. It was really hard, but I got it correct."

"You are so smart, my little professor." Laura puts her nose against Kelly's and rubs it. The little girl giggles. "What do you say? Should we eat tacos to celebrate?"

Kelly's loud yes is evidence enough of how good of an idea it is, her imagination showing me Kelly filling a taco to the brim proves how perfect of an idea it is.

As my happy family walks back towards the car, Frank observes us. His emotionless expression tells nothing, but his eyes burn.

Kelly notices it too. And she knows.

Tomorrow will bring even more pain.

# Chapter 13

It is getting late. Too late. There are nightly shadows crawling outside the windows. They are eager for the moment when all lights go out, and their feast may begin.

*Nightmares*

The whispering inside my head has force-fed me the word all night, each time louder than the last. The beautiful singing of a thousand voices has toned down to a soft mumble under the whisper.

They feel it.

The monsters outside feel it.

I feel it. It makes me hungry. The angst. All the troublesome thoughts of a young girl sitting between her parents. She pretends to do her homework, but her mind thinks about so many more important things. The life of a little girl is so stressful. Her troublesome thoughts refocus on the monster named Frank and how she can possibly avoid him tomorrow. The question remains unanswered. Then her thoughts wander to this night's main act; Her two parents sitting on each side of her spitting words at each other.

The at first calm discussion quickly derailed into a loud argument. Laura's subtle attempts to keep the argument down never stood a chance. To Milton this never was a discussion, he was armed for a fight. He has been since he came home. He never noticed the situation they put their daughter in, no matter how many times Laura glanced in her daughter's direction.

Within Kelly's thoughts, the argument turns into lions roaring at each other, every word is a bite, and every silence is a scratch. Among their roars, Kelly's voice mumbles the squeak of a scared mouse. She wishes they visited the horrible house of grandma' after all. If they did, her parents would never have gotten the chance to argue, but grandma' became sick with an enervating cold, one of those colds only grandmas get where they sneeze the teeth out of their mouth. When Kelly's mind tires itself on wishing, she blames herself for everything. All her parent's unhappiness is after all her fault. They were happy before she sucked it out of them, and they had money before she ate all their food away.

"What if I run away?" She picks up her pen, nothing happens.

The shadow monsters outside cover the windows, blocking every ray of light that possibly could find its way in from the street. Their shrieking laugh is almost enough for me to leave my safe place inside Chester and chase them down one by one until I die. The fraction of my thoughts capable of rationality is alone what convinces me to survive. But they are slowly drowning in Kelly's depressing thoughts and the blood-thirsty instincts I will regret so much tomorrow.

"What if I just disappear?" Kelly drops her pen on the table again. She sighs. "Would they notice it?"

The sounds are numbing. Laughter. Screaming. Whispering. And mumbling.

"I could live in the hiding place. No one would ever find me." She picks up Chester from the table. "What do you think, Chester?"

She moves her fingers around his neck making him nod.

"Good." She yawns loudly.

Outside the shadows have begun their fierce chant. "Pain. Pain." The choir is so loud, the argument sounds like nothing more than static.

"Tomorrow," she whispers. "It is too dark outside."

I agree with her, there is nothing but darkness outside.

"Mom, I think I'm too tired for homework."

Her two parents stop midsentence.

"Of course, honey," her mother says. "Go up and brush your teeth. I will be right with you."

She kisses Kelly on the forehead. It is a lazy kiss, but just enough to abrupt the negative spiral Kelly's thoughts have begun. Just, not enough to get her crawling up from it.

The screaming continues the second Kelly walks up the staircase.

"You never scream at me, Chester. You are too kind."

If Chester would scream at her I would tear him up from the inside. Lucky for him, dead toys don't scream. The laughter grows intense as we walk past the window in the middle of the staircase. The chant has grown into an inaudible mess. They are ecstatic. They slam the window unable to break through no matter how much they want to get past it. One Nightmare dies slamming its head against the window into a bloody, fanged popsicle, all while laughing. I am glad their chants are only for my ears and not Kelly's.

"We are lucky dad hasn't taken his juice yet. It makes him so much angrier." She hugs Chester. "And then he gets mean." A memory forces its way into my consciousness. Milton Marcsinzky holding her by the ankle. He screams, Kelly and Laura cry.

"Do you want her to be like you?" He spits in Laura's face. "Do you want that?"

The memory comes to me in a punch through all other thoughts.

"No, you don't get to run away from me!" Kelly's mom screams downstairs. For a moment I still think it's Kelly's memory.

"I do whatever I want!" He screams back.

Kelly stops on the stairs for a moment and listens. A door slams. Kelly's mother continues to yell through whatever door it was he slammed in her face.

It comforts Kelly. It is one more door between her father and the juice cabinet.

"Remember to brush your teeth, Chester. Tomorrow is a big day."

On some level, she knows it is only a child's promise. Nothing more. She will not leave them, not yet. Every day, she will continue to go home hoping for the better and each time she will realize that they will never change. I know this because, behind her words, her thoughts are running wild with all the times they have let her down.

The argument between her parents becomes furious as we enter the bedroom. They are in the same room again. Milton slammed the door open so hard the windows rattled. Kelly pets Chester over his head and ears and hides under the covers as if lightning bolts struck beside her bed. Her petting only stops when her eyelids finally become too heavy and not even her tornado of thoughts hold her up anymore. As her dreams reenter her mind, a new door slams open downstairs and glass bottles clink against each other. Her dad empties the bottle, her mother screams at him, tells him the bottom of the bottle solves none of their problems. He tells her he will stop drinking when she stops shopping her problems away. She cries, she has not bought anything new in years, everything is for Kelly. Kelly and her father's drunken desires.

Then, there it is, the sound of flesh against flesh. A fist hitting a face, and screams turn into cries.

Kelly's sleeping mind captures it all.

# Chapter 14

Every punch echo in Kelly's dreams. Every word spat by a father thunders from grey clouds above the playground where she just last night danced with hedgehogs, foxes, and a blue teddy bear. Tonight, the little girl stands alone in the thunderstorm with a thumb in her mouth.

"You lying whore!"

A mother's tears rain heavy on the little girl's hair. The little girl hugs herself hoping for her warmth to keep her safe.

The screams from the bedroom right under Kelly's own bed breaks the playground in two. The little girl falls down the emptiness crying for help.

And then the silence paints her whole world black.

"No," Kelly whispers as her dreams reach out to her physical world.

Outside, the Nightmares laughs as they feast on every ooze of suffering.

The gates open as soon as the sobs of a hurt mother fall silent. The dark twisted creatures pour in as if the windows gradually become permeable from the top down. If I did not know any better, I would have been convinced they were only one organism, falling to the floor in one steady dark stream. Their chant never stops, not even for a second.

"Pain." It is a celebration fueled by the hurt of a young child. "Pain. Pain."

The first ones hitting the floor cushions the fall for the ones following. Their bones crack from the other's weight, a chilling shriek leaves their dying bodies as the pain becomes more than just a chant. A sound reaching the core of my spine. I love it. They are hurting. Instincts beyond my control take my body in its possession. Hunger fuels me. A hunger only to be quenched by silencing their chants and choking their heartbeats. I push myself against the window built into Chester's eyes. Fresh non-poisonous air hits my face. This is air meant for nightly creatures. Air for monsters. I take a deep breath. It energizes every fiber in my body. My mouth waters and the drool crawls out into long tendrils.

I am ready.

Kelly turns around under the covers. Her mind still echoes the punch delivered through a caveman's method of winning an argument against someone physically weaker.

I look to the window to see tonight's victims continuing their march.

I am not a murderer, my regret whispers as a pinch of discomfort. My hunger quenches it, pushing it back into the deepest corner of my being. The monster is in control. I am now a complete set, a monster through and through. A horrible being created to kill.

And I kill with pleasure.

"Come on!" I roar.

The first one stretches its ugly head up over the bed end. One second later its blood gushes all over Kelly's sheets. It is a wonderful sight. Black on white. I lift the headless body over my head and pour the remainder of its blood over me and into my mouth. It tastes so good, but my hunger only growls stronger. I throw the empty body to the side as it dissolves into the air. The first wave is already on the bed, moving slowly. I throw myself into the horde, everyone within my reach dies instantly as I tear up their chests with my claws. I eat their lungs and hearts right from their ribcages. The gurgled sound from their throats, their pulse against my tongue, fills me with a sense of complete peacefulness. A peacefulness only possible through their screams.

The second wave charges from every side of the bed, the third and fourth are directly after it with no interruption. Their mindless march tackles me to the ground. Their bodies block all light and leave me blind. I don't mind. I am born in darkness. I only need my claws to rip them apart and the taste of their flesh on my tongue to guide me. In the darkness, my world becomes screams and roars. And blood, darkness, and blood.

It is not the laughter or the frenetic chant that finally scares me out of a slaughterer's frenetic trance. It is the sighs of relief followed by Kelly's scared cry when all horrors in her dreams penetrate out into reality. One after another I hear them, monsters pushing their poisonous hands into her dreams and sighing in the climax. A chock runs through my body as every cell reacts. A new instinct overrides all else. Bodies fall in pools of blood. Light once again seep in through the thick mass of Nightmares. Their hands are still inside her head when they die. I never pull them out, I just attack the next one, and the next one, and the next one until I once again can see her beautiful blond hair under the dark mass. I continue until my body is the one thing between them and her and the only way to her is through me. They shove their hands into my chest without success in hope of reaching her dreams through me.

"Pain." They chant between every repeated punch, and I feel my bones giving in under the pressure. "Pain."

I grab the closest head and drags it closer to my face while burying my teeth deep into its throat. It wheezes as air escapes its lungs.

"Pain!" I roar, partly from my body screaming in agony, partly in rage. I show a mouth full of sharp teeth and blood slowly vaporizing into the dark fog of my enemies. I roar. I grab the next one pushing itself into the dead one's place. I growl as it dies. The creature's dark fur light up from my eyes' yellow glow. Its dark eyes glimmer from the shine. In one move I swing my arms in wide circles and force every Nightmare away from Kelly. The unlucky ones staying within my grasp are dead before they have the chance to react.

"Pain!" I roar again. I stand on all four, wheezing between my teeth. In the light that is emitting from my eyes, they are all forced to show their hideous appearance, their long noses, and whiskers, their small eyes. They fear me now. They realize they are outnumbered, and I am not leaving my place between Kelly and them, I never will. Suddenly one of them raises its ugly nose to the air. Shortly after the others do the same. Then they simultaneously burst into a terrifying screech.

"Pain!" The scream changes into the chant I have learned to recognize all too well under these short days. It is a war cry. I prepare myself for the upcoming attack. My muscles tense up as they get ready to burst into action. I scan every one of them, spotting every weak link. No one will get past me.

There is never an attack. Instead, they disappear, and their chant slowly dies to nothing but a breeze.

For hours, I stand reacting to every little sound my imagination makes up.

It cannot be this easy, I think There has to be a catch.

*Home.*

The whispered word thunders.

# Chapter 15

Laura Marcsinzky is masterful in her ways of covering up all traces of abuse. Her bruises are invisible under the make-up layered even thicker today than before. Her eyes seem to glisten from happiness and not from dried tears, her smile feels truthful, her voice seems to burst with happiness.

Kelly's father is still asleep.

"He didn't sleep well." Is the only explanation Kelly gets, and the more Kelly asks the quicker her mother changes the subject.

"Do you want jam on your sandwich? More milk? What fun will you do in school today?"

"We're having PE today," Kelly proudly answers her mother's last question with jam covering her whole mouth.

"Great!" Kelly's mother says with one of her smiles I now know are false. The smile never reaches her eyes and dies almost immediately.

"We will play soccer!" Kelly continues with a new bite of the sandwich stuffed into her mouth. "This time I will score."

"Yes, you will honey. Yes, you will." Laura pulls out a hair that accidentally followed the sandwich into Kelly's mouth, a movement on autopilot.

Kelly giggles the most innocent giggle I have ever heard as the hair tickles her lips. The sparkles leaving her mouth layers on top of my already bursting heart. Traces of a smile play on my face. If she could see me, her giggle would immediately fade, everything about me would terrify her. Sharp fangs ready to bite deep into her bones. Narrow eyes with a predator's glow. Luckily, she sees Chester's hollow eyes and his friendly smile. He makes her smile even wider.

"Did you hear that, Chester? I will score!"

"Yes, honey and the crowd will go wild as you celebrate." Kelly's mother raises her hands above her head and mimics the cheering sound of a crowd going wild. Even such an act of celebration is only a shadow of the real deal. Laura stops in the middle of one of her woaahs. Her hands still raised above her head. She heard a sound from the bedroom and froze. Her heart stopped mid-beat. My own breathing stops. Then it comes again, the sound of her husband's feet dragging across the bedroom floor.

The wife-beater releases a load moan.

Laura breaks free from her paralyzed state. She is focused, not even pretending to be happy for Kelly's sake.

"Come on Kelly," she says and lifts Kelly out of the chair. "Mom has to get you to school now before it is too late."

"But mom, I'm not finished yet."

"Hush, Kelly. We don't have time for this. We're already late."

They are not. In fact, they are early, but Kelly is bad at keeping track of the time. Kelly's father is late though. Loud curses penetrate through the bedroom door as he realizes what time it is. At the sound of her father's voice, all Kelly's arguments go mute.

"Daddy is angry." Kelly's thoughts bring up a memory of her father punching her mother, there is blood everywhere.

Mother and daughter leave the kitchen in the quietest way a mother and daughter can. They leave the table in a messy state of jam and bread. They almost forget me and Chester, but Kelly grabs us in the last moment.

"Bye, daddy," she says and slowly waves in the direction of her parent's bedroom.

Her stressed father bursts out through the door in a whirlwind of clothes as we leave the house. He catches a glance of Kelly and her waving hand but wastes no time in answering it. He sprints to the front door and wrenches it open as hard as he can. The shear force pushes Kelly and her mother out on the lawn. They stumble and fall. Kelly hits the ground with Chester cushioning her fall. She avoids getting hurt but she screams anyway, as do I. Laura hits the ground headfirst.

"Where are you going?" Milton yells.

Laura rubs the dirt off her face with hands so shaky they smear the dirt, and her make-up, all over her face. She scans the area around herself until she finds Kelly. Her bruises come clear to the world. At this moment, she cares little for her looks. Her only thought is her daughter.

"Are you okay, Kelly?" She whispers, slowly caressing the back of Kelly's head.

Kelly nods anxiously holding back her tears with all her willpower.

"Where are you going?" Milton repeats. He walks out to us. Kelly smells the juice on his breath as he leans closer. "Don't think you can run away from me."

"Please don't hurt mom," Kelly thinks.

Milton grabs his wife by the arm. Hard. Laura screams. In a reflex of self-defense, she drops Kelly on the grass, who lands on her back and momentarily loses her breath. The chock forces my body to lose its ability to breathe too.

"I'm dropping her off at school!" Laura yells back with tears in her eyes.

"Do you really think I believe that?" He screams the words, spitting saliva all over his wife's face. He shakes her in his hands. "Do you really think I'm that dumb?"

"I'm dropping her off at school," Laura repeats the words between her teeth. Her arms are firmly positioned between them to cushion his shaking.

"Do you want Kelly to grow up without a father? Do you?" He throws her down to the ground again. Her face hits the stones spread out on the entrance and leaves an ugly scratch across her cheek.

Laura touches the scrape and flinches. She looks up at Kelly, who now has put her thumb in her mouth to find support in it. The tears on Kelly's face tell her mother the attempt is unsuccessful. Kelly's shame spreads in my gut.

"Only babies suck their thumbs," a child laughs in her memory.

"Is everything okay?" The deep voice startles me. It comes from behind Kelly.

Kelly turns around. I cannot see the source, but the voice is unmistakable. Milton gets caught off guard and stares at the man for a long moment before recognition crosses his face.

"Everything's okay, Mr. Reston," he says, lingering on the words like snake delving in his thoughts. "There is no problem at all."

"Are you sure?" Mr. Reston's steps sound against the asphalt as he enters the Marcsinzky's yard.

"Absolutely sure. Laura just tripped on the stairs."

Mr. Reston is so close, I can see him with his wiggling mustache, and round shape.

"I see. That's an ugly wound you have there, Laura. You better let someone check it for you." He stretches a helping hand to her. "Here, let me help you up." The bruises on her face, he never mentions even though they glow against her pale skin.

Laura nods. She accepts Mr. Reston's aid and lets him lift her up. A rebellious act both she and her husband know will cause her more harm later.

"I was just telling her that. We have some alcohol inside to clean it up." The lies Milton tells come so easy. Small wonder Kelly learned to lie so well. "Why don't you come inside Laura and let me check it for you?"

Laura looks at him, then at Kelly and Mr. Reston. She shakes her head, a choice cementing the high price she pays tonight.

"It will have to wait, I'm in a hurry." She walks over to Kelly and picks her up. Chester and I are left on the lawn. "Kelly here must get to school in time. Shouldn't you also be on your way, Mr. Reston?"

Mr. Reston laughs one of his signature laughs. I have missed them so much these few days, I did not know it, but they fill an empty hole in my heart I only now realize exist.

"Not today. You see, one day every now and then I have to let the younglings be alone in my shop to learn how it will be when I retire." He picks up me and Chester from the ground. I get a glimpse of his grey car on the pavement. He must have stopped the car as soon as he saw us laying on the ground. "And this, my young lady, I think belongs to you. It would be a shame if you lost one of the finest teddy bears I've ever seen."

"Thank you." Kelly hugs the teddy bear tightly. She giggles under her thumb. Her tears glister in her eyes. "I will never let him out of my sight."

"Good." Mr. Reston gives Kelly a soft punch on the chin. "And make sure your mother keeps herself on her feet for me, okay?"

"I will do." Kelly's thumb releases its comforting grip over Kelly and finds its way out of her mouth, as it should always be for little girls.

A hint of the smile I saw on Laura's face in the toy store appears again. One look in her husband's direction destroys it and her flight reflex kicks in. Her grip around Kelly tightens in an instant.

"I'm so sorry, Mr. Reston, but we really have to rush."

"No worries, I have to randomly drive by my store and see that it is still not in flames anyway," Mr. Reston laughs in an excuse to follow Laura out of the Marcsinzky's lawn. "If you want, I have something in my car that might help you with that scrape?"

One look between husband and wife, one terrified look.

"No, she's okay."

"We can look closer at it when she gets home," Milton continues.

"Okay, then," Mr. Reston says thoughtfully and turns to Kelly. "Hopefully I will see you and Chester again soon, and you can tell me all about the adventures you two have had."

Kelly giggles again hugging Chester close to her chest. Inside Chester, I scream for Mr. Reston to save us from this home, but he cannot hear me. He never hears me.

"Have a nice day, honey," Milton says as Laura runs with Kelly to Sedan as fast as she can.

Laura finally allows herself to breathe when she has put several blocks between her husband and Sedan. She turns on the radio. She drums along to the song, but she hears nothing of the song playing. She is completely drowned in heavy thoughts.

"Mom, why is dad angry again?"

Laura interrupts her drumming without answering her daughter. She bites her lip.

"Mom."

"Yes." She pauses. "Honey." She takes a deep breath. "It's just that, mom said something stupid, so dad is going to be angry for some time now."

“What did you say?” Kelly continues to play with Chester like if she was talking about nothing.

“Mom said.” Laura hesitates. “Mom said that dad has to stop with his juice.”

There is a silence between them. Laura inspects how deep the scrape is in the review mirror. She sighs, it is clearly too much to cover up. Her bruises though, those she can fix again.

“But dad should stop with his juice,” Kelly says. “It makes him stink.”

Laura laughs. It is a nervous, tense laugh. But she laughs, nonetheless.

“Yes, honey. Dad stinks when he drinks his juice. But we can’t tell him that. It will make him sad.”

“And angry?”

Laura glances at Kelly. “Yes, it might make him angry too.”

“Okay.” Kelly restarts her play with Chester jumping back and forth between her legs. Within her mind, her thoughts continue the discussion.

“We can’t run away today, Chester. Mom needs us.” Chester stops jumping and looks at her then at Laura. “That’s right. We can do it another day.” Chester nods.

“How many goals do you think I will do today at PE mom?”

“A hundred! No! A thousand!” Laura Marcsinzky is drumming the steering wheel again.

“I think so too,” Kelly says bursting in excitement. “And you will meet Bo again, hopefully, he doesn’t get a splinter this time, so you can continue being friends.”

I have got to admit it. Meeting Bo is the most boring part of the day. His splinter is also one of the few things not worrying me because I know Kelly will not score in football. She will never even get close to the goal. Frank will make sure of that.

# Chapter 16

"You know what?" Timmy proudly crosses his arms over his chest. A posture he has most likely seen his father take on after a long day's work. "I think I will use the biggest soccer ball today."

Two netted white metal frames rise in front of us as the duo walk towards the sports field. Kelly thought of a giant green ship when she first saw it. They have changed to shorts and t-shirts in the school's blue and white colors. The same colors Chester wears every day. All the little sailors running around on what her imagination painted into green deck made her giggle. Timmy even got blue and white shoes, though they have faded into a greyish color.

"No way!" Kelly says. "I would be too scared to trip over it."

Timmy blushes. "I bet you wouldn't trip on it. You are too good at football for that."

"It's just because I practice with the football dad bought me." Kelly looks at her shiny shoes, another item that pushed them to the brink of ruin. "He likes when I play football with him."

"Did your dad buy you a football?" Timmy almost falls on his nose as he halts on the spot.

"Yes, he does stuff like that sometimes when he is in a good mood. Like when he bought Chester for me."

"Oh, I wish my dad would be more like your dad."

Kelly flinches but Timmy never notices it, the sudden shift in her thoughts hits me in an electric chock. From a father cheering his daughter on while teaching her all you can do with your feet, with a bottle of juice in his hand, to her all too fresh memories of this morning painted in blood and bruises.

"No, you don't," she thinks. "Maybe he is waiting for the right moment," she says.

Timmy looks weirdly at her and shakes his head. "No, he buys us food instead."

"Oh, my mom does that for us," Kelly says with an astonished look on her face. Her dad never buys food, only juice. "Didn't your dad buy you Bo?"

"No, it's my brother's. But he is my best friend anyway."

Kelly gives Timmy a weird look as she processes the possibility of a family of more than one child and two parents. No matter how hard she thinks it all just seems impossible.

"Do you think we will be on the same team?" Timmy continues. "It would be so much fun."

"Yeah! If we stand with someone between us maybe Mrs. Danderby will divide us into the same team."

They agree on the planned heist, and I would have believed in it too if I did not see Mrs. Danderby looking at them with one of her rare stiff smiles.

All the little sailors grab a football at Mrs. Danderby's command. Timmy, to my surprise, takes up on his promise and grabs one of the largest sizes. He clumsily kicks it around on the field unsuccessfully forcing it in the right direction while Kelly cheers him on.

"Come on, Timmy! One more time."

He stumbles and falls on his nose.

"Shit!" He says awkwardly. "I almost had it."

"Language Timmy." Mrs. Danderby gives him a strict look that makes Timmy blush.

"That's right, Timmy." I clench my claws harder around the grips in the wall at the sound of his voice. I abhor him. "Sissies are not allowed to curse."

A burst of resounding laughter rises from the crowd, if the Nightmares laughed like that, they would have been so much more terrifying. Mrs. Danderby pretends not to hear him. She looks in the other direction to not see him, or what he does. But she knows, it is clear on how she suddenly gets a rash on her arm and how focused she gets on two other kids passing the ball between each other.

"I actually think Sissy-tear Timmy should stay on the ground and eat the weight of his words in grass," Frank continues. "Don't you think so?"

He gets appreciating nods from his gang.

"Come on Timmy, eat the grass. Just taste it for us."

"He doesn't want to Frank," Kelly breaks in. Her heart is pounding from nervousness, but she can't do nothing.

"And what do you know about that?" The intense change of focus to Kelly startles her. Her nauseating tension spikes in an instant. It makes me want to throw up.

"Don't you dare hurt her!" I scream. My clawed hands dig into the dents hard enough to rip them apart from the wall, any ordinary wall that is. I once again see Frank in blood. I am a murderer of demons, and I am ready to show this child-like abomination the monster that lurks in the darkness. I will drink him dry. I will listen to his final scream die out in his last breath. I will...

I will stand by and watch Kelly's daily torture continue. I am useless in every single way.

"I know, he doesn't like vegetables," Kelly says hesitantly, her grip around Chester turns into a nervous choke hold.

"But has he tried grass?" Frank walks so close to her I can see his freckles.

Kelly stands paralyzed without saying a word. "Don't hurt me," Kelly's inner voice repeats. Her mouth remains shut. "Don't hurt me."

Frank's eyes burn into hers until she cannot stand it anymore and looks away.

"Don't hurt me."

"As I thought." Frank pushes Kelly so hard she falls onto the ground. She drops me and Chester, all while her inner monologue screams. "Why don't you join him?"

I am furious. Furious with Frank, furious with my inability to aid the only one meaning anything to me. This demon deserves to be haunted by the Nightmares for the rest of his life. I wish for the monsters of darkness to visit him in large armies with no one to guard him. I want to hear him scream in terror and pain under their chants and sighs of relief, his scream would be barely audible, but it would be so worth it. I look at Kelly. Her shorts are stained from the grass. Her elbows are red from catching the fall. But she is not scared, not anymore. Her thoughts are swirling around developing pictures of her father hitting her mother until her mother could not stand anymore. Memories from long before me, and Chester.

"He hurt me. You don't hurt me. No one hurts me and mom," Her thoughts scream.

"No!" She raises up. "You can eat grass."

Frank looks startled. Then his face shifts into an evil grin. The gang whistles with anticipation. The gest passes Kelly without notice, she pushes him and forces him one step backward. The evil in his eyes flares as he rubs his shoulder where she hit him.

"You will pay for that," he whispers, he will enjoy every second when she does.

"Okay, now children," Mrs. Danderby interrupts just in time to stop Frank from launching himself at Kelly. "Line up so we can divide you into teams."

Frank looks up at his teacher. He smiles and then shifts his focus to Kelly.

"You're dead," he says. "See you on the field." He turns around and walks away. The walk of a predator awaiting a wounded prey.

I am terrified to my core. Kelly on the other hand is angry, she stands in the same spot. Her anger has drowned every part of the little girl Frank scared into submission. She would have pushed him again. She is her father's daughter as much as she is her mother's, and her father 'never takes shit from anyone.' He hurts people who wrong him. She wants to hurt Frank more.

"No one treats me like that," she mumbles. "Not anymore."

She picks up Timmy's football and puts it in front of her. Her thoughts of reason are replaced with anger. It pulsates within me in a steam of fire and thunder. But in contrast to her, I can still think, and the consequences will be ugly. She takes charge and kicks the large football in Frank's direction with all her force.

"No," I whisper, but it is too late. It is a bull's-eye. The football hits him right in the back of his head and throws him to the ground. Adrenaline rushes through Kelly's body, she is thrilled. Finally, she stood up to the bully. Finally, she did what is right.

"You eat grass!" She screams triumphantly so everyone can hear her. She raises her fist to the air.

"Kelly, what are you doing?" Mrs. Danderby says with a controlled voice colored from stains of fear.

Frank slowly rises from the ground. He rubs the back of his head. Then he turns around, and we get to see it. Fury and cruelty. Kelly stops her internal celebration, and, in an instant, her mind clears.

"What have I done?"

Her mind fills with images of a girl, pushed to the ground. Every time she tried to get up some one pushed her down. The same girl was forced to run naked the day before she left school.

"I will miss you, Timmy," Kelly thinks. "I will miss you, mommy." Her eyes meet Timmy's who still lays in the grass, scared out of his senses. His mouth forms one word.

"Run."

"How dare you?" Frank roars.

Mrs. Danderby turns around and focuses on the other children. Her rash turns into a serious problem. She wipes a tear of her face.

Kelly turns around and she runs. She runs as fast as she can. From the bumpy view through Chester's eyes, I see Timmy getting further and further away from us. Frank gets closer. Kelly takes off towards the hiding place, not home, home is not safe enough. Frank growls behind us. Mrs. Danderby divides the two teams. Kelly will not be on the same team as Timmy today. We reach the end of the field. Frank catches up to us.

I am terrified, truly terrified. Those eyes, they glow with all wrong in this world. He catches Kelly's hair and drags it towards him. The pull forces Kelly to trip. She falls headfirst and screams. Hair rips from her head as his grip holds her up. It hurts so badly.

"How dare you?" Frank roars again.

"I- I- do-," Kelly stutters.

"I will make you pay for this!" Frank lifts her up and then slams her down to the ground once again. Kelly screams, both in pain and fear.

I just stand on the other side of Chester's eyes watching the cruel act. "Please," I beg to no use.

Frank is worse than the dark Nightmares. He lifts her up again. Kelly is silent this time, she uses all her energy to hold back the tears running down her face.

"I will make your life so painful, you will wish I treated you like Ana," he says. "Do you understand?"

Mrs. Danderby is finished dividing the teams. The two teams are walking to their separate side of the field. No one and everyone look in our direction.

Frank throws Kelly to the ground again. His anger pulsates through the air. He is not finished yet. The view from Chester's eyes changes, and Frank's face gets closer.

"Your silly teddy bear will be the first to suffer."

His face gets so close his breath condensates against Chester's eyes.

"No, not Chester," Kelly cries.

Frank ignores her plead. He sinks his teeth into Chester's face. His bite creates small dents on the inside. And pain. A screeching pain in my chest. With both my hands I reach for the pain, and I lose my grip.

"What is happening?" I ask before hitting the ground. The teeth-shaped dents grow as Frank tear the fabric apart. Kelly's cry grows louder. Light burst through the seams holding Chester's head and body together. My heart is ripped in two. I scream. Kelly screams. Frank wheezes through the cotton.

*Home.*

The tear grows slowly seam by seam until the head separates completely from the body. I scream as my heart seemingly bleeds out inside my chest. Frank spits out the head.

"Chester!" Kelly screams.

Frank smiles down into the body, giving me a glimpse of his perfect teeth. All he sees is the white cotton stuffed into a teddy bear. He laughs and throws me to the ground. Kelly instantly lifts me up and reaches for the head but Frank kicks it further away from her. He forces Kelly to the ground. Kelly cries into the body. Her tears smear out on the cotton as I lay on the floor fighting to control my breathing and my pain.

Frank throws himself down on Kelly's back. "This is what happens when you make me angry," he says between his hyperventilating breathes.

He grabs her shirt and tears it apart. I get new memories of Ana from when Frank tore her clothes to pieces in front of everyone on the playground. How he then stood up and put his dirty shoe on her back and says.

"Guys, she is not even pretty enough to look at." He cleaned his shoes on her naked body.

"No, not that."

What monster is this? I think.

Frank leans closer to Kelly's face. His face gets between Kelly's and the hole in Chester's body.

"Do you know what dad calls girls like you?" He whispers in satisfaction. He inhales, I can almost see the sparks of tension in his breath. "He calls you sluts. You hear that? You are a slut. Just like Ana."

He arises, clearly satisfied with the result in front of him. "Just like Mrs. Danderby." Then he kicks her before running back to the others. "I will see you later."

And Kelly lies there with the cheering voices of kids in the background. One of them scored. She will not score a thousand goals today. Not even a hundred. Not even one. Kelly cries. Her thumb goes into her mouth. She crawls for Chester's head and hugs it with the body. I lay on the floor in Chester's body and feel the pain slowly decreasing. This is the worst day of my entire life. And worse is yet to come.

The toxic air slowly sips in through the hole. It burns, just not as much as the tears landing on the cotton where Chester's decapitated head used to be.

Mrs. Danderby blows the whistle to tell everyone it is time to pack up. Kelly hears it, she thugs Chester closer to her body. She arises and then she runs. She runs so no one has the chance to catch up to her with Chester close to her body and her thumb comfortingly in her mouth.

"Only babies suck on their thumbs." It is Frank's voice again, only this time as a memory.

Kelly runs to never come back. Never ever.

# Chapter 17

"Chester, I'm so sorry." Kelly tries to force Chester's head and body back together without success. "I'm so, so sorry."

Her tears drench the cotton that is Chester's intestines. None of them reach me. Only her world's poisonous air pours in through the opening in my once protective room.

"Don't be sorry," I say with a breath hurting all the way down from my lungs. "It is not your fault."

My comforts never reach her.

*Home.*

"What do you want me to do?" I scream weakly. I cough. "I am trapped here. Just like I've always been."

The voice answers with silence. As usual I must figure it all out by myself. I stand myself up, a feat far more devastating than it has ever been before. My pulse races inside my chest. Every beat creates a new wave of pain resonating through my body. I focus on each slow inhale and every steady exhale as I slowly adapt my body to the pain.

"He didn't mean anything he said," continues Kelly. She has buried her face in Chester's head.

Yes, he did. I look out through the hole and see Kelly's back through her torn shirt. Frank meant every word of it. What is worse is what more he meant. He will come after her for the rest of her life.

"We just hide here forever. We don't need anything, anyway. We got everything we need." Kelly mumbles into her teddy bear, but I do not believe her. Forever is a long time.

Mrs. Danderby yelled after Kelly as Kelly disappeared into the woods. She will be the first one to search for Kelly, and I am certain she knows were to search even though Kelly thinks her hiding place is so secret.

"See, we can even have a school." Kelly takes a notepad out of her backpack. "Today's word was miracle. We spell it like," She scribbles with big letters in the notepad. "Em-I-Are-A-Kej-EL." She checks the correct answer. "No, that wasn't right." She hesitates and touches the letters while she loudly spells them out. She stutters when she reaches C and bursts out crying. "I want Mrs. Danderby to be here and help me."

No one can help you, my dear angel. I clench my fist around my chest as a heartbeat throws a new set of razors through my veins.

I must do something, I think in panic. Anything.

As Kelly lays down in a pile of leaves and thinks about everyone she misses, I curl into a ball in a desperate attempt to ease the pain, but it only gets worse.

*Home.*

The floor warms. The déjà vu is too striking to be a coincidence. Heat, it seems to be the only way the whisperer knows how to communicate without repeating the same words over again. I lay still and feel how I slowly cook to death. Is this how you want me? Fried inside the prison you put me in. Flames burst close to me to scare me into action. The flame that burns my face actually gets my attention.

"What do you want?" I scream as I throw my body away from the stinging heat. "I can't do anything. I can't help anyone. I can't help her. Don't you understand!" I cry between my forced breaths. "I am useless."

The walls turn red from the heat except for where the dents in the wall create a ladder up. The ladder looks exactly as grey and dull as it always does. The floor gets hotter, and bursts of fire close in on me to push me towards the only place of safety. I throw myself at the dents just as the fire is about to burn my feet off. The dents are cool in contrast to the heat radiating against my back. The fire quickly covers the floor and pushes me upwards. It chases me up faster and faster, and I climb with the pain in my chest raging and my breath becoming heavier the higher I get. My sight blurs as the world slips away from me. The cool air from the outside brushes against my face, a welcome change to my stinging burns. Up here the air is only toxic, and the welcoming breeze gnaws in my lungs.

I reach the top where Chester's head is supposed to be but now Kelly's world begins.

*Warrior of the snake, save your home.*

Instinctively, I raise my hands towards the opening. The fire licks my feet in hunger for my flesh. The moment my hands touch the border between Chester's inside and the other world, a force pulls my hands closer and locks them in place. A tingling pain wanders through my hands, like small needles piercing through my skin. Panic berserks its way through my mind, overriding every other thought residing in my brain. I pull. I yell. I bite my hands to tear them loose. I do everything I can think of to escape, but nothing succeeds. Then my eyes widen as a clear blue liquid releases from my hands. My body goes numb as the liquid stretches for every corner of the hole.

*Blood.*

I register the whisperer's word, but it never breaks through my shocked mind fighting to regain control. My yells turn into screams. The more I scream, and the more I rip my hands away from the force locking me to the outside, the number I become. Suddenly I no longer feel my hands. Then, all my body's signals go silent. My body becomes nothing more than an empty shell hanging sloppily from the blue liquid. The blue liquid connects to all corners of the hole. The fires around me fade out. Everything turns back to the sterile cold room it once was and the blue liquid releases its grip on me, and I fall.

I hit the ground at the same time as I realize my breathing once again is painless.

This is too much, I think. As I think the words, a voice breaks into my home from the outside. Not Kelly's. Not Mrs. Danderby's. Not any girl's, or woman's voice.

"What are you doing here?" He asks.

# Chapter 18

I never noticed the sound of branches breaking, or feet stumbling through the woods. Neither of us did.

"What are you doing here?" he asks again.

A blunt feeling of exhaustion has spread itself into every limb of my body. I breathe, I am alive, but I am too tired to move. I look up through the blue tainted window which spread out from my hands only a few seconds ago. My whole view is Kelly's beautiful hair entangled in Chester's cotton.

"Hey, little girl. What are you doing here all alone?" I recognize the voice. My fight or flight reflexes curl back to where all my other bestial reflexes hide. I close my eyes and dare to let myself focus on surviving.

Kelly's head turns towards the voice. She sees him, the man doing what she considers to be impossible. He stands in her hiding place. This is a place where all turns invisible. She wipes away the tears on her arm. He is too big to fit through the pipe.

"What are you doing here?" She returns his question instead of answering. "How did you find my hiding place?"

The man laughs. I imagine his mustache wiggle with each chuckle.

"I'm taking a walk in the woods," Mr. Reston says. "It's such a beautiful day. I wouldn't want to miss an opportunity like this for anything in the world." Branches crack loudly under his feet as he moves closer. "Your hiding place you say?" He pauses to inspect her creation. "Quite amazing what you've done here. Are you sure you didn't get any help?"

Kelly shakes her head. "No, it was all me."

"Wow, you're quite the architect, aren't you? I would never manage to build something like this." He now stands right beside Kelly, and I get a glimpse of his shoes. His brown, comforting leather shoes.

A quick glimpse of pride shines through in Kelly's eyes, just to be smothered the next second by memories.

"Why are you hiding here anyway?" Mr. Reston continues when his question remains unanswered. "Shouldn't you be in a class by now?"

"I will never go to class again," She answers. "I will not go anywhere where Frank is. He hurt Chester." Kelly picks up Chester's head and hugs it. Her tears fight their way through her barricades once more. "He ripped of Chester's head. He is so mean."

"Oh." The joy in Mr. Reston's voice disappears. The view changes from Kelly to Mr. Reston's face as he picks up Chester's body to investigate the tear. "Frank Fuller." He gets a concerned look on his face. "That's truly one mean kid." He looks Kelly's way, and for the first time the joy runs of his face.

"Someday that kid is going to get the worst beating of his life," He sighs. He leans forward towards Kelly. "Don't cry dear. Everything will be okay."

"No," Kelly sobs. "Chester was my best friend."

She cries into Chester's face while Mr. Reston silently watches.

"You know what Kelly?" He says and caresses Kelly's cheek. "I can fix Chester at my workshop back at home. If you want me to?"

Kelly flinches in response to the caring touch. Mr. Reston immediately removes his hand from her face and puts it on his lap.

"You can?" She asks hesitantly.

"Yes, and I can armor him so Frank can never rip him apart again. Doesn't that sound great?"

Kelly nods. She takes Chester's lifeless body from Mr. Reston and hugs it with the head as if the hug would magically fuse them. She dries her tears off her face on Chester's fur. A spark of hope light up within her, warming the heart under my scales. I want to thank Mr. Reston for his ability to ignite it. I could kiss him if he let me close enough. A weak fanged kiss.

"Come, Kelly," Mr. Reston says. "Let us fix Chester. It will be like an adventure."

Kelly looks hesitantly at the reached-out hand before she grabs it. Mr. Reston lifts her up in one single movement and carries her away from the horrible hiding place. And as we get higher up, I can see the school on the other side of the road. It was never a good hiding place. Someone would have found her eventually, but gladly the one who found her was Mr. Reston. His car is parked not far away, not more than a hundred meters.

"Do you want to sit in the front seat?" He asks.

In Kelly's head, her mother's voice preaches, "Never enter a stranger's car."

Mr. Reston is no stranger. He is the owner of the toy store. He gave her Chester. He gave me Kelly. He is the kindest there is.

Kelly and I nod.

"Great," Mr. Reston continues and removes a small screen from the passenger seat, he taps on it and the screen goes black. "But you better buckle up because this car is like lightning." He puts her in the seat and makes sure the seat belt is buckled before he walks to the driver seat. "Do you know where I live?"

"No." Kelly shakes her head. She thinks the car smells funny. Like newly painted houses.

"Okay, then this day will be the best day of your life. Because my home is so amazing you won't believe it. It's just outside of the town. Two right turns and one hill away." He starts the car.

"There, there Chester," Kelly whispers to Chester's head as the car leaves the pavement. "Everything will soon be okay." Her mind pictures Chester after Mr. Reston has fixed him. A fur made from shining armor.

"One right turn," Mr. Reston says as he steers the car away from the school. "Only one turn and a hill to go."

We drive past Kelly's empty house. Not even her father is home anymore. Kelly stares at it until it disappears on the horizon. Her mind's eye sees her mother laying on the grass where her father pushed her. She cries again but continues to look out of the window, so no one will see.

Mr. Reston sees it though, but he never says a word of it for the entire trip.

# Chapter 19

Mr. Reston's house is not amazing. It is better. It is outstanding. the timbered walls and the round windows give it the look of an enormous ship, and a timbered ship is what Kelly sees, a large timbered ship made into a castle. Noah's ark, she thinks imagining the colorful drawings from one of her books, and I agree. Only the animals are missing, but Kelly's imagination puts them all into place on the ceiling and behind the curtains. I get the feeling her imagination is unnecessary, the animals are all there, stuffed with soft cotton awaiting all the happy children, just like in Mr. Reston's shop.

The drive here took a little more than half an hour. Fifteen minutes before Mr. Reston's car reached the second right turn and another fifteen minutes before we reached the hill. For most of the ride, all our views were trees and if Kelly would not have been occupied with processing her horrible morning, she would have considered each of them as beautiful as I did. Before Frank attacked her, she considered everything beautiful. An ability which in itself should be considered a miracle. Frank destroying it, should be considered a crime.

"I'm sorry but lightning isn't as quick as it used to be," Mr. Reston said excusably when Kelly asked why the trip took so long. A normal day, such an answer would have resulted in a giggling Kelly, but not today. She looked away drying new tears from her face with Frank's, and her father's, words echoing in her head.

"Do you know what dad calls girls like you? He calls you sluts. You hear that? You are a slut."

Her dad calls her mom slut.

Her eyes wander hesitatingly over the house towering in front of her. It really is enormous. Much bigger than any of the houses on her street.

"Do you live in a castle?" She asks.

It must be, I think. This building is not built for one man. It is built for his court.

Mr. Reston responds with one of his trademark chuckles. "Yes, I do. I even have a tower where a dragon guards princesses until the day a knight in shining armor comes along to save them." He points in the direction of a tower in the left-wing of the house. "But the day I have a princess to hide up there she won't want to be rescued. I will be her bravest knight in shining armor."

Kelly's imagination catches a quick glimpse of Mr. Reston's large mass in an even larger golden armor glistering in the sun. "Do you know who your princess will be, Mr. Reston?"

"Oh, I have my ideas of who it could be." As he answers he opens his imagined visor and winks at her. "But I have been fooled before. That's why I need a guarding dragon and a dungeon to store all my prisoners." He puts his hand on her shoulder and laughs as he sees her flinch. "Don't you worry. The dragon won't catch you. It captures those who want to hurt me, and you are the kindest girl in all of Vesterville. I'm so happy I get to show my home to you."

Kelly looks at him, and she actually smiles. It disappears quickly though. Quick enough to suffocate the warm light before it reaches my heart. Mr. Reston looks at her with a smile telling the world her joy is all he needs, and even though his smile gets notably smaller when the sadness grabs her once again, his shine never fades.

"Can I tell you a secret though?" He leans closer to Kelly with a comforting arm around her shoulders.

Kelly nods.

"You can't tell anyone about this place," he says. "You see, if people would find this place, they would try to take it from me. Could you keep this place secret for me?"

Kelly nods again. Her imagination has already built a picture of strangers tearing Mr. Reston's house apart, log by log. "I would never want for anyone to take your castle away, Mr. Reston."

"Great!" Mr. Reston continues to describe everything magical about his house with a tone indicating nothing other than energizing happiness. He is such a beautiful man, Mr. Reston.

"I have my own workshop right there." He points towards the rightest window. Threads in different colors hang from a bench blocking the view behind them. "You will get to see it later when I fix Chester. But prepare to drop your jaw because it is an amazing room."

Kelly nods, she scratches her jaw to check whether it's still there. Just in case.

"And if you look to the left you find the kitchen where I make the most delicious sandwiches." Mr. Reston continues and moves his finger to the window next to the workshop, and Kelly's imagination catches a glimpse of Mr. Reston in a chef's hat.

I observe his guidance from the floor in Chester's body. Everything gets a shade of blue from my blood. He tells Kelly his dad built the house for his big future family that never became big enough, and how Mr. Reston inherited it when his parents passed away.

"Do you want to come in?"

Kelly looks down into the hole where Chester's head used to be unknowing of how she looks straight down on my tired and lifeless body. My eyes meet hers. The blueish nuance from my blood colors her face. She is the prettiest there is, even through the filter of myself.

"Yes, Chester needs surgery now!" She says, a soft tremor makes itself known in her voice when she thinks of Frank putting his teeth to Chester's soft fur. "We can't wait much longer."

"Okay then!" Mr. Reston chuckles, his energizing happiness seems to increase even more as he opens the door. "Let us hurry to the workshop then."

The inside of the house looks almost exactly like the outside. Walls made of logs and circular windows. Photos hang on the wall with wooden frames melting in with the surroundings. They portray a mother, a father, and a small boy. A young Mr. Reston with his parents. The resemblance to his father is uncanny. All the faces look seriously into the camera. If I had energy left in my body for it, all the faces staring gravely at us would have sent a chill down my spine. Not a smile except the one hiding under Mr. Reston's mustache makes itself known in the room.

"Come here." Mr. Reston pushes Kelly in the direction of the workshop.

He opens another door. Kelly halts when she sees the wonders hiding behind it. Mr. Reston is already inside the room he calls his workshop, humming a song I have never heard before.

"Don't be scared, little child." He interrupts his humming to say. "The most dangerous thing in this room is me. Not even the needles can hurt you. Just do as I say, and everything will be fine."

Kelly steps over the threshold. She halts again. I only see the ceiling. But it is astounding, just like his store. It is covered with all kinds of planes, birds, and dragons hanging in strings. The colors are mindboggling even though I only see them from the blue filter of my blood. The view from Kelly's eyes leak into my vision and I get to see plush animals in all sizes and all colors. Zebras, snakes, lions, wolves, penguins, all build a wall of welcoming smiles.

"Is this a workshop?" Kelly asks. "It is bigger than my room. It is even bigger than mom's and dad's room."

Mr. Reston stops humming again, he chuckles. "Yes, I need a room like this to handle all my ideas. You see, this is where I create all my toys. Some of them I sell in my store but most of them I keep here at home. Even Chester here is one of my special creations."

Kelly looks down at me once again. "He is?"

"Absolutely! He is one of my dearest creations." Mr. Reston's face appears next to Kelly's. He grabs his hands around the belly of the teddy bear, letting his fingers stroke carefully over it, right about where the bulge is positioned. Kelly follows his every move, afraid to lose her precious teddy bear. "The plushies I make always tell me when those who choose them are in danger. That way I can always save you when you need me to."

"They do?" Kelly looks up at Mr. Reston without trying to mask her surprise. "Is that how you found me? Did Chester tell you I was in danger?"

"Yes, he did." He claps her on the back. "Chester wants to make sure you always stay safe here with me. After all, you chose him, and he loves you with all his heart for that. Just like I do." A shimmer in his eyes flare up, it makes him seem so happy. "Let's see if I remember this correct."

"But if you made Chester, aren't you angry Frank hurt him?" Kelly asks.

"Frank..." Mr. Reston sighs, his joyful flare briefly turns into ashes. If it would not have been the defense system Milton Marcsinzky had taught his daughter, I would never have noticed it. Every change in mood could mean danger, so goes the rules. The sight of Mr. Reston's eyes darkening spreads like an electrocuting shock through Kelly's body.

"I'm so sorry," she says with her hands instinctively raised to her face, just like her mother defends herself from a husband's punches. "I didn't mean to make you angry."

"What do you mean little girl?" Mr. Reston says, startled by her reaction. "I'm not angry with you." Mr. Reston glances down the headless teddy bear. "No, I only become angry with those who hurt my creations or me." Mr. Reston shakes away the shade of anger from his face. "But Frank will one day get what he deserves. You see, kids like Frank always get just that. Besides, I can fix this damage, and now I get to show the prettiest girl in the land my house." He takes a deep breath of excitement. "I'm so lucky you chose Chester. Do you mind if I take him for a minute?"

Kelly nods and hands me over. "I didn't want Frank to hurt. I just got too angry. Just like dad, I forget how strong I am when I'm angry. I once threw a chair across the kitchen." A quick glimpse of her lifting a chair when she tripped over it flashes by in my head. She lifted it way over her head and threw it away.

"You did?" Mr. Reston shifts his attention to Kelly and looks at her in amusement. His contagious smile manages to seep through Kelly's wall of sorrow but in the constant stream within her, it drowns as quickly as it breaks through. "We'll have to work on that temper of yours, don't you think so?" He ruffles her hair. It makes Kelly giggle. Her giggle makes me happy, tired but happy. "You really are a pretty one, aren't you?"

Mr. Reston's careful investigation of Chester's body continues. "Yes, we need a blue thread for this. One a little thicker so someone who tries to hurt Chester will break his teeth first."

I get to see the walls and a bench as the view changes. The walls are covered with drawings of a toy creator's ideas. Each drawing looks happier than the last. His bench is covered with different threads in all kinds of colors. His face blocks the view again as he takes a closer look at Chester's cloth.

"Have many kids have been here to visit you?"

"Only five. Six if we count you." The shade of his eyes turns grey again as he inspects the tear closer. "Sadly, very few have chosen to visit me yet. What happened between you and Frank anyway?"

"He was mean to Timmy." Kelly hesitates. "So, I kicked a football to the back of his head. Then he got angry and chased me. He pushed me and ripped my clothes." Kelly just now realizes how her shirt still has the back open. She tries to force the ends together, but they fall back down her sides. "Then he called me a slut and pushed me down like he did with Ana."

Kelly's thoughts get heavy as she relives the terrible moments in her head. Mr. Reston stops in the middle of pushing a blue thread through the eye of a needle.

"He did?" He asks. "Do you know what he meant by that?"

"No." Kelly sobs. "But it is not a nice thing to say. My dad calls my mother that and she always cries."

Mr. Reston puts down the needle and the thread and looks at Kelly. "No, it is not a nice thing to say at all. No one should ever have to be called a word like that." He picks up the needle again. "Not a single soul should be called that."

"I hear him scream at her some nights. He uses the word often when he thinks I'm asleep." Kelly's trip downwards memory lane deepens as she awaits Mr. Reston to finish working on Chester. "And afterwards mom goes to the bathroom and cries. Once I sneaked down to her, I didn't want her to be alone, but she screamed at me and told me to go to bed again. Dad doesn't know, he always falls asleep afterward."

Her voice dies of into silence.

"I'm so sorry you had to live through all that my child." Mr. Reston succeeds in pushing the thread through the needles eye. He puts a comforting arm around her shoulder. "My dad didn't treat people well either. That's why I am the way I am today."

He puts Chester's head on top of the body. Everything goes dark, then he removes his hand from Chester's eyes and two light beams form on the other side of my blue wall. Mr. Reston pushes the needle through the fabric as he stitches the head and body together. The needle tears through Chester's thick cloth and reaches into my home. The pointy end comes in and then disappears again. And it hurts.

So much.

My weak heart pumps the little blood I have left faster through my body. The needle goes through Chester's skin again. I scream. It goes through my blood wall and out through Chester's head again. I hyperventilate in the short break I get before the needle reenters Chester's skin.

"The way you are?" Kelly asks. Her voice is only just audible through my numbing pain. "But you sell toys. That's the best one can do."

The needle stops while going through Chester's neck.

"Please," I beg. My nerves wind together in a tense ball. Everything within me screams in pain. "Don't stop."

"Yes, I do, and yes, it is. Especially when I get to meet children like you. When you choose to be with me, I am as happy as a toy store owner can be. Just as my father was happy when I chose to spend time with him," Mr. Reston says and continues sowing. "I will always be grateful for those moments, and what he taught me about living my life."

"What did he teach you?"

Mr. Reston stops again, he let the needle stay in Chester's fur for far too long before answering her question. "To always wait until someone chooses to come. Just like I chose my father. I must wait until someone chooses me before I can be truly happy."

"Who chose you?"

Mr. Reston ignores her question and Kelly lets her curiosity go in favor of studying Mr. Reston's craft.

The sowing gets faster. The breaks I get are now so short I don't even get the time to breathe. Kelly waits patiently for her teddy bear to become whole once again. Mr. Reston sticks the needle one last time into Chester's neck. I am completely numb, biting my tongue just to stay afloat but it doesn't help much. He pulls the thread and ties a tiny knot over the last stitch.

"There you go!" He bursts out enthusiastically.

The blue wall shatters, falling in raindrops back to me. They are rejuvenating against my scales. Without thinking I open my mouth to catch them. It tastes like metal. I laugh. It feels so good. Every drop falling over me is new energy exploding into my body. The drops missing me, guide themselves to my skin as if there was one collective consciousness guiding them. My skin absorbs every drop greedily with small stings every time they penetrate my scales. The stings are pleasant and awake me with shocks of euphoria.

I gasp for air. I am whole again. Chester is whole again.

"See, you can't even see the stitches," Mr. Reston continues proudly.

I rise from the ground, full of new energy, and I climb, no I jump, up on the dents. I want to see as much as possible of Mr. Reston's world in my new chance of life. Kelly's smile, I want to see her smile.

I reach the stitches between Chester's head and body. They have become one with the wall. They could as well have been there from the beginning. I celebrate in loud shouts of happiness. Somehow, I survived. We survived, I tell myself. Both I and Kelly survived.

Thanks to Mr. Reston. The wonderful mustached man saved us.

"Wow," Kelly says with her sweet voice, it has never been so beautiful before. "No one will ever notice it. I can't wait to show mom this."

I stretch my head to the windows just in time to see the view bounce up and down as Kelly jumps while hugging Chester tightly. She throws us in the air and catches us again. A joyful rollercoaster I'm more than willing to experience again and again. In the corner of the window, Mr. Reston stands. The wonderful man who saved Chester and me. I want to kiss him. Preferably without scaring him to death. His smile... I missed it. I missed all of it. My euphoria suddenly runs off me. His smile is not the one I'm used to seeing. His attention is all directed towards Kelly with a black fire in his eyes. It's haunting. I focus on him with the small glimpses I get before Chester flies again.

I put it in all the plush animals I create. His voice repeats in my head along with a nagging feeling. It lets me know if my creations ever are in danger. He was out driving early, much earlier than he ever has been in the toy store. Much earlier than anyone ever has been in the toy store.

Kelly's cheering slowly dies off as she also notices it. He seems to be nervous with anticipation. But for what?

"Why aren't you happy?" Kelly asks.

Mr. Reston's smile grows bigger, and his fire burns stronger. "I'm happy my little girl. The happiest man there is. Maybe you want to take Chester for a stroll around the house while we make sure the stitches won't go up."

"What a great idea! Come on Chester let's go for a walk." Kelly's happy voice sounds like shimmering bells in my ears, she immediately forgets Mr. Reston's odd behavior.

"What should we look at first?" She asks.

"Oh, if you take look over there you will see the dragon guarding my tower." He points in the direction of a plush dragon standing on a pedestal in front of a door. "Don't you see how fearsome he is?"

"No. Chester is not scared of dragons. He knows how to make any dragon a kind lizard."

"That's great! Every girl needs a hero who can fight dragons." Mr. Reston's trademark chuckle shows no sign of the weirdness his face could not hide. "And if you look over there, you will see the door to my dungeon."

Chester stops walking. I look straightly at a door just next to the one to the tower.

"What are you hiding in your dungeon?"

"All my trophies, and the shining armor of the knights who have fallen while fighting my dragon."

"That sounds scary!"

"Even for Chester?"

The view changes to Kelly's face. She makes Chester nod. I also nod.

"Yes, it scares him."

"What do you think of the tower?"

"I think it must have the best view in the world," Kelly says. Except from the view from my window, she thinks.

"I'm glad you feel that way, my little princess." Mr. Reston walks up to the door. His haunting smile still on his face, his eyes with the same charring fire. "Because you have chosen to live there." He opens the door.

Both my heart and Kelly's stop. What did he say?

"I won't live there," Kelly stutters. "I live with mommy and daddy."

"I'm sorry Kelly." Mr. Reston sits down on one of his knees, so he is at eye-level with Kelly. "But you can't live there anymore." He is serious. That's the haunting in his eyes. They are glimmering. He is nervous but happy. "You've chosen to live with me."

"No, I haven't!" Kelly picks up Chester and hugs him, and me. The joy sparkling within her suddenly turns heavy. "Mom and dad will miss me. Chester wants me to be with them."

"Chester wants me to be happy too, and I'm only happy if you are here," Mr. Reston says. "Isn't it so, Chester? And, your parents, they won't miss you, my dear Kelly. They never liked you." He pauses, thinking and searching for words. "And besides, you see, they are dead."

Kelly stops breathing. Her mind goes into a paralyzed state. She falls. I fall. We both hit the ground.

They must be alive, I think. They were alive this morning. But the look in Mr. Reston's eyes tell me different. He smiles.

They are dead now.

"You see, Kelly. You only have me now, me and Chester." He leans forward and puts his hand on Chester's head. "I beg you to do as I say because if you betray me, I have to hurt you. And Chester doesn't like traitors."

Kelly stares hollowly into Mr. Reston's smiling face. Her mind pictures her mother's bloodied body she remembers from so many times before, but this time the blood is not because of her father. He lays beside her with the same bruises and scratches he gives his wife. Kelly's heart breaks. She cries. She tells herself it's impossible while she knows all too well what people are capable of.

"No don't cry, my dear little girl." Mr. Reston leans closer to us and hugs us.

Kelly flinches from the touch. She tries to break loose, but he pushes her closer. He kisses her on the lips. He is the first one except her parents to do so.

"Don't try to run away from me, darling. You will learn to like it here, and you will learn to like me." He puts his hand on the back of her head and pushes her closer until her head rests on his shoulder. "I'm sorry my child but you chose this life. We have to live up to that deal, okay?"

Mr. Reston smiles, his glimmer is now a full glow. He enjoys the hug he forces upon Kelly.

I realize what I see is his true self that has been hiding within him. It is the devil behind the mask.

# Chapter 20

The truth is laid up in front of me, but the more I understand the less comprehensible it gets. The pieces are too uneven to fit. There has to be an explanation.

Kelly's father killed her mother and shot himself, I think. That has to be it. From what I've seen, he is more than capable. That must be the truth. Mr. Reston spares Kelly the horror of coming home. Mr. Reston is kind. He has to be. Then I think of Mr. Reston's smile and his kiss, and it tells me another truth.

"Did you kill them?" Kelly tries to push her head away from Mr. Reston, but he holds her firmly against his shoulder, not letting her move anywhere.

The heavy silence speaks a thousand words. Kelly screams when she realizes the meaning behind his silence.

"No," I mumble.

"I did what was necessary."

She kicks with her feet and punches with her hands to get lose from him. Nothing she does loosens Mr. Reston's grip on her, it only tightens until she can't move anymore, and every attempt results in nothing but small spasms.

"Hush, my child. It is no use to fight it." He rocks her back and forth. "Hush now."

"Why?" Kelly cries into his shoulder, desperately.

The pointers on the clock behind them wander over the board as minutes become hours, and Mr. Reston rocks Kelly like a mother rocks her newborn child.

"Hush." He continues to say and slowly caresses the back of her head.

"No," I mumble the word so many times it loses its meaning. It is just a word to express the tangled mess of thoughts in my head. Kelly's sorrow layers on top of the mess in a loop going deeper and deeper. The whole time Mr. Reston heartlessly comforts Kelly for what he caused her.

"If you only let me, I can give you a better life than what your parents could have given you. We can be so happy."

It is a promise neither of us believes.

"You are not my mom!" Kelly cries. "You are not my dad."

"No, I am better."

"Why did you kill them?" Kelly asks again.

"Because I wanted you."

"Why did you want me?"

"Because you choose me."

The heaviness within Kelly instantaneously bursts into flames. Her tears dry out from the heat now rampaging freely under her chest.

"I never chose you." She yells into his ear. "I want to be with my mom and dad. Not you."

"No, you chose me." He kisses her on the forehead. His mustache scrapes against her skin as thorns of a rotten rose.

"NO!"

The boiling rage is contagious.

Do it, I think. Do it! Let him feel the pain he has caused you.

My encouragement is unnecessary.

She bites him in the neck as hard as she can, just as he is about to declare she chose him. Instead, he roars. He pulls her away, but she has bitten into his skin. Drops of metal leave him for her tongue and she bites harder. He grabs her by the hair and loosens his grip around her body. At the same time, she releases him. His hand releases her hair and moves to the bite mark she left him.

She is free. That's all she needs. She runs towards the front door. It is locked. Both our hearts sink in our chests. But she continues along the hallway until she reaches the door to the workshop. Her heart beats so hard it drums in my head. It makes it harder for her to breathe. The door opens when she moves the handle. The sound of Mr. Reston's heavy steps echoes across the hallway. He yells after us.

"Where?" She thinks through the noise of her heartbeat and her heavy breaths.

The panic thunders as every hiding place she finds is a bad one. His steps get closer. She runs to the table and hides under it among all the small pieces of cloth. She tugs Chester and me closer to her.

"Everything will be okay. Chester." She whispers. "I promise. I chose you, not him. You will save me. Please tell me you will save me. Please tell me you won't help him."

I reach to the window and press my hand against the cold surface to get as close to her as possible.

"Yes, I will save you," I say. "Everything will be okay."

It is desperate, I know, but I must do something. He closes in on the door. I force myself against Chester's inside and push myself out. I hold my breath. Kelly never looks up. She cries into her dear teddy bear, convincing them both everything will be okay. I run between the cloth, to the door, and beg for this to work. I force down one poisonous breath.

"Blood." I push my hands in front of me, using nothing but my hope on it to work.

The stinging sensation wanders over my hands. It numbs me as the blue blood spreads slowly. I need it to be bigger than before, much bigger. It reaches the size of the hole it covered in Chester. I force it further.

"Blood." Every vein in my body screams, every organ shuts down from blood loss. "Blood!" I scream, pushing more blue out of my empty shell of a body.

His steps sound outside the door. He knows Kelly hides in here. I push the covering shield further, and feel my knees give in from weakness. He slams the door open.

"Kelly!" He screams.

"Blood!" I roar.

The first step he takes inside the room goes right through my protecting shield. I fall to the ground with a sigh and the shield shatters.

"Kelly!" He screams again. He goes silent, listening for Kelly's mumbles of comfort. "I know where you are."

The words scare me. They also fill me with energy, and when the blood slowly recollects in my body I get up on my feet.

"No!" I run towards him screaming.

I climb up on the cloth, standing between Kelly and him, pushing my hands against him again and force my blue blood to create another force field around Kelly and me. It has become red just like the blood dripping from Mr. Reston's neck. He stretches his hand through it without knowing it. Kelly is not mumbling anymore.

"Everything will be okay!" She cries, loud and scared.

Mr. Reston shoves all the pieces of cloth to the side and throws me across the room.

"Everything will be okay."

"I told you not to make me angry!" Mr. Reston screams into Kelly's face.

He smacks her, just as her father used to do with her mother. The little girl's tears spread across the room. One of them lands by my side.

"You will pay for this scar." He lifts her up in the hair, shaking her. "You are just like the rest of them! You don't deserve my tower!"

Kelly screams. She remembers all too well that this is how her father used to treat her mother. Mr. Reston will drag her to the bedroom. He will punish her, he will scream at her, he will call her bad words even though he said he didn't like them. She cries, she knows her life is over. I know it too. But I can't let myself believe it. Mr. Reston drags her across the workshop. In my dizzy state, I chase after them with nothing but toxic air in my lungs and in my veins. I reach them and claw myself to the shield around Kelly's foot protecting her world from mine. I climb up to Chester and throw myself up to his head. I am close enough to touch Mr. Reston's hand. I stretch for it.

But Kelly drops us.

Right outside the door to Mr. Reston's dungeon, she drops me and Chester. Leaving us and forcing herself to go through Mr. Reston's hell alone.

"Chester!" She screams, then she sobs. "Save me."

Mr. Reston lifts her up, so she looks straight into his eyes.

"Do you think he will save you?" He spits. "He is my creation. He always helps me. Who do you think gave you to me?"

He opens the cellar door and throws her in front of him. And no matter how fast I run, I don't reach them before he closes the door.

My sight darkens from too much toxic air, but I won't go back to the safety in Chester. I will always stand by the door, fighting to save her. I succumb and fall to the ground. Drowning in the images of how Kelly's life is forever destroyed and her pain while Mr. Reston throws her on a table. The pain fills her mouth when her teeth hit the hard surface. The metallic taste fills her mouth again. Her fear rampages when he rips the last pieces of her clothes off. First the already torn shirt. Then the shorts, her shoes, and her socks. Somehow, even though she has never seen what her father does to her mother, she knows what will happen. Pain strong enough to break bones strikes when he punches her almost unconscious as she tries to cover herself. Her cries become a whimper. Her fear gets numbed as she drifts into unconsciousness. She is ready to die now. She is ready to join her parents, in whatever place Mr. Reston put them. Mr. Reston rips away the last piece and his own clothes. And Mr. Reston pushes himself towards her. Into her. The pain is worse than death. And still, it gets worse, even when it seems impossible, it does. The pain is endless until he spread himself in her, and she finally faints. The last terrifying thing she hears is his sigh of relief.

Everything is dark, and I'm convinced this is the end. I await it. The end for both Kelly, and me. In the background, a blue ghost screams at me.

"What are you doing?" He says. "Did you really think you stood a chance? You must be out of your mind to believe something like that"

The blue ghost drags me away to the fangs of the dragon and all my senses of reality fade away.

# Chapter 21

I never realize I pass through the dragon's plush wall. My fogged thoughts grasp at every tiny straw to make sense of what just happened, but they never succeed. I am dying, I must be, with all this pain flooding my brain, how can I and Kelly be heading anywhere else than the afterlife? My body hits the floor. The pain changes form, from explosive and devastating to constant and numbing.

"What were you thinking?" It is lecturing me, the blue ghost from my afterlife. It has turned grey. "Did you really think you stood any chance in saving her? You are completely moronic, you know that?" It gives off a loud sigh. "But then again you are just like the rest of them, aren't you?" It walks off into the blurred shadows, then it comes back again, and then it's gone. My vision slowly refocuses and forces the shadows back to my periphery where they belong and finds the light which shouldn't exist among the dead. The ghost continues pacing back and forth. It takes shape. The two-legged creature gestures at me all while constantly screaming at my face, it condemns me. Its face takes shape, grey scales form out of blurred contours and yellow eyes emerge from two cavities among them. My consciousness awakens with a shock that forces my body into reaction. I awake, startled and terrified, and back away from it as far as I can, all while screaming my heart out.

"Finally!" The ghost declares triumphantly, but it is no ghost anymore. He is a lizard on two legs, with sharp fangs and clawed hands. The same horrific monster haunting me in all my reflections now stands in front of me. My back hits a wall. I continue my escape just to push myself harder against the wall.

My feet slow down as my thoughts catch up with me.

"Feeling like leaving already?" The monster asks. "Go ahead, run out to your cute teddy bear and hide."

In reflex, I look up and find the two light beams that connects this room to the outside world. My breathing slowly returns to my control. I look back at the reptile who studies me from afar. He smiles.

"Yes," he says. "But the faster route would be straight through the wall."

"Where are we?" I ask, my mind immediately throw a more urgent question into my mouth. "Where is Kelly? Is she dead?"

My tongue halts as one last question lingers on my thoughts. "Are we dead?"

The other gives me a long look then he nods, and calmly sits on the hard floor.

"Kelly is alive," he says. "She's not feeling good, but she's alive."

"How can you know?" I ask hesitantly. "Have you seen her?"

"No, I just know," he answers. "And, besides, if she was dead, you wouldn't be feeling as well as you do either."

Well? I think. I am not feeling well. I am in pain. I glance at the light beams and the freedom they symbolize. Pain must mean she is alive. I turn and scan the wall. Curved, just like Chester's.

The other sits completely still until I once again meet its gaze. I flinch from the sight of him, and my heartbeat once again breaks out of my control.

"Let me guess," he continues. "You don't know if you can trust me. After all, I'm just like you, and who can trust something like us. Beasts in snakeskin, completely under the possession of our animalistic instincts. Is that correct?"

He glares at me in what I only can translate as contempt. My pulse slows down a couple of beats. I nod.

"Great," he says. "Just so you know, instincts fade. And if my word isn't enough for you, just look into yourself. If she's alive, you'll feel it. If she isn't." He shrugs. "I guess you will feel it too. The other ones did at least."

"Other ones?" I ask.

"Other ones," he confirms while he turns away from me. "Go on, see if she is alive. I know you want to."

I close my eyes, fighting the instincts to not lower my guard around the monster in front of me. I search in my mind and my heart for any connection. I find it immediately. Her heartbeat, and her breathing. Under it, I also hear the deeply hurt thoughts processing what just happened to her, taking their form in haunting nightmares of Mr. Reston's satisfied sighs. It is all there, just hidden under all the pain running amok.

"Are you convinced?"

I open my eyes only to see the other standing so close to my face that I can taste his breath. I flinch and instinctively scream. A smile tears his face apart as he sees me fail to run further into the wall.

"Why did you do that?" I ask with my breath caught in my throat.

The other leans closer to me. He smiles. Our scales touch.

"Because I wanted to see you up closer." His smile disappears. "Will you trust me now?"

I don't answer. Not with him this close.

"Fair enough." He says interpreting my silence as a no, which it is. "Raphael did not trust me either."

Once again, his mention of other ones like us startles me. The horrifying confirmation that I'm not the first one this lizard has encountered in Mr. Reston's residence.

"Raphael?"

"Yes, Raphael. You are the fifth to cross my path." He studies me. "And I guess I'm the first to cross yours."

I nod. "Did they all come in a toy with a child?"

He looks at me with a thoughtful expression. "Yes, they all did." He walks away to the other side again and sits calmly on the floor.

"Did you also come here with a child?"

His eyes go wide open. For the first time, he hesitates. "Yes, but not like you. I and my child moved here when the house was built a long time ago." He sighs. "I, and little Richie. For you, that is Richard who just threw Kelly down the stairs, and... Yes, we both know what happened next." He closes his eyes and looks away. "I'm sorry for that by the way."

"Mr. Reston is your child?" The reveal hits me surprisingly hard, I should have seen it. It's Mr. Reston's dragon after all. "But he isn't a nice child. He is a cruel man."

The other flinches. "I wouldn't say that again if I were you," he wheezes.

But he is cruel, I think. I force myself to not utter the words.

"And Richie was a nice kid once," the other continues. "The nice kid is just hidden under all the other layers that have drowned his better self."

I find that hard to believe, especially after what he just forced my Kelly through.

"Who are you?" I ask instead of ventilating my thoughts.

"Me? I am a warrior of the snake just like you. I am Sariel. And your name is?"

"Gabriel." How long have Sariel warrior of the snake guarded someone who brings darkness to children, I am about to ask. I instantly realize what a bad idea that would be.

"How long have you guarded Richie?"

Sariel frowns.

"Not as long as you may think," he answers. "At one point the guarding became pointless."

"When he began destroying other children?" I ask before I can stop my mouth from talking. I regret it instantly.

Sariel gives me a sharp look.

"No, it was earlier." He looks away. "One day you will stop trying too if you are unlucky. The other ones never got that far."

"Me giving up on Kelly?" His words strike trough me in boiling pulses. "I will never stop protecting her!" I spit in his direction.

My words bring a smile to Sariel's face. "How cute. I hope you are right. I have only heard that too many times before. Four times to be exact." He walks over to me. I don't back away from him this time. I wish for him to dare a little closer so my fangs can reach him quicker.

"But you are always proven wrong." Sariel sighs. Just like Mr. Reston's chuckle, the sigh must be Sariel's trademark sound. "Just like I was a long time ago. The Pain-screamers here always wins. They break every warrior and destroy every child. Those lucky get to die. Those unlucky get to see their Love twist into the man downstairs. Just imagine, your lovely girl somehow surviving this hell just to become the very essence of all she fears. Just imagine her hurting others, all in the name of love."

"My Kelly would never hurt anyone!" The burn in my veins bursts me up on my feet. Sariel is thrown back and he loses his balance

She is nothing like the monster your Richie is," I scream into his face.

Sariel looks at me, startled. Then his face turns ash grey.

"She is," he whispers. "If she somehow survives long enough for the Pain-screamers to get to her, she will become the worst murderer imaginable. And you will do nothing to stop it." He stops and looks to the wall.

"I think you should return to your dear teddy bear now," he then continues and turns to me. "Richie is waking up and now, when he has calmed down, he might give Kelly her teddy bear back. You know, something to comfort her when she is alone in the dark."

I stare at him with my claws ready to carve in between his scales. The bitter expression on his face is toxic just like everything else about him.

"Come on now, leave," he says and points towards the wall. "Your teddy bear is that way. Come on, I know you know how to do it. Or do you want me to throw you out? I can, but it will hurt a lot more."

Down the cellar, Mr. Reston's heavy steps echo against the stairs. The sound pushes the blood thirst back into my spine.

"Kelly." I turn to the wall and push myself towards it.

"Just remember," Sariel says. "Kelly will die here. Both of you will. Do yourself a favor and just let her go."

I glare back at him.

"Never," I say and continue to push myself out.

# Chapter 22

I hold my breath and run all while I promise myself to never look back at the dragon and the traitor living within it again. I jump down from the platform on which the dragon resides. Air involuntarily leaves my lungs as I land, and for a short moment, the shock silences Mr. Reston's echoing steps.

As Chester's blue cloth rises in front of me Mr. Reston exits his precious dungeon and crosses the floor, but not in the direction of Chester. No, he walks towards his dragon. Not even a glance is given to the teddy bear.

"Did you see her?" He says and picks up the green dragon. "She is so beautiful." Mr. Reston hugs the dragon, and from where I stand, just two steps away from Chester, I see the love between a child and his favorite plush shine through. "I think she can be the one. Did you see her face? She loved this place. I think she likes me too." He hesitates. "But she hurt me... and I hurt her. Can I really trust someone who hurts me?"

The love that must be Richie looking out through Mr. Reston's hide glows. Sariel looks out through Dongo's eyes. The lizard looks back at him with adoration radiating from him. The same adoration I feel every time I watch Kelly, and every time I get to be a part of Kelly's hug. Sariel notices me, he shakes his scaled head while closing his yellow eyes. He loves little Richie back with all his heart, and yet he seems to not care for the hurt Mr. Reston inflicts on others. He cares little for protecting little Richie from the Nightmares.

He cares for nothing of it.

"What do you say Dongo? Do you think we should give her the teddy bear back? Yes, you are right, we should."

Mr. Reston puts Dongo back on the platform. Sariel disappears. He has refueled on love from the monster he himself has created. I run the few steps left and push myself to safety. I immediately fill my lungs with new clean air. I am briefly relieved, but the feeling is quickly forgotten as my worries for what Mr. Reston is about to do eats it all up. He lifts us up until he and Chester are eye to eye.

"Do you wish to see our dear Kelly again? Of course you do. Maybe you can make her better."

Is it tears on his face? The ugly tears of fake sorrow as he convinces himself he is sorry for the pain he caused her. He loved every part of it, nothing he does can ever change that.

I hate you.

Mr. Reston gives us a hug.

If I could, I would rip his eyes out and feed him with them. Then I would force him to puke them up and feed him with them again. All while I slowly cut his body into pieces. I want it so bad. I hold my breath and push myself out. I lean out through the window and point my fangs towards his throat. I can't hurt him, but the satisfaction of pushing my teeth so close to his life is all I need. Seeing Sariel watch me through Dongo's eyes makes it even better. At least now he feels the same for me as I do for him.

"Will you please tell her I'm sorry for hurting her too?"

I reach my claw out, and scratch the shield protecting him.

"Never," I whisper.

He releases me and Chester and looks at us with tear dripping happiness. He hides it behind what he thinks regret looks like, but it is happiness.

"Thank you," he says.

"I will kill you," I whisper into his ear. "And you will suffer through every second of it."

He looks at me with the delight of thinking he manipulated Chester into believing he didn't love every minute of hurting the little girl in the cruelest way possible. Not even Chester is that dumb. That's right, not even a hollow teddy bear without a brain or consciousness is stupid enough to believe the lies he tells it. He fooled us once, but it will never happen again.

"Not even him!" I scream in his face, hoping some of my spit gets through to him. "You don't even fool him!" My spit falls against his shield. When not even conscience sticks on him, how could spit?

"Let's take you down to her, okay? She might wake any second."

She isn't awake, she isn't even close to awake. Her mind is so deeply spun around the nightmare she just lived through she won't wake up for long. Her screams haunt every moment of her dreams. Dead parents float around under Mr. Reston's sighs. His happiness reaches its climax. It repeats itself. The scenes start over, and over, and over again. In the center of it all Kelly cries uncontrollably.

Her hurt, her trauma and her destruction. All in a constant stream.

Kelly will never truly understand what happened to her. When she does not understand how much he wronged her, when she does not understand how much hate she is allowed to feel, I will hate for her. I will find a way for revenge.

He lifts us down the stairs.

"Here's your little princess," he says. "She is so pretty when she sleeps, don't you think?"

Pretty. Beautiful. Cute. The words have a different meaning when he says them. For him, they are an expression of perversion. The words are filthy now. The innocence in them is forever spoiled. He walks up to her.

Don't you even dare to get closer to her, I think.

He does anyway. He touches her. He caresses her cheeks with traces of her dried tears still visible on them. He removes hair from her face.

"I'm sorry," he says. "I never meant to hurt you, but just like you, I lose my temper. I hurt people when I get hurt." He studies Kelly's face under her wet hair. "We are supposed to love each other, you know. You will learn that one day. When you do, you will like everything about me and my home. Then, we can be happy together. Just like when I learned to love my father."

I'm about to scream at him. I want to run on Chester's arms and scream so close to his face as I can get. I want to scream so loud his shield no longer manages to block the sound. But the view of Kelly interrupts me. The pool of blood between her legs. The traces of him diluting the red color. The bruises on her body. The bruise on her eye from one punch she got when she resisted him. She had no chance, but she tried anyway, and it only caused her more harm.

"No," I say with tears dripping from my face. "Oh, please no. My little Kelly, please no."

This must be a nightmare. Nothing else fits, but I never have nightmares. I never sleep. I only faint, and that unconsciousness is dreamless and empty.

"Take good care of her for me, Chester."

I look at him with tears still dripping from my face. I will take care of her, but not for you. He nods believing he and I have an agreement. He then puts me, and Chester on Kelly's naked chest. He moves Kelly's arms into a hug around Chester and me.

"You will forgive me one day," he says and then walks up the stairs.

I immediately leave Chester's inside and run over to Kelly's face. I hug it. I don't know what to do. I want to tell her to wake up, but the reality is worse than her dreams. I can't tell her to stay asleep either because her nightmares will drive her insane. So, I just hug her watching my tears dripping down on her face and run down her shield. I will never be able to truly comfort her. I am nothing. My lungs give in. I consider the thought of letting myself die by her side, but the thought of leaving her alone with the Nightmares tonight, or any other night, makes me want to live. I run back to Chester and breathe for as long as I need to restore my strength, then I run back out to her again. The cycle is repeated more times than I care to count.

Upstairs, Mr. Reston whistles. I thought it was a new level of her nightmares, but it isn't. It is Mr. Reston whistling upstairs while dancing with heavy steps across the house. Monsters like him should not be allowed happiness.

Kelly finally wakes up when I am into one of my recovery sessions. In the middle of one of my inhales, I hear her. It starts with a subtle sob. Nothing more. I'm not nearly as recovered as I need to be. Yet, I strain myself, and once again push against the wall. She screams. It is the heart-wrenching scream of terror when she realizes her worst nightmare was real. Her scream escalates as I enter her world. She tries to cover herself with nothing but her hands to aid her. I run up to her, crossing the pool of her blood she now sits in.

"Mom." She screams in one dragged-out word. Her voice cracks both from pain and the realization that her mom never will answer her call again. But she continues to scream for her savior anyway.

"Please," I say, wasting the little air I have on useless words. "I want to help you."

She notices the blood when she accidentally puts her hand in its sticky pool. She knows it is her own, she felt it leave her when Mr. Reston violated her. She stands up in a reflex to run away from all her problems. Her sudden movement throws me across the table, and I fall. Kelly's pain as her body stretches out is excruciating, something breaks inside her, and the pool under her fills with more fresh blood. Her screams fill the room as I hit the floor.

I force myself to stand and climb back on the chair. The air in my lungs is not close enough. In truth, my lungs are empty. Kelly's scream turns into a scrambled mess as my brain fails to process the information. Its only goal is to survive long enough to reach Chester.

I crawl the last few steps. During the last steps, my sense of the ground disappears. My world becomes Kelly's mumbling screams. With her heartbreak screaming in my ears, I stretch myself towards where I remember Chester sitting and I go through his skin. My muddled numbness slowly dies off and my brain reawakens. The panic Kelly transfers through our connection grows into a storm. I let myself take on more breath. Then I prepare to run out one more time.

*Blood.*

The whispered word startles me. I look at my hands, remembering the last time the word was spoken to me. It created a shield protecting me from the outside. I raise my hands and push them in front of me. I force the tingling feeling. The blue color spreads slowly. I take one deep breath and push it. I order the wall to bend with my thoughts. Kelly's feelings rampaging freely between my thoughts motivate me to push even after I should give up. It bends. The blue slowly wanders down my scales and up my arms. It bends over my head and under my feet. My sight flickers as my body adapts to the decreased blood volume flowing in my system. Click. The sound in the back of my head echoes as the blue blood connects behind me. I condemn the voice for not telling me everything from the start and run through the wall. I breathe. Nothing burns in my lungs. I breathe again and then I know, it works.

Kelly has fallen back on the table, with her back in the red pool and a new one spreading under her. She holds her hand on her lower stomach and bends in response to the pain. I freeze at the sight of her. She has smeared blood all over her body and face.

What can I do to help her?

She looks at her blood again, then she drags her hand between her legs and looks at the blood now coloring her fingers. She suddenly stops screaming, she just looks at the red color. Her thoughts go from a screaming mess to complete silence. The crack when she breaks is loud as an explosion. She lays down doing nothing but looking at her fingers. I walk up to her and put my hand on her hair. It is two firm walls against my hands. My own blue wall, and the one separating me from her world. I push myself closer until it resembles a hug.

"I'm sorry," I say. "I'm sorry, I couldn't be there for you."

"Chester," she says.

The movement her hair makes when she talks pushes me away. I stumble as I regain my balance.

"Where are you?"

She is met by silence.

"I'm just here," I whisper, "right next to you."

She moves. Her bloodied hand supporting her weight while she painfully sits up.

"Where are you?" She repeats. She looks around. Her eyes wandering right past me and lock on the teddy bear.

"Chester, I need your help."

"Do you think he will save you?" Mr. Reston had said. "He is my creation. He always helps me. Who do you think gave you to me?" The words are still fresh in her memory, but she chooses to believe none of it. She needs her bear in shining armor to comfort her. She puts her faith in the traitor who put her here.

Chester's stone face keeps its mouth shut. She sits up on all four. The expression on her face is one of total pain.

"No, Kelly," I beg.

Her bleeding worsens. But she crawls. The crawl drains all her powers. Her fight is heart-wrenching to watch. She stretches her arm to the blue teddy bear and grabs him by the foot. She falls flat on the table still holding it. I walk up to her. I touch the shield covering her hair. Her face is drenched in sweat, tears, and determination. She pulls him towards her one weak pull at the time, and he slowly curls in her direction. For a moment she stops to catch her breath. I get my hopes up for her to realize she should save her strength and not waste it on a useless teddy bear. Then she pulls him one more time. Chester is close enough for her to reach him with both her hands. She curls into a little ball with him entangled between her arms and legs.

"Chester." She stains his blue fur red. "Please help me."

She hugs him harder. His head twists as her arms almost decapitate him, but Mr. Reston's threads hold, just as promised. For the first time I agree with her. Chester, please help her. She really needs the hero who can drag her out of this hell. We both know he can't do anything. He is just teddy bear.

I walk up to Chester's strangled head. I put my hand on him.

"How can we help her?"

He is crying. It is Kelly's tears running down her face, past his blue fur, and down his glass eyes. But his tears are real. We both are crying.

And as we all three cry Mr. Reston whistles one of his favorite tunes. He breaks into song. The cellar door opens. His steps echo through the room while he slowly walks every step down the stairs to visit Kelly once again.

# Chapter 23

His steps sound like a doomsday clock. Twelve steps, twelve loud, haunting chimes.

"Chester please help me," Kelly begs.

Her plead will be unanswered. Chester won't help her. He is Mr. Reston's creation after all.

I want to help her, but I am just as useless. All I can do is stand in the monster's way and watch as he walks right past me and assaults the only one I love. So, that's what I do. I stand up, look one last time at Kelly's face pushed into Chester's neck, and put myself between her and the demon now walking across the floor. He holds a serving plate in his right hand, the left he hides behind his large body. What he wants us to believe is his walk of shame looks pathetic.

I put my hands up and redirects my blue shield to protect Kelly. It breaks immediately as he puts down the plate behind me. I fall back, not allowing myself to catch my breath.

"How are you feeling little girl?" The demon asks.

"You don't touch her," I wheeze while I regenerate my blood.

Kelly answers with silent sobs. She is scared that anything she says will make him angry.

I force my blood out one more time. I put all my energy into the blue formation creating in front of me. I don't allow myself for a minute to believe the truth. The truth is that all my attempts are pointless.

"I hope, you have the power within you to forgive me." Mr. Reston changes his mask of remorse to the more pathetic face of sympathy, but behind both masks, the charring glow still resides within his eyes. It carefully investigates Kelly's naked body, making sure not to miss out on a single detail of the devastation he left behind.

"I truly hope you can." Mr. Reston continues and stretches one of his hands to caress her cheek. Kelly flinches. She whimpers, but he continues without even for a second considering if he overstepped. My shield shatters. I jump the stretched arm and bite it. The covering surface between him and me keeps me from the satisfaction of penetrating his flesh. But I continue. I continue for as long as Mr. Reston strokes his finger over her cheek. An eternity passes before his hand moves away from her. An eternity of me failing to protect the one most important to me. Mr. Reston stares at me with glee while imagining all the horrible things he can do to a little, defenseless girl laying helpless in front of him. Kelly's thoughts scream as she lays paralyzed.

"Please! Please!" Her breath vibrates, but not a single word leaves her lips.

Mr. Reston's hand slowly moves over to her arm. The glow in his eyes burns brighter. It is a fire in which his soul loves to burn. My biting gets less furious as thoughts of hopelessness break through my barriers and suffocate all instincts of saving Kelly from the monster I cannot touch. I just stare into his eyes while they wander over her body.

Why are you like this? I think. Why do you want to hurt her?

His eyes fixate on Chester. His hand stops moving. I release it and fall to the table. With my last small molecules of healthy air in my lungs, I run back to Chester, broken.

Monster is the only word I can think of. The truest description of the creature in front of me.

Mr. Reston's hand touches Chester. He pets the back of the bear's head and scratches it behind its ear.

"You chose me," he murmurs.

No one chose you, I think as I sink back into Chester to catch my breath and restore my powers. I am certain of it. No one in their right mind would ever choose you.

"I made you a sandwich." Mr. Reston says.

The plate scrapes against the wooden table. Kelly's internal voice screams when it touches her leg. For a moment, her scream drowns all rambling pleads for help bouncing in her head.

"You need to eat, my little girl."

"Stop," her thoughts cry. Then her voice goes silent.

The sudden absence of sound hits me in an electric shock. I can't stay inside anymore. It's too dangerous. I force out a new shield around my fingertips and run out just before it seals behind me. He stretches over to her again. His ugly face is so close his mustache touches her cheek. He slowly moves away from the kiss he considers gentle. His kiss sets root in her mind and spreads in a web of darkness to every corner of her thoughts.

"Mom." The word breaks free through the silence. "Please save me."

"You really need to eat something, sweetie." He pushes the plate closer to her, and it touches the pool of blood underneath her. It catches his eye, an eye that catches fire, and the true nature within his soul reaches out through the small window. He lets his index finger go through it, then he rubs it on his thumb.

"You need to eat otherwise you will be like Esther," he says.

Without any further explanation, I know she died. She died a horrible death in blood and tears.

"I will need to check up on you further if it doesn't stop." It sounds like a mental note for himself. He looks down at Kelly, who luckily haven't looked up from Chester's neck, and spared herself the horror of seeing him go through her blood. I walk up to them and stand in the pool between them. I need to see the demon up close. The burn in his eyes fades when he looks at Kelly who cries into Chester's fur.

"Maybe I have something that can help you eat." The sudden change in tone startles me. It becomes what I remembered from the toy store. The happiness and kindness turn horrific in combination to the blood and mutilation he admires in his creation. "I've brought someone who always helps me when I'm feeling down."

He stretches out his left hand, which he hid until now. In it, he holds the plush dragon where Sariel lives.

"Dongo here is the greatest dragon of all. He is the guardian of princesses and savior of all gentle souls. He might even be able to help Chester convince you about the importance of eating."

Mr. Reston pushes the dragon over me into Kelly's face to cheer her up. The fact that Kelly instead hides her face further into Chester's neck is proof of his failure, at least for me. The fact that she cries into her own blood is proof he will never cheer her up. Mr. Reston sees nothing of it, instead, he imitates the voice of his imaginary dragon.

"Hi, my name I Dongo. And I want to be your best friend."

All while Kelly's inner voice is completely silent.

I know that inside the green plush dragon Sariel looks out through its eyes. He probably enjoys the view of her golden hair against his windows. I hope the bloodstains among the gold make him aware of the damage his little Richie has caused this little golden-haired girl. I hope he cares. I hope he is ashamed.

Mr. Reston sighs. He finally realizes how pointless his attempts are. He sits Dongo down on the table in front of us.

"One day you will long for me to cheer you up, and I will be the only happiness you know. Then, you will thank me for all I do for you."

I highly doubt that. I highly doubt we ever will be thankful for anything he has done for her. I also doubt he will be her only happiness. He will be her worst fear for the rest of her life. I look up into the eyes of the green dragon now standing in front of me and yes, Sariel hangs there looking at me. He disappears at the first glance of me and hides himself in the depth of the dragon's belly.

Mr. Reston once again stretches over me to caress Kelly's cheek. Just seeing him touch her is too much.

"Please," she says. "Leave me alone."

He withdraws his hand quickly as if her sudden response burned him. The fire in his eyes turns red and dangerous.

"I can touch you how much I want," he says.

He raises his hand but stops the impulse just before he smacks her over the head.

"You chose me, remember that." He stands up and walks towards the stairs.

"Hopefully Dongo, and Chester, can talk some sense to you."

He slams the door behind him, leaving us on the table. Me, Sariel, Chester, Dongo, and Kelly. And a plate of sandwiches that won't be eaten.

"Thank you, Chester," Kelly says. "You saved me."

She thugs him in between her legs. Her thoughts slowly reawaken their terrible course down into darkness. Pictures of dead parents with blood running down the edge of their lips, just as her mother usually has after her father has passed out drunk. Kelly sobs. Images of the nightmare she just lived through interrupt the family portraits where the happy smiles have been exchanged for dead faces. She cries.

"You are my friend Chester," she whispers. "You are nothing like he says."

# Chapter 24

A loud grumble echoes through Kelly's body. My first thought is that she finally gets to die, my second is desperation over her leaving me behind in this godforsaken world. But it isn't her body telling the world it is giving up. Kelly is hungry. She never moves in response to her stomach's calling. In fact, nothing has moved since Mr. Reston left. Kelly still has Chester wrapped between her arms and legs. Dongo still stands in front of us commanding Kelly to at least taste the sandwich his owner put out for her. The radiator still slowly pumps with a distinct growl back in the furthest corner of the room.

Visions of Kelly's mom laying on the floor flashes before my mind's eye. Kelly's father lays beside his wife. They both look hollowly into the emptiness. They are both dead.

"Mom," Kelly sobs. "Dad."

"Preparing for tonight?"

A hideous body suddenly stands beside me. Scales, claws, and sharp eyes. Sariel. The devil's assistant. He observes me with the same judgmental look on his face he had when I left him in Dongo. In this light, the bleakness of his scales comes clear. Their once noble blue color has turned grey from years of service, or betrayal depending on which one of us you ask.

"At least you should," he continues as I don't answer him. "If you really want to fight for her that is. But I understand if you have realized how pointless it will be. She will die anyway."

There it was again. Him pushing the exact right buttons to make me boil. The next thing I know, his pulse pushes against my fingers as I hold him over my head by nothing but his neck.

"Don't ever say that again!" I roar.

My claws scratch against his shield, I want it to break just to feel his pulse flow down my fingers. He laughs hoarsely and grabs my wrist. He squeezes until my blood pushes against my scales. I focus on my shield not breaking. My shield pushes harder against my wrist. I will not let go. The pain around my wrist reaches crushing levels. I am no coward, I think. I never give up. I am nothing like him. Still, the strain against my wrist forces my hand open. He twists my wrist to the side, holding himself up with nothing but my arm and his grip around it.

"It's so easy to get under your skin," he says putting himself down to the ground. "What makes you think she will survive?"

He throws me to the ground and puts his knee on my chest. He leans closer until his mouth touches the blue by my ears.

"What makes you think she is any different from the others?" He wheezes, slowly raising his voice into a guttural growl. "What makes you think you will be able to fight away the Pain-screamers any better than the others did? What makes you think she will be able to resist them any better than the other children who were protected by failed warriors? What makes you think her dear Chester won't end up on the shelf together with the other ones?"

With the last question, he lifts me over the table edge and leaves me hanging with my neck in a firm grip between his claws. He forces me to look out over the room towards a small shelf hanging on the opposite wall. It is a hand-made shelf, from the look of how unstable it is, built in school by a little boy. On the shelf, five haunting plush animals silently sit and watch all the horrors happening in the basement. They are nothing but empty eyes and thorn cloth in colors that once were happy. A faded blue elephant with a silent nose, a pink monkey with a smile gone stale, a dirty green fox with a nose a few strands from breaking loose, an orange owl with wings no longer strong enough to lift into the air, and a purple giraffe with a neck broken so many times it in no way could lift a head proudly ever again.

"Do you see them?" Sariel whispers into my ear. "The corpses? They were once like us. Then their Loves died. Sarah survived two days, Uriel died the next. Carl survived for five, his protector Michael seven. Nikki survived four days, Camael died hours later. Esther couldn't make it further than one day, sadly the wise owl was empty when I arrived. Ethan died after seven days, both he and Raphael were in so much pain the last days of their life that they took their last breath within the same hour. They both smiled when death finally took them."

He points me in the direction of every plush animal as he mentions their owners' names, starting with the elephant and finishing with the giraffe. Five children have already died in this house, all of them suffered. Just as Kelly will have to suffer if she stays alive. Tears build up in my eyes. Every warrior fought with all their might, and none of them succeeded. Sariel throws me back on the table. His look of disgust now diluted with fear.

"Do you now see there is no hope for you? Whatever you do, you both will die."

I look at him, then at Kelly and Chester together embracing their horrifying fate.

"Even if you are right," I say while rubbing the pain from my wrist, "she deserves someone fighting for her. Isn't that what we are supposed to do? Save them from the pain during the night?"

"You will only make her life worse!" Sariel screams at me while clawing his head. "She will die! What is the use of prolonging what is already painful? The Pain-screamers here love to see us bleed. They love to break us. And when they have broken you, then they go for your Love."

Sariel stops his rampage hyperventilating. Screaming at me has drained him of the last colors on his scales.

"Just don't give them the satisfaction of breaking you before they break her," he whispers between his breaths. "Force them to focus on her and let her give up before they use Richie to do something even worse."

"So I am supposed to just let them attack her? Without helping her?"

Kelly's body grumbles again. She whines and thugs Chester closer to her body.

"She needs me," I scream into Sariel's face.

Sariel sighs into his hands while shaking his head. "You are all so noble when you haven't seen the depths of this hell yet. Then I have to pick up the pieces when the Pain-screamers leave you to die in the sun. After the first night, you won't want to walk out again." He pauses briefly to look at me, then at Kelly. "What do I have to do for you to understand me? No one gets out of here alive. Everyone suffers. You are just giving them what they want by facing them."

Sariel's voice fades out. "You are just hurting here more.".

I look at Kelly again. She shivers and tries to hug herself warm. My eyes wander to the graveyard and then to Sariel. Kelly's flashes of dead parents mix in with my own imagination picturing her dead. My view blurs as my tears break free.

"You know," Sariel says. "Camael told me, her last memory before waking up in her green fox was the snake's voice foretelling how she would move on to another place once her child was safe. A place full of happiness where we later get to meet our Loves after they pass away. So foolish she was." He sighs. "Michael remembered words about how his and Carl's soul would meet after death if he could protect him. He called it heaven. Raphael said he was told we would meet our children under the tree of life and the fruit growing on its branch where only happiness and peace coexist. But the snake didn't tell them about the other way we go. If our Loves die, we die too. And all the warriors who have died here faced a painful death. A so painful death. But what they found worse was the emptiness within their hearts when their Love wasn't there fill the void anymore. We die when our soul can't handle the loneliness anymore and we just fade away like the pain-screamers. And if our Loves survive, they become like my little Richie because no soul in a child can handle the kind of nightmares this place gives you. One day their soul dies but their bodies keep walking the earth. You will wish they died after that."

In front of me the shell of a warrior wages back and forth. I see that now, a shell is all he is, nothing more. Just like the corpses on the shelf. I glance at our dead audience. Chills travel across my spine creating a shiver all over my body. Chester would be a perfect corpse with hollow eyes. Just as the monster upstairs wished for him to become.

"How about you? Do you think someone will find you and fall in love with your cute and cuddly fur? Of course, someone will! You're too cute for anyone to ignore." The jolly voice I was met by on my first day in the toy store says under Kelly's nightmares. "Today is the day. Today is the day someone falls for you."

If she had not picked Chester, if she had not picked me, she would never be here. She would live at home with her drunken father and her abused mother. She would have been better off without me.

"How long ago did he make Chester?" I ask as the thought settles in my chest.

Sariel looks at me. "A year ago. A long tempting year. The waiting was always part of the thrill. But the last years he has become more impatient."

"And all those plush animals, they are nothing more than trophies for him? Nothing more than successful hunts!"

Nothing more than baits disguised as warriors, I think.

"No." Sariel shakes his head. "They are so much more. He made them himself and he takes personal pride in every one of them. When Kelly showed him Chester's ripped-off head, he got furious."

Kelly moves. For a moment, all my attention shifts to her and the sudden abruption in her dreams. The pain runs through her stomach as the small movement rips a vessel. She grins. The depressing realization of what the future Kelly most likely faces roots itself inside me.

I love you, I think. I love you with all of my heart. Sariel's words echoes in my head. She will die. She is better off dead.

"She won't survive for long," Sariel says. "If she fights for it, she might survive for a couple of days but those will be painful days."

"I know," I say and rub my temples with the palms of my hands. I smear the tears over my face.

But someone might find her, one hopeful part of my brain says. The realistic part of my brain knows no one saw Mr. Reston take her. No one except the man who's going to kill her knows where she is. And if the choice is between death and staying longer in this basement, then maybe death is the better solution and the quicker it comes the better her end will be.

But someone could still find her, my egoistic brain shouts. We must at least give her the chance.

Sariel looks at me fighting with myself, he sighs. "The Pain-screamers here, they are... They are worse than anything you have ever seen. And no matter how hard you fight, they will overpower you both."

A memory of the Nightmares crawls up in my thoughts as they did by Kelly's bed. The darkness in their eyes. Their long noses, their sighs as they force their way into her dreams. I hardly think they can become much worse.

"Don't they attack Mr. Reston anymore?"

Sariel shakes his head and looks at me with pain written all over his face. "They live inside him now. I hear them whisper temptations in his thoughts every day."

It should come as a shock to me that these monsters can live inside their own victims, but it fits with their nature too well. The Nightmares are nesters.

"And we are here to make sure their minds survive these crucial days," I say continuing my trail of thought.

"And we who fail are condemned to for the rest of their life watch our children destroy the life of others. In this house, we are all condemned," Sariel continues in a whisper.

And I nod.

# Chapter 25

Somehow Mr. Reston convinces himself that Kelly can forgive him. He considers his violations against her body and soul as such a minor overstep that it takes mere hours for it to be forgotten.

"He plans how he will swipe her off her feet," Sariel says as he describes what is going on in the darkened hive-like mind of Richie.

Just moments ago, Sariel described how Mr. Reston's next plushy already left the drawing board, a tiger this time. A fearless tiger by the name Mike with red fur and blue stripes. It will be his most beautiful creation yet. The children will fight over it. They will fight over being the one following Mr. Reston home.

"I hope you are hungry because I brought you an even better sandwich this time," he says and interrupts his jolly singing.

Beside me, Sariel flinches. "He sees the untouched sandwich."

Instinctively, I run to Kelly, but Sariel catches my arm.

"There is no use," he says.

"I know!" I scream in his face and rip my arm away from him. I run until I stand between Kelly and her assaulter. Mr. Reston stands stunned at the end of the stairs. His paralysis slowly fades into dark flares in his eyes.

"You haven't eaten the old one." Mr. Reston growls. "Don't you like what I'm doing for you?"

He throws the new plate on the table, smashing it into shards flying across the room in sharp arrows. The projectiles push my body to the ground and hit Kelly's already tortured body. Each shard digs into her skin like knives tearing her up on the outside, so it matches her already torn inside.

"You should be grateful for what I'm doing for you." He slams his hand over her face in one single movement and throws her across the table.

"No," I say.

Kelly is silent through the whole flight, only to let her breath leave her mouth in a silent moan as she collides with the hard surface.

"No."

The scream inside her head is painfully numbing. Just like how the punch ripped her wounds open, her silent scream tears her world in pieces. I try to crawl my way back to her and Chester who still lays in her arms, but her heart wrenching scream holds me fixed. A painful grin spreads over her face. She opens her mouth. But there is no scream. Filtered through her mental screams, small snippets of her mother on the kitchen floor make themselves visible. Laura's hands cover her bruised face. Kelly's father stands above her. The juice hangs fresh on his breath. He has the bloody traces of Laura's face on his hands. And she says the same words leaving Kelly's lips.

"I'm sorry."

Mr. Reston stops himself in the middle of another assault. His fire dampens. Blood is once again running down Kelly's thighs.

"I don't want you to end up like Esther." He says and recollects all the shards, he glances out through a small window directed to the backyard where five small crosses are planted in a line. "I want you to stay with me longer than she did."

Esther only survived one day, Sariel's haunting voice clarifies in my memory. I glance at him, and he nods in confirmation to my suspicions. She starved herself, or whenever she refused to eat Richie got angry and killed her with his anger.

"I will make you a new sandwich, but you have to promise me to eat this one, okay?"

Kelly nods without a word. The few words that calmed him down were enough to drain her of all strength. He disappears again. Kelly, who had not dared when he was around, cries. I do too.

Sariel grabs my shoulder in an awkward attempt to give comfort.

"She did well," he says. "Maybe he will let her live today."

I nod. Is it worth it? The pain and cost of surviving?

"You need to rest. Tonight will be the worst you've ever faced."

"Will you help me?" I ask.

"No." Sariel's grip around my shoulder hardens. "I could never do that."

"Why?" I ask more in a reflex to his cryptic answer than of actual curiousness.

"Because I've already lost, and they know it. With me there, you would never stand a chance of surviving." He helps me up on my feet. "Richie is on his way down. If your little girl eats, he will let her be tonight. But if she pushes the sandwich away, she will probably not survive the hour. I don't know what you hope for, but with what I know today, I would have hoped Richie resisted his father back when he was Kelly's age."

"His father treated him like he treats Kelly?"

Sariel gives me a look telling me I am balancing on the border of questions I can ask him.

"Worse." He pulls me towards Dongo. At the same time, the door upstairs opens, and Mr. Reston walks down with a new sandwich.

"Wait," I say.

Sariel stops without questioning me. He sits beside me, and we both look at the plate now placed in front of Kelly. Kelly looks up at it, she meets Mr. Reston's observing eyes. The fire burning behind his lenses ejects heat.

"How can he be so cruel?" I ask.

"This is not Richie," Sariel answers. "It's the Pain-screamers. They are pushing him. Cheering him on."

Kelly chooses life over death. She slowly gets up on all fours and crawls her way to the plate. Every slight movement forward creates waves of pain forcing her to stop and breathe. With every stop, she meets Mr. Reston's fierce look waiting for her to give up. The terror when seeing the cruelty behind his eyes, is enough on its own to force her one step forward. She will survive, the notion fills me with both ease and dread.

"Are you sure he will let her be if she eats it?"

"Yes," Sariel sighs. "As long as she follows his rules she will survive."

Kelly falls flat on her bare stomach during one of her strides. She weeps as the pain from her inside gets too intense. She screams internally over all the pain. She stretches her arm for the plate but only touches the edge with her fingertips. The pain is too great for her to get up again. She is stuck at the finish line. She looks at Mr. Reston, his eyes burning darker than ever with Nightmares and desires.

"Can you please stretch me the plate?" She asks. "I'm really hungry."

Mr. Reston looks at her with nothing even close to kindness in his eyes. The man in the store has drowned in the darkness's egoistic agenda of pain.

She stretches for it once again and fails.

"Please."

Mr. Reston stretches over and pushes the plate just a little bit closer to her. Then he falls back, showing her that it is all she gets.

Kelly forces herself one last time to the plate. She stretches. Her fingertips slide over the edge, and she drags it towards her. The movement completely exhausts her. Still, she forces herself to pick up the sandwich.

"Good girl." Mr. Reston smiles. I want to kill him slowly for how he says it, I want to rip his skin off piece by piece.

"Now eat it all so you will grow big and strong." He continues and pushes the sandwich she now holds in her hands towards her closed mouth. She opens and closes her mouth around the small piece fitting into her mouth. Mr. Reston follows her every moment as she chews, and finally swallows. The dry pieces go down like sandpaper against her throat.

"Now another bite," he says.

Kelly does as he commands, forcing every crumb down her throat.

"Can I have some water?" She asks.

"Later, when you're finished eating."

Kelly nods without an argument. She forces every piece of the dry bread down to her empty stomach. She camouflages the ache it gives her by hiding her face in another bite. With each bite she has to force herself to not throw it up again. Mr. Reston's face only displays pleasure.

"Come. He won't hurt her tonight," Sariel says to me as the last crumb has entered her stomach. "I'm sure of it now. The Pain-screamers are satisfied."

Mr. Reston gives Kelly a soft pat on the head like she was a pet fetching his stick. “Good girl.”

Kelly hides her face in her arms, she is scared of looking up at him and show him the tears soaking his table. He might punish her for destroying it, a risk she is unwilling to take.

I look up at Sariel and nod. I want to force myself to look at this torture, but I can’t, not anymore. Sariel stretches out his hand and I grab it, glancing one last time at Kelly. Her tears have created a small pond under her nose, but she makes no sound. She wants to live, even if it’s just for a day longer.

One day might be enough for her mother to find her, she hopes. And I tell myself she is right.

# Chapter 26

Every second under Dongo's thick hide is nerve-wrecking. I keep expecting Mr. Reston to walk down the stairs one last time to prove Sariel wrong. On the other side of Dongo's hide, Kelly forces the sandwich to stay in her stomach. She is also scared of him coming down one more time, and if he comes down the consequences of him seeing the sandwich floating around in her vomit absolutely terrifies her.

But the perverted old man goes to bed without even checking in on his little prisoner.

While I spend my minutes and hours fixed by Dongo's eyes keeping watch for everything and anything capable of hurting Kelly, Sariel sits on the floor like a statue waiting for the rot to eat through his bones.

"It will soon begin," he says calmly. "Richie is finally asleep."

My body relax just to immediately preparing for the coming battle.

"They break free." He continues and sighs. "It will not take long for them to catch her sent." He pauses shortly. "They just did."

From upstairs, the chant grows from inaudible to the massive force I have learned to recognize.

*Nightmares.*

The singers repeat the words in a choir accompanied by an orchestra of teeth rain and door scratching.

"Did you hear it?" I ask hoping that the whisperer's voice awakened a dormant instinct within Sariel.

"Of course, I heard it." He screams back at me to be heard above the chants of pain. "Like that has worked on me for the last years."

I sigh.

He has to feel it too, I think. He has to feel the hunger feeding every impulse to throw himself at them.

But he just sits still not moving a limb, breathing calmly through his nose in slow, long breaths.

"What are you planning to do?" He asks with his eyes still shut and his breathing still in harmony.

"Everything in my power to protect her."

"What a clever plan." The contempt in his voice soaks the room. "I wish you the best of luck." He turns silent, in what must be his approval of me to kill myself. His disapproval would only encourage me to throw myself at them with an even fiercer force.

He probably knows that.

Kelly's thoughts drift deeper into the nightmares of today. I walk out and let the outside night air hit my face in a refreshing breeze. The toxicity only itches inside my lungs. I fill my lungs through my nose in a long breath. The scent is intoxicating, their dark blood flowing through their veins waiting for me to set it free. They are all uncountable hearts pumping in a dance of death.

How can Sariel even want to resist it?

My non-animal side knows the answer, it always does, but it is drowned in the instincts storming through my brain not leaving a single thought unaffected. It is addictive. The ever-growing chant feeds the beast within me even further. It is as if they want me to notice them. I walk up to Kelly, and Chester. She finally falls into her once happy dreamland. Tonight, her dreams portray a distorted world where everyone she loves is dead and only evil thrives. Above it all, a tower bell echoes with Mr. Reston's climactic sigh foretelling impending doom.

The Nightmares breakthrough. They fall down the stairs and the window and hit the floor. The first ones are left in a bloody mess. Screams of death mix with laughter and haunting chants of 'Pain' in chorus.

I breathe.

I will not fail, I tell myself with my last capable thought. They will not get to Kelly. None of them will create the nest in her they built in Mr. Reston.

Nightmares attack from every side of the table at once. The tumultuous war cries drown into static under the soul-slitting screams coming from the stairs and Mr. Reston's Nightmares. Not even my reptile brain manages to hold on to its killer instinct when hearing their screams. The screams turn into painful yells as these Nightmares make their way up from the floor. My thoughts freeze. The first normal Nightmare reaches me, I grab it by the throat forcing my brain to focus on their ever so tempting scent of darkness. I bite and feel its pulse slowly fill the empty hole that is my hunger. With one eye, I focus on the stairs awaiting whatever is released from Mr. Reston's inside. I glance at Dongo's eyes but am only met by hollow emptiness. No matter how hard I focus, the unease never lets go of its grip on me and my instincts never really kick into the level I need to fully protect Kelly.

A bleak hand stretches up on the table. It resembles in no way the clawed paw I expect from these horrid Nightmares. It is a small human hand, a child's hand. I freeze as the little creature crawl up on the table. Black blood drip out of my mouth. A child shows its horrible grin and greedy eyes in search of a victim. It finds me. The grin widens, displaying more of its teeth that should be cute white children teeth, the same teeth smiling at me from Kelly's mouth every time she looks into Chester's eyes. These smiling teeth are sharp fangs built to rip everything and everyone in its way to pieces.

"Pain!" He screams and bursts into a burst of laughter that makes my soul crawl as far into my body as it possibly can.

No, my thoughts whisper in despair. I don't want this.

The boy-like monster looks back over the edge and screams the word once again to welcome its many brethren who stretch their countless child-like heads over the edge. Each of them looks me into the eyes and laughs. One of them licks her dark lips. I recognize one of the faces, the most common face, from the picture in Mr. Reston's hallway. The disfigured smiles of little Richie biting eagerly in my direction. The tanned skin has turned pale, and the brown hair has blackened, but it is him. The others... I swallow as the realization sinks in. They are his victims staring at me with the Nightmares' dark eyes. All Mr. Reston's Nightmares laugh in a horrible howling choir.

While all other Nightmares never saw me as more than an obstacle, these run right at my paralyzed being. I take the wave right into my face. Their child-hands grab me and throw me around like a lifeless doll. They bite and twist my limbs. One of them successfully bites into my arm and my pulse leaves me for him. The pain forces me out of my paralyzed state, and I throw a little Richie across the table in one circular motion. It laughs constantly until it crashes and loses its breath. They all lose their grip on me during the sudden movement and fall to the floor. Thousand small faces stare at me for a long moment with nothing but the chant of the normal Nightmares sounding through the room. Then the Richie laughs and rubs his thin arm over his mouth. He shows my blue blood as a trophy for the others. They join in on the laughter, screaming their favorite word in a long ecstatic cheer. The horde of ghost-like children attacks me once more.

"Chester, help me!" Kelly whisper from her own nightmares as her attackers give out sighs of relief.

I am failing, I realize as I fight off all the monster children now encouraged by the sight of my bleeding. Kelly will be lost if I do not do anything soon.

I back slowly towards her. For each step I take, I have to avoid being eaten by the wave of fanged children surrounding me. I grab a girl and raise my fangs to bite into her throat. Her pulse breaks through between my fingers. The skin looks just like Kelly's. It feels just like I imagined it to, smooth and soft. The fragile skin of a child which should never be broken. She twists her head, facing me. The evil grin spreading across her face reveals all her teeth in their horrifying glory. The little child laughs. She knows I cannot kill her. They all know it. Sariel could never do it, and neither can I.

She throws herself at me, aiming her teeth towards my throat. It stings when they hit, but my scales withstand the pressure. The monster gnaws its way further in. The others attack every open part of my body and build a dark mass on top of me and drown me under their child-like beings.

"Please," Kelly whispers again, and the tear she cries sounds through her voice.

I must save her, I think as I stretch my arms for the girl biting into my throat, only moments are left before she reaches through my scales and punctures my veins. I look into her eyes, the beautiful eyes of a girl who never grew up. She looks back at me, and the evil joy she shows could have paralyzed me once again if I let it, but I fight on focusing on Kelly's voice to push me forward. I grab her body with one of my arms, and her head with the other.

"I'm sorry," I whisper and twist her body until her neck crack from breaking. The monster laughs hauntingly all the time until only a gurgle escapes through her throat, right before the neck gives in and the body shakes in death rattles.

I cry while grabbing the next and rip it off my arm so hard its teeth stay buried in my scales. New children attack at the first moment they get when my scales once again become free. The new ones I shake of the moment their teeth hit me. I scream and bite one of them so hard it dies. I spit the blood out, the thought of tasting it disgusts me. The child vaporizes in front of me, just like the nightmares I had to face before, with a laughter like it has already won. And they have won. The shame in killing what we are supposed to protect is too much for my soul to bear, and too much for my instincts to drown.

I force myself to shut my eyes to not see their faces and tiny bodies. Now, all I see is darkness, and all I hear is the Nightmares ecstatic breath against my scales as they try to kill me and their laughter as they succeed. I claw them of me focusing only on what I must to save Kelly. Their breaths suddenly stop when I tear their bodies in two. I imagine the normal Nightmares rugged fur in my hands and force myself to ignore the softness I claw into pieces.

Slowly, I succeed to back towards Kelly and the nightmares haunting her. The next time I open my eyes, my back is against the mountain of Nightmares piling on top of Kelly. I shrug all the tiny hands of me and turn around before I get a chance to see the faces who should be innocent. The dark mountain rises in front of me with all the demons sighing in relief. Small hands grab for me, but I'm already buried inside the bodies. Nightmares scream, and I kill all who are standing in my way to Kelly without hesitation or remorse. The satisfying hunger grows inside me again. A child's hand touches my foot and it's all gone in an instant.

Under all the dark bodies, I find her. Her beautiful hair shining through all Nightmares. The laughter is all behind me. I grab a normal Nightmare and allow myself the celebration of swallowing its blood as I rip its neck from its body. Beautiful blood energizing me. Behind me, the laughter from one of the children breaks through the walls of their comrades. The other Nightmares rush at Kelly, and consequently me, and try to punch through me to reach her. With every punch, the real Nightmares come closer. I fight myself lose just to get fixed at her head once again. At the same time, sighs erupt from the other side of Kelly's head where I cannot protect her.

Behind the darkness, the faces of Richie and his buried prisoners slowly get closer. One Richie grabs a nightmare standing in his way and opens a big hole in the body with his teeth. He throws the dead body to the side, laughing and enjoying every drop of the same blood running through its own veins. His dark eyes lock on me, and the laughter goes into a falsetto. They rip away the creatures pinning me to Kelly's head. I prepare myself for the wave of their teeth coming only for me.

To my surprise, their sharp teeth never hail down on me. Instead, the punches are exchanged for countless small hands. They all hold me fixed to Kelly's head and force me to stand in a cross-like stance while one of them climbs up to my face. It leans towards my neck and smells it. Its saliva dripping down on me.

"Pain," Richie whispers with a growl, then he laughs and sinks his teeth into my neck.

Every muscle in my body rages to break free but my fight only results in small shivers. The teeth slowly dig deeper into my scales until they crack. I scream with all my lungs until only wheezing remains. The child's laugh gurgles as blood fill its mouth. My veins slowly drain themselves, one beat at a time.

This is the end, I think. I'm finally going to die.

The sharp teeth let go of me. Richie raises his head and bloodied mouth until we are eye to eye. The little boy's darkened eyes stare right into mine. He smiles and looks out through the mass of nightmares crawling around us and towards the dragon behind all the darkness. He laughs.

"Pain." He screams, but I know what he really says. He calls for the coward hiding behind the dragon's eyes. They know he will not save me no matter how much they taunt him, and they know it hurts him more than any physical pain they can cause him. Richie tells Sariel what a failure he is.

Richie looks back at me and the grin swallows the beautiful boy's face. He grabs my head with his hands and twists it to the side in one quick motion. The break stays absent. He takes no notice of it, maybe he does not care. Instead, he bites into my throat one more time and rips my scales away.

"Just take me," I whisper with what energy I have left. "Take me away from the shame of not being able to protect my Love."

The boy stops his furious butchering of my throat. He looks at me, and then at the other children eagerly standing in line to kill me. He laughs, again. All the others raise their voices and align their laugh with my butcherer's. The boy turns his attention to me with his laughing army behind him.

"Pain." He whispers over, and over again with an ecstatic look in his eyes and the charring fire I remember from Mr. Reston's eyes.

He puts both his hands on each side of my face and leans closer until our face almost touch, then he kisses me. The smile grows bigger as he sees my confusion.

"Shame." He whispers and kisses me again before repeating the word.

All the others join in, forcing me to watch them call on my weakness. The one in front of me removes one of his hands from my face, he raises it and then punches me quickly over my face and chest.

I drift away, and slowly grow numb from the punches. He grabs my throat in a chokehold. He shakes me, then he says one word and pushes me into Kelly's hard surface. The surface gives in, and I fall backward with his hands guiding me down.

"Shame." The word lingers on his lips before the monster releases me into the darkness.

# Chapter 27

The fall only lasts long enough for me to hit the floor. The crash from my body against wood echoes through my bones. I lay still and await their last bite and my final breath.

Just breathe, I think. it will soon be over. One breath, cherish it, cherish every breath you get. I catch a familiar scent. A scent that tickles the part of my brain connected to Kelly's world. Death is truly merciless if it places me where I was the happiest.

"Who are you?" The voice also sounds familiar, yet so distant. She should not see me. She never has before. I belong in the sidelines, outside of her grasp.

Echoing laughter drowns the room in dark emptiness. I open my eyes. Breathing hurts. Everything hurts. I stare at the ceiling of the room Kelly calls her bedroom. Between the wooden cracks, darkness slowly seeps its way in. I support myself on my arms just to see more of this room. The fatigue presses against my drained body like heavy rocks. Under me, a small pool has been created on the floor from the blood still dripping from my throat. It colors the pale wood clear blue. I slowly turn my head from side to side, focusing on not draining my powers too quickly. It really is her room, the same bed, the same little table with a proportionally sized tea set. Everything is the same. The only difference is me. I am a part of it now. I can lay on the bed and sit on the chairs. I can fake drink tea with Gleason. A new wave of laughter thunder through the room and I flinch involuntarily. Is this the hell death has sent me to? A place where I am always reminded of the pain I caused her.

"Are you like them?" The beautiful voice says.

I turn my head as far as the pain lets me, but the owner of the voice never enters my periphery. It is just the same toys that used to fill her bedroom.

The ceiling lamp is the only light source in the room, everything else is dark. In the lamp's flickering light, the dark view outside the window come clear, dark bodies and white teeth biting against the window creating a sound imitating heavy rain. I force myself up. The tea table rumbles in response to my movement. A chair wobbles back and forth from the sudden movement from someone moving further away from me. I focus just to see the golden hair reflecting in the lamplight.

It can't be anyone else. My heart skips a beat. A small voice in my head knows it can be the nightmares messing with my head. It can be their way of breaking me even lower down the ladder of shame and disgrace. The risk is still not enough to deny me the chance of ever talking to her. I crawl closer. She crawls further away from me.

"Kelly," I say with a voice too weak. "I want to help you."

She crawls one step further away from me, ensuring herself we have a safe distance between us.

"You do?"

The laughter floods over us again. Kelly's breathing stops. She looks worryingly out the window, then at me. Nightmare's eyes burn through the window scanning the room for all living. I ignore their murderous stares and focus all my attention on Kelly.

"I don't want to hurt you," I say.

"I don't believe you. You are a monster just like them."

I flinch, and the metallic taste of my last blood fills my mouth. It hurts hearing her say the words I tell myself every day. It hurts more than the destroying wounds on my neck.

"No, I'm not a monster," I say with words sounding hollow even to me. "I am Gabriel."

"Gabriel?"

"Yes, a warrior here to protect you."

Every second, I expect to see her burst into a smile and reveal her sharp teeth before jumping towards me and take my last living moments away.

"Shame, shame," she would say.

"A warrior?"

"Yes," I say, in almost a whisper. "The others, they are nothing but nightmares."

I fall to the floor, exhausted from holding myself up for so long. I breathe, then I force myself up again to continue my crawl closer to her. She does not back away from me this time.

"They are scary," she says.

"Yes, they are." Above me, a drop of dark saliva falls to the floor. Laughter. I look up and see dark flesh pushing the wood to its limit.

"They came into my room before," she says. "And I hid down here."

"You did?" She nods. "Why aren't they here now?"

"Because they didn't find me."

They didn't find her under a small table where one easily can see her. I look at the window and the bulging ceiling. Their anticipation seeps through every crack in a rotten stank.

"Do you want me to hide with you?"

She looks at me hesitantly, debating within herself whether I am safe enough. Then she nods.

"I have room here by Gleason." She puts her hand on the plush fox.

I sit by her, pushing the little fox to the side until he falls out from the safety under the table. If this is all a lie for the nightmares to break me, I am buying it. This must be Kelly.

"Do you think they will find us?" She asks.

"No," I lie and shake my head. "This table is a too good hiding place."

"I think so too."

She puts her head on my shoulder.

I must fight the urge to flinch. This is all I ever wanted, it is even more. Her head seeking comfort on my chest. I put my arm around her shoulder. It feels like home. In a perfect world, this is where I always would be.

"You have a pulse." Her voice cracks as her head vibrates against my chest.

"Yes, I have."

"Do you think they have a pulse too?"

Pictures of their blood pumping out through their veins as I rip the limbs off their bodies flash before my eyes. The dark liquid quickly evaporating into thin air.

"No, I don't think they have a pulse. I don't think they have a heart either."

She smiles hesitantly at me. To my surprise, there are no fangs hidden behind her lips, only perfect human teeth in a smile of perfect cuteness. Her smile disappears as quickly as it came, and she cries.

"I don't want to be here anymore."

It catches me off guard and I stare at her for what feels like eternities as her tears drip down my chest.

I hug her, putting my face against her hair. Her scent is heavenly. I hold my breath and savor it for as long as my lungs allow me.

"Everything will be okay," I say. The comforting words mean nothing, but it is the only thing I can do. It is all I ever wanted throughout these dark days I spent in her teddy bear.

The wood squeaks as nails fail to withstand the pressure from Nightmares pushing themselves against the ceiling. The teeth raining against the windows grow in intensity. She pushes herself harder against me, and in that moment of being trapped in this room of terror and anguish, I find true happiness. It's such a complex feeling, choking me and at the same time bringing joyful tears to my eyes.

"You are safe with me." I want to tell her, but I stay quiet and hug her tighter.

The squeaking turns into breaking when the fibers slowly give in. The teeth tapping against the window turns into screeching as the Nightmares rasps them against the surface. I smell her once more. It might be my last breath, and if it is I want it to be worth it. The ceiling breaks and the window crashes in. Splinters and glass shards explode into the room. I and Kelly become one ball as she crawls closer and buries her body in my scales. Dark bodies fall to the floor, and all light disappears as the lamp breaks under them. Then the ceiling ignites from the sparks bursting from the broken lamp, and light once again dances victoriously across the walls. The nightmares who survive burst into devilish laughter as they see the corpses bleeding out around them.

"They can't find me here," Kelly whispers into my chest.

The Nightmares look around with their noses in the air. They sniff for the scent of their victim, my Kelly.

A little boy walks up to the one closest to the table. Little Richie Reston with his dark hair, pale skin, and sharp smile. He leans forward and grabs the clawed paw of the monster closest to him. He pushes it against his belly until all claws break through his skin. He smiles. He rips the claws out of his body and tears the skin on his belly apart.

"Pain." Richie screams and laughs until he is opened from the beginning of his chest down to his crotch.

I force Kelly's face to lock against my chest, I cannot allow her to see this. I don't want to see this. Yet I stare at the boy tearing his body apart.

Richie digs under his organs until he finds the stomach. He holds it out in front of him, admiring its beauty while laughing. He rips it away from the rest of the body with the esophagus dangling like a rope from his tiny hands. He does not scream, he just smiles a haunting smile of joy. Then he pours the content out on the floor. The blue content, he swallowed not long ago from my throat. My blood creates a small pool on the floor. Richie leans over it filling his lungs with the scent, the same scent dripping from the holes in my neck.

Little Richie lifts his face to the air and inhales. Then his eyes lock onto us, he looks right into my eyes but somehow deep down I know, he can't see me. They are blind here. He has caught my scent and now he knows where I am. He grabs the monster whose claws were used to access his stomach and pushes its nose into the pool. The monster involuntarily inhales the scent of my blood, all while Richie looks me dead into the eyes.

I am the bait, I realize. They could not find her, not as quick as if I found her for them. The mole-like monster howls painfully when it realizes I am close to them. It drags the attention of all other monsters and among them the other pale children. All of them walk slowly towards the pool while the stomach-less Richie walks towards us, he limps from blood loss. A choir of howling breaks through the wall of dark bodies behind him. The little

Richie crawls under the table towards me. He pants with every movement. I stop breathing. He leans over me and inhales me passionately. He stops by Kelly's hair and takes a deeper breath through his nose. Kelly shakes as she his breath hits her neck. Richie smiles.

"Pain." He screams with his last long breath and falls to the floor.

The others freeze, they all know her hiding place.

"I'm sorry," I whisper in Kelly's ear. She cries. "I'm so sorry. I wanted to help you."

The Nightmares throw the table across the room with ecstatic screams. They step over their dead brother and throw themselves over me. Within seconds they have caught her smell, and she can never hide again. I cover her with all my body, barely withstanding their attempts at tearing us apart.

"Please, save me," she says.

How can I? My thoughts whisper through the pain. I'm the one who condemned her. Their claws rip on my unprotected skin. I bleed out on the floor and her. My blue blood smears all over her chin. It glimmers prettily against her beautiful skin.

"Blood," I whisper. It has been the solution so many times before.

I push my palms against her skin and force the last blood I have access to out through my fingers. It connects with the smeared blood on her chin and becomes one spreading shield covering her. First her, I think, then myself.

If I can.

"What are you doing?" She asks with tears dripping down her eyes.

"I'm protecting you." I pant as my last energy leaves me.

"Will you be okay?"

"I will miss you Kelly," I whisper. My muscles are too weak to hold us together and I let her go.

She sobs but lays her hand on my chest. It is a shield between us, but her warmth still reaches through. "I will miss you too, Gabriel," she says. "Thank you."

It is comforting to know that in my last dying moments she realized my sacrifice.

I hit the floor, still alive. I must stay alive. Just long enough to keep her safe this night. The monsters immediately throw themselves over her, but none of them can touch her. I focus on breathing. I focus on her golden hair in the sunlight and her laugh.

"Pain." A Nightmare whispers into my ear.

A child's hand grabs me by the throat and drags me away as the others continue pummeling the shield I built around Kelly. Kelly cries, it is a good thing, it means she is alive. Close to unconsciousness, I am dragged out of her mental room. Little Richie drags my body over the table. Around me, children gather to feast in screeches of excitement. He throws me. And as I land, they all attack. I cover my unprotected skin, but I am too weak to resist. They throw my empty shell around with their teeth. They enjoy every moment of my torture.

Breathe, I think, just breathe. One more day might be enough for someone to find her.

They tear my limbs off one by one, but I no longer feel pain. I only feel numbness. They laugh, but I do not scream.

As the day gets closer, their goal shifts to killing instead of torture. Their teeth dig deep inside my stomach. They dig through my intestines, enjoying their new-found toys. They scream in laughter. Their hands dig inside me for all organs they can eat. The morning light shimmer through my otherwise dark world. My breathing gets weaker, but not from them having a go at me.

Morning is coming. I let myself take one last breath. I imagine her smell filling my lungs who are now outside my body. I smile, at least I think I do.

It is not their laughter I hear last. The snake wheezes.

*Gabriel, warrior of the snake. You failed our creation. You failed your Love. Your death will not be in vain. Rest in peace Gabriel, warrior of the snake.*

With the horrible reminder thundering in my ears, I give in to death.

# The Boy & The Dragon

# Chapter 1

The worst part was never the teeth, neither their sudden transformation. When I first saw them, I thought it was. They turned what I loved the most into the incarnation of evil. Just raising my claws against them left me with an unease reaching down into the nerves in my spine, when I touched them, I found myself unable to kill.

I know better now. What came afterward terrified me more. The fanged smile on their faces when they looked into my eyes. The awareness behind their dark irises. A consciousness had awakened under the darkness, and they had become thinking creatures.

Hell truly began after that day.

One of them took my hand and kissed it, I will always remember it because Richie's father did the same thing before fun-time began.

"Come sit here on my lap. I want to show you something." Then leaning closer to the little boy and whispering into Richie's small and impressionable ears. "Remember, don't tell mother. She'll only be jealous."

The other Pain-screamers attacked me. Not the ones who still looked like hairless moles from hell, but the ones who looked like my Richie. The Richie's pinned me to the ground. The pack leader, the one who kissed me, sat on my chest and dragged his hands over my chest. Somehow it hurt more than claws. They got to me, he knew it, they all knew it. From that day, they were victorious. The pack leader then dragged me to were little Richie lay and threw me right into his head.

I awoke in a basement looking too much like the basement Richie spent his nights, the same basement he later began trapping other children in, all in the name of love. The painful order Richie created around himself to keep his life together was nowhere to be found.

I met Richie.

He did not hide under the bed. He lay by the wall, with the bed's splinters scattered around him. He was hairless except for a couple of patches. His scalp was red where his hair had once been.

"They found me." He repeated.

"Who?" I asked.

The child looked straight at me as if he until now had been unaware of my existence in the room with him.

"Who are you?" He flinched. "Please, don't hurt me!"

The fear in his eyes broke my heart that night. I had fought for him for years without an end and when he saw me, he flinched at the sight of his savior.

He thought I wanted to hurt him.

"I won't hurt you. I will never hurt you." Just me saying the words calmed him down. The laughs echoing through the room tore him up beyond repair instantly afterward.

"Don't let them take me." He cried. "Please, help me."

When the Pain-screamers appeared from every side of the room, he became hysterical. They jumped him, and I got to see how they pushed their teeth against his skin and how they bent his limbs in all the directions they should not be bent. I listened to his limbs click back into place, and his screams in pain, and his desperate call for help, and all the laughter.

All the horrible laughter.

I did nothing to stop it. I only studied the thought-out process of pain as his shadow clones crawled all over him.

The pack leader kissed me on my hand before dragging me back out. He left me outside to rot in my grief. I sat where he left me for hours until the morning arose, and the air began to hurt. When my vision blurred, I crawled my way back to Dongo, and sat paralyzed, listening at their laughter as they hoarded around the one I had sworn to protect.

Much like I do now. I stand by and watch the Pain-screamers jump around in an orchestrated dance processing the cruelty they are capable of. Their laughter creates a song only fitting for the cruelty hiding between these walls. No other haunted mansion could host this kind of concert, no other also inhabits the world's worst nightmares.

They did it, I think. For the first time, they killed one of us.

All the others they left outside Dongo mutilated and hardly breathing for me to see their horrid capacity. Each time they grew bolder, picking the warrior apart a little more. Uriel they left with her scales peeled off, Michael they left bleeding out without hands in front of my hiding place, Camael lost both arms to their hungry teeth, Raphael they cut open from his belly button to his neck. All of them they left for me to admire. All of them I crawled out to rescue in the break of dawn with the Pain-screamer's laughter following my every step. I dragged the bloodied bodies back to Dongo and watched their breathing and pulse with every step I took. I used my blood to stop their bleeding. They never fully healed from their wounds, and only Uriel rose to fight again. They took her hands and ripped out her teeth the night before her Love Sarah died, and I crawled back out for her again when the morning sun rose. The others sat by my side for the rest of their Loves' lives only capable of listening to the cries for help and the laughs of pain.

But tonight, the Pain-screamers kill. I always knew they were capable, but somehow, I convinced myself I never would see it happen. Their warfare has always been more psychological since they realized they can hurt us. Since they got to Richie. Since pain became their way of life and not just a word.

An arm flies across the table and one of the Ethans run after it like a dog after a bone. He takes the arm between his teeth and throw it around like a toy. With one glance he looks into my eyes. The cute face of a pale child disfigures into a pain-screamer's grin.

I am a survivor, I think. I survive against unspeakable odds while all others around me die.

The sight of the children feasting on Gabriel is still not worse than what they have done to the wiring in Richie's brain and the thoughts I am forced to listen to every day.

On the other side of the table, a horde of dark bodies forces themselves on

Kelly, she lays completely still. Not a sound leaves her lips. She should not be calm, not with them crawling all over her.

Pain-screamers in the skin of Sarah, Nikki, and Carl lift what is left of Gabriel's body over their head, the torso with the head, one arm, and one leg. The trio's brothers and sisters follow them while dancing, jumping, and laughing at their creation. Now I see the short disturbing contractions on his chest. Gabriel is still alive and breathing, barely. He fights to stay alive for as long as he can, without fighting back.

And the Pain-screamers doesn't mind the extra hours of fun-time.

The three demons put the body down in front of me and Dongo. All the child-like faces look up at me. They smile at me while they drag their teeth over Gabriel's body. He shivers. His breath is so weak.

A Richie tears his teeth across Gabriel's body until he reaches the stomach, he then digs so deep under the skin that he reaches the intestines. Gabriel's body breaks out in involuntary spasms. The pain-screamer rips out all the intestines by quickly jerking his head back. I shiver from the satisfaction in the child's eyes.

But I cannot look away. Greedy children throw themselves over what will be Gabriel's corpse. They fight each other for the best piece. The morning light breaks through the cellar window, and Gabriel's breathing stops.

A loud scream bursts out from the horde of nightmares. Kelly. Whatever Gabriel did disappeared the moment he passed. The pain-screamers scavenging his body look at her with big smiles. They cheer and jump around in a circle around Gabriel's body. All but one Richie, the one who ripped Gabriel's intestines out. He stares up at me with the intestines hanging from his mouth. When the others run to join the feast, he climbs up Dongo's body coloring it with Gabriel as he gets closer.

Why does Gabriel not vaporize as the others did? I think to myself as panic hijacks my brain at an exponential rate.

Richie reaches the neck, and my pulse stops. He smiles and drops the intestines behind. He reaches the nose and then sits right in front of my windows and stares calmly into Dongo's eyes. The dark hair falls over his face. The innocent eyes disappear behind the darkness, leaving only the horrifying mouth visible. He leans towards me and pushes his face against the window. It is what separates us, a window shaped like a glass eye. The little mouth twists into the fanged smile that always startles me no matter how often I see it. Between the teeth, Gabriel's organs twirl into a mess of tissue and blue blood.

I am a survivor. I force myself to breathe slowly. In and out. I am a survivor.

The Richie backs away from the window, he rubs the teeth clean with his small fingers, then he drags the fingers across the window and writes with smeared, unsteady letters. Before he finished the first letter, I know what it will say. It is all they think about.

PAIN

He laughs while writing the last letter and repeats the written word as he finishes.

I know he wants to trigger me into letting my instincts free. Instincts I've successfully muted throughout the years. They try every night. Nights like this, with body parts of a warrior in their arsenal, always become more difficult. I close my eyes. I need to control myself. I am a survivor. When I open my eyes again, Richie has picked up the last of the organs, Gabriel's heart, and juggles it with his hands. He stops to cut his hands with his teeth. Then he smears his black blood all over Gabriel's heart. The scent reaches into Dongo's inner dungeon. It ignites a spark of instincts in the deepest corners of my cells.

Breathe, I tell myself, you don't have to look. Yet I do. I don't even breathe.

Richie uses the heart to smear his blood over his mouth like lipstick and kisses the window right above the I. Black and blue mixes into a glimmering onyx. The scent mixes with rage.

I throw my arms through the window and grab his neck. Blood smears over my arms and head as I pass his written word. I twist my hands tighter around his neck, blocking all air. But he shows no fear. No, he smiles and follows the word written over my face with fascination. I try to crush him, but my hands weaken their grip on him and let him go.

Richie grabs my arms with his small hands and pushes them away from him, looking at me the whole time with a smile of superiority. He leans forward until our noses touch. The dark eyes blister with fire and evil.

"Shame," he says.

He throws himself at me, biting into my face. I scream in agony and throw myself back into Dongo. The glass stops him with a thumping sound. Blood runs down my face and I stare at the monster on the other side biting furiously at the window while laughing maniacally. All while Kelly is tortured to the brink of insanity by the others. But they let her live. Just so they can come back tomorrow. And the day after that.

The Richie on the other side of the window calms down. He won. They have all won. And we all are lost.

Shame, we should all feel ashamed.

# Chapter 2

Shame. The word lingers on me, as I stare out at the sun rising behind the cellar window. They are evolving. First in their appearance, then in their words.

Did they find it in Richie's vocabulary? And if so, what else did they find in there? What can they find in the corners of what Richie is and was when they killed his inner self?

The shallow wounds from the Pain-screamer's assault decorates my reflection. They still feel sore, but they will meld in with my scales as esthetical cracks on my once crystal blue face. The scars will make me look tougher, as tough as I need to be in this life. Gabriel hated how I look. He did not attempt hiding it. Raphael hated me too, the way he scanned me from head to toe showed nothing but disgust. Even with his organs on display for all to see and only my blood protecting them from the outside world he feared what our scales meant. He looked at me with disgust in his eyes to his deathbed. Michael and Uriel showed no reaction, whether they liked their scales or not I could never tell. Camael smiled at the first glance of me.

I sigh in disbelief even though I am all alone. Letting the sound out feels better than forcing it all to stay inside my head.

They are all so lucky to already be out of this world, I think, and mumble to myself. The future has always proved to be grimmer than the past. None of them has to live through the trauma of their Love's thoughts slowly distorting into a reflection of the Pain-screamer's cruel nature. None of them has to see memories of horrific actions get twisted into grotesque, yet thoughtful, teachings.

"You don't want to get in trouble, okay?" Said with a firm grip around a crying boy's arm turns into a parent's caring words.

"I love all, but you are the only one I can touch. You are the one protecting dad from doing something really bad." Said with the convincing voice of a wise adult with a soft touch on the boy's back turns into rules.

"Remember you chose this life with me."

Don't get in trouble. You only touch those who choose you. Thoughts getting more convincing when a child grows up into a young adult. Memories so easy to twist into darkness.

The morning light illuminates every corner of the basement. The few greedy Pain-screamers still holding on to Kelly scream hoarsely in panic when their bodies give up from suffocation. The others have disappeared into the shadows outside, and Richie's nest. None of them can stay in Kelly. Not yet. The nest is not near complete. They must kill the soul.

But first, there is torture. I guess the Pain-screamers don't want to miss that part.

But the biggest question for their nest-building is whether they can make Richie keep her alive for that long. I don't believe they can. He finds her too pretty. Just like he thought of Esther as the prettiest of them all.

The Pain-screamers crawl inside the nest they built around the corpse of what once was Richie's heart and soul, they stretch their backs and lay on the cement floor satisfied with their craft. It is an itch inside my head scratching through Richie's otherwise pitch-black dream world.

There is never a sound when Richie awakens, not anymore. Just a sudden flash of light hurting like a migraine. His thoughts go from nothing to breakfast in under a second. Then he remembers what day yesterday was. Pain-screamers awaken from their break and shift their focus to pulling levers.

Yesterday was the day his waiting finally paid off.

Again.

The scenes from the basement repeat themselves throughout Richie's memories. Her hurting, him feeling so, so complete. His happiness, and her thankfulness after he forced her to eat. He thinks about how much they love each other and all the ways they can prove their love. After all, she chose him, she wants this life.

The first time these thoughts of darkness hit me was the summer Richie turned 18. Without a soul, his body moved on autopilot through the days. It was enough to get him through school, not enough to make him any friends. Memories of belts to hold him tight while his father did his business left him no impression. His mother's funeral was a stale memory behind a bench without tears. She broke her neck after a misstep down the stairs. Richie didn't cry the night after the funeral either when he had chosen punishment instead of a reward.

"Thank you." The finishing words Richie later learned to respect were only an anecdote at the time.

The words came just as a slight divergence in his otherwise sterile thoughts. She was a small ray of light in a shaded world. Richie sat on a bench in a park made beautiful by the spring sun, Richie saw nothing of it. He saw a ball bouncing towards his feet. A little girl laughing while running away from the mother who stopped chasing her the moment the child stopped looking back. The little girl shone in the grey place Richie lived in with her colorful dress. A quick glance in the mother's direction. The little girl caught the ball right by his feet.

"Maybe I could", a voice whispered in his head over the Pain-screamers mocking laughter.

Maybe I could, he thought.

One thought nothing more, hinting at how he always found children wonderful. They were the happiness in a darkened world, he chose his father, so they could be safe. The thought drifted off into nothingness as soon as it sneaked up on him. It was the beginning of maybe I should, and maybe I will.

I kept hoping for way too long that the thought would stay there, as nothing but brain cells short-circuiting. I explained him building a toy store with what he told himself, it was not because he wanted to get closer to them but because no child should have to live with only one toy as he did, the dragon still in his backpack to that day. He loved them and wanted them to have a better life than he had. When he stuck the first needle through the fabric of what would become Trevor the elephant, I believed his dreams about how happy it would make the child who finally fell for it. I ignored how nightmares of his father got twisted into an idolization and how fear turned into thankfulness for creating Richie's stronger self. I ignored the laughs in his head when Sarah found everything she could ever have wished for in a blue elephant, I only focused on the joy Richie felt and explained it with his dreams coming true. Then he followed Sarah home. He took her away, and the horrors truly began.

Even then, I continued hoping it was the first and the last time. That the second would end it. And then the third, the fourth, the fifth. I hoped Gabriel would see the meaningless in saving Kelly. The cause would only result in more pain. He never listened to me. Now his corpse lies on the table where the Pain-screamers left him.

I am running out of hope.

As Richie gets out of his bed and prepares breakfast, he makes two sandwiches, I push myself out of Dongo and climb down to the corpse.

"Why won't you disappear?" I whisper. "The others did." The answer nags in my head, and I don't like it. The others didn't die by their hand.

He has no pulse, for some reason it was important for me to control it. His death was without question. His heart is far outside his ribcage.

Kelly moves restlessly. She awakens from her nightmares that only will get worse from now on. Upstairs, Richie imagines Kelly's smile when he delivers her a plate. He flips an egg, places it on the plate and inspects with glee how perfect it became. As soon as Kelly hears his steps, she pretends to be asleep again. In his fantasies, she will jump up as soon as he opens the door and hug him thankfully. The Pain-screamers feed him with positive images, fading out all the blood and carnage he created. I grab what is left of Gabriel on my shoulders and carry him back to Dongo. He is not heavy.

The door opens. The laughter in my head goes ecstatic as the Pain-screamers notice Gabriel's absence. Richie looks out over the horror room. Kelly's breathing turns into hick-ups. The Pain-screamers change their feeding plan from happiness to anger. She does not want to see him after all. She disrespects him. They never overdo it, they just feed him enough to make him imagine her paying for ignoring him. I hold my breath awaiting the horrors. But he puts the plate down in front of her, leans over, and kisses her on the cheek.

"See you tonight," he whispers.

The anger brewing within Richie and the images of her bleeding to his satisfaction make me want to scratch my brain out. I curl up against the wall.

"This is not Richie," I mumble. "It is the Pain-screamers."

Inside my head, my own voice whispers questions.

But what if he always has been like this? What if I just choose to ignore it? What if the Pain-screamers only use what was already in his library?

# Chapter 3

Every day is an uneven battle. Me fighting for the last of my sanity versus the Pain-screamers constantly whispering temptations into Richie's ears. It is a battle getting worse every time a new victim steps into one of his traps. Or when the child chooses him, as he convinces himself to oblige his father's made-up demands. The most difficult part of the day is after school hours, and the worst days are Saturdays and Sundays. Children fill the store during all hours those days. The Pain-screamers feast on every moment, and Richie struggles to stay put. His conviction to follow his father's rules fades with every new child entering the store.

There is no plush for them to choose today, he thinks.

"Pain." The Pain-screamers laugh in his ears.

"Rip them away." The inner voice terribly similar to his own translates for him. "No one will notice. It is about time you got to choose one."

To endure, I focus all my attention on Kelly who hugs her now empty teddy bear. There are so many similarities to what already happened five times before. All of them held their plush animals close when the pain grew worse. They all cried for help in the ears of their loved, and dead, animals. They all died under excruciating pain.

Kelly cries out as she thugs Chester closer to her. Her movements have grown stiffer and slower. The pain in her inside will continue to get worse until her last breath. She forced down all the content on the plate Richie left for her with tears dripping down her face. With each chew she looked out the window afraid to see Richie's car on the driveway before she had the chance to finish it. He will reward her for that. She will never understand why he continues to punish her.

"It's only you and me now, Chester." She mumbles to her teddy bear while stroking his ears. "Only you and me."

If she only knew her parents were alive. They look for her with posters around every other streetlight. Laura Marcsinzky with heavy make-up poorly covering her bruises. Milton Marcsinzky heavy under the eyes from all the alcohol he drank last night. The stank is still fresh on his breath.

Kelly clearly has it better with me, Richie thought when he saw them. That's why she chose me. To get away from them.

With time, she will get over that he claimed he killed her parents.

The thoughts drowned his frustration over her sleeping when he gave her breakfast. She will never know about their attempts anyway. No one has found Richie's prisoners this far.

As a buzz in the back of my head Richie's brain tells me he looks up from the scribbles he wrote on the back of a receipt to look busy. His thoughts are too cluttered for him to do anything important on a day like this. In front of him, a boy comes up asking for the toilet.

"Just choose one, this once. You can take care of two." The voice inside his head translates laughter of pain.

"Please," I say and flinch. "Don't do it."

A sickening excitement creeps on to me as Richie takes the child away from the others. He touches the boy's lower back. His pulse races.

"We have one in the back," Richie says. "Just you come with me this way."

He leads the boy behind the counter towards the office. No one can see them. No one even noticed them leaving. Richie made sure of that.

"Just once." A whisper, nothing more, but it thunders through my head in the heaviest of storms.

Richie stops breathing from excitement. The Pain-screamers go silent. Everyone waits for what comes next. I scream from the pressure of all horrible impulses lining up inside Richie's head.

"Remember." The familiar voice of an old man breaks through, the excitement. "I only hurt you because you want to hurt. I am not a bad man. I am giving you what you want. I hope you have learned that much. We in this family only give people what they want. Nothing more."

Richie quickly removes his hand from the boy's back.

"It's right over there," he says while hyperventilating. "Please don't touch anything when you get back out. If I don't have the papers in order, I can't sell all the toys in the store."

I fall into a pile on the floor next to Gabriel's body. Richie's father's words. Back then I would never have believed I could be thankful for them. The Pain-screamers burst into an echoing laughter. They have tried to break the barrier they built for many years. No translation is needed for this celebration. They are getting closer. Next time might be the breakthrough they have been waiting for. In truth, if the child would have been a girl, I'm not sure his father's words would have been enough. The temptation would have been too much. I catch my breath just as Richie does before he goes back out to the store.

"I need to bury you," I say and look to the body parts next to me.

I know it is impossible. Every attempt to alter the world around me has been a complete waste of my time but letting Gabriel rot here next to me is not an option. The store's doorbell chimers as a new group of children storms in. Children laugh unknowing of the danger walking among them and unaware of how close their friend was to be forever lost, but all is okay, for now.

I would love to visit the store once more, just to see with my own eyes how much it has changed since the days when Richie brought me along and let me sit in the office. Back when I still convinced myself everything was well with him. Before it became the hunting ground for the Pain-screamers' sick fantasies. Watching him by the counter for hours, smiling at every child passing the store with their favorite toy in hand. That was good times. Times that grew dark awfully fast.

I lay still and breathe while listening to the Pain-screamers' celebratory laughter. A new gang of children enters. The laughing voices shatter in an instant. Everything turns red. I never got a chance to prepare myself for what was coming. Neither did the Pain-screamers. I scream as the intense anger fills every corner of my mind, quenching all my thoughts relentlessly.

The Pain-screamers scream too, but it is all in ecstatic joy. The red glows brighter for every second. I cover my eyes, but it is all in my head. In the red, pictures of a teddy bear in two pieces, one body and one head, outline themselves. Chester. Memories of what Richie felt while he sewed them back together. Anger over one boy. The boy who just entered the store with his friends. Frank Fuller. Richie's mind boils and the pain-screamers waste no time. They feed the fire with images of the boy twisting in death rattles as his last breath leaves the body.

"Kill."

"Hi, Mr. R," Frank says and walks by the counter.

His gang always looks at the football cards in the furthest back of the store where the shelves protect them from Richie's glaring looks.

"Thank you for letting me borrow the toilet, Mr. Reston." A child's careful voice says in the deepest end of his subconscious. "I made sure not to touch a single thing."

"Please, Please," I whisper. But I know, the battle is already lost before it started.

The red slowly fades only to give room for the planned killing. Frank comes up to the counter with a pack of cards and a smile twisted by Pain-screamers into a grin.

"I'll have these, please," he says and puts the pack on the counter as he does once every week and hands Richie his dad's plastic card.

The boy has been carrying the card around for as long as he has visited Richie's store. The only trace of the boy's father came in the money transferred. Just like the money the child spends, the child never created much interest for the father. The father only cares about power and fear, which everyone crossing his path knows from experience, including Richie. For Richie, the experience came from one time when the child wanted to return a broken toy. The memory of the bruises in themselves is enough to infuriate him, the memory does not add much but the Pain-screamers throw it into the fire anyway.

The fire burns big and bright, and they all admire its horrendousness.

Richie focuses with all his strength on this moment and the teddy bear the boy broke. Small divergent strands of thoughts wander off in murderous fantasies.

In one divergent strand, Richie punches Frank to the ground and then stabs him with the colorful airplane hanging from the ceiling. The corpse lays on the tiled floor bleeding out while coloring the happy propeller and the wings in red. Behind Dongo's thick cloth, I scratch my scales to not have a meltdown.

"Oh, new cards, I see." Richie stutters. He takes the card pack and shoves it into Frank's eye. My breath stops for a moment as I mistake the action for reality and not being a divergent thought colored by Pain-screamers whispering in his ear. "Don't you have the whole collection yet?"

"No Mr. R, they make new cards all the time, so I will never get them all." Richie breaks Frank's fingers one by one while enjoying the sound of Frank's screams to the fullest. The gang following Frank's every step actually cheers Richie on, or is it the Pain-screamers laughing behind their faces.

"I see," Richie says. He punches Frank unconscious, just like the boy's father did to him. Teeth drop into the boy's throat choking his unconscious body to death. "Isn't Mr. Fuller, you father?"

Frank stops mid-putting the plastic card back in his pocket. He nods.

"Great!" Richie's fake smile feels slimy into my backbone. "He came by and asked me to fix up a package for him earlier today."

"He did?" The tension in Frank's voice fades away as he lingers on the words. He smiles. "What package?"

Richie leans over the counter towards him. He strangles Frank until the eyes roll back into the skull, and then they pop. "I don't know if I'm supposed to tell you. It was a pretty big one. I think it was supposed to be a surprise."

The excitement sparkles in the boy's eyes. "A package from dad? He has never done something like that before."

"No," Richie contemplates while taking the card reader back behind the counter, "I've actually never seen him here before. But God what an order he made."

"What?" Frank goes from sparkling to bursting, never noticing the blatant lie. "I want to see it."

Richie catches him mid-jump and snaps his neck. The crack before the life disappears in the boy's eyes is so satisfying. "I don't know," he says. "He wanted to get it himself."

"Okay," Frank says, the shining burst in his eyes fade, much to Richie's joy.

The pause coming next gives me a short moment to breathe. Then I scream again, as pain-screamer's cheering becomes a terrifying flood.

"You know what?" Richie asks, and the boy's hope gets re-ignited. "If you just were here an hour later you could have asked him yourself."

"I could?" He looks at Richie with curiosity. He thinks hard for a while. "Maybe, I could stay here until he arrives."

Richie's adrenaline is pumping, Frank is nibbling the bait. Just real it in slow now.

"Maybe you could," Richie says. "But are you really going to let your friends wait for you all that time?"

"My friends." Frank looks at his gang as if he had forgotten they even existed during those short minutes.

"Guys. I think I will stay here for a while to see what dad's been doing behind my back. You better go somewhere else or else he might suspect something."

The gang nods back at him.

"We'll be at the playground. Remember the cards." One of the taller in the bunch says proving like so many times before that Frank is the only one among them with access to money. The Fullers are the only ones in Vesterville with money.

Frank answers with a comforting, "Sure, I will."

Frank has bitten. He caught the hook from which there is no return, Richie dances on the inside with all the laughs as his only music.

"If you want, you can wait in my office. I even have my own binder full of these cards."

"You do?"

He never had any cards, just as he never has been interested in any sport. "Yeah, but the players might be too old for you to remember."

"Don't be so sure Mr. R, I know an awful lot about football."

Richie laughs, it synchronizes perfectly with laughter inside his head. They are all thinking the same word. Kill. The pain-screamers sound their encouraging chant.

Pain. Pain. Pain.

"We will see about that. I'm a lot older than you can imagine."

Frank laughs too. He follows Richie back to the office, Richie glances at the store and makes sure no one looks in their direction. The beauty of children is how they never notice anything around them when they are focused on something they like.

"Let's see where I have it." Richie fake-looks through his binders on the shelf. He grabs one, the largest one marked Taxes 2010. He grabs it with both his hands. One glance out the door, still no one looking. Frank sits down on the office chair.

"Here you go."

Frank's eyes get bigger as he sees the large binder. Then he sees the binder flying towards his head. The hit is not enough to knock him unconscious. He falls off the chair clueless about what just happened. Richie launches at him before he gets the time to puzzle it all together. Richie's hands tighten around Frank's neck. The boy's breathing turns into wheezing and then into nothing. He tries to scream for help, but no sound passes his lips. He kicks furiously but the carpet muffles the sound. Richie leans over him putting all his weight on Frank's throat. It crunches under his fingers.

"You deserve to die," Richie whispers. "For what you did to Chester."

The last shimmer of life leaves Frank's confused eyes. He dies unknowing of the reasons justifying his killer's judgment. Chester was after all only a teddy bear, a teddy bear he probably forgot the moment it left his hands torn in two. Frank's kicks slowly lose intensity as the body redirects all energy to keep the vital organs alive. His heartbeat slows down under Richie's fingertips, each beat is as clear as the ticks and tocks of a clock. I focus my breathing around the beats to withstand the pressure. Tick, inhale, tock, exhale. Survive, I think. Just survive. Tick, inhale, tock, exhale.

The death rattles kick in. Quick twitches all over Frank's body. Richie waits them out with his fingers still tightly locked around the boy's neck. He smiles, a quiet chuckle leaves his tightly closed lips. His fingers still flare in blue and red on the boy's neck after he lets go. Richie corrects his clothes, making sure the trousers cover the bulge from his crotch. It was arousing. The twitching, the pulse under his fingers, the last breath, the breaking of his father's made-up rules. He crossed the edge he has been balancing on for so long and fell down the pit filled with Pain-screamers welcoming him with open mouths.

And it felt good. I smile even though I am terrified. So, so good.

I turn to Gabriel. "Help me," I mumble. He answers in the same way a corpse always answers unspoken questions.

I want to continue hoping, but am I capable anymore? I should not be. Not when Richie in full erection receives the next unknowing customer. The child smiles, she laughs at Richie's jokes but if she knew what the store owner hides behind the counter, she would run screaming for her father by the door. Richie thinks about what excitement one more would do; would it layer on the already present excitement? It would be exhilarating.

I cry. Not because Frank died, death is long gone from affecting me much. I cry because my last hope fades.

"Please help me." I cry. "Please Gabriel, help me."

He stares me into the eyes with his own empty dead face. Mouth open and tongue hanging out. It should be scary, but I find it comforting.

A new wave of horrid thoughts flood over me as Richie clasps his hands around Frank's throat again hoping to relive the fascination of Frank's pulse fading under his thumbs. What hits me the hardest is the frustration when the attempt proves unsuccessful. He slowly turns flaccid, only the imagination keeps him going.

Pling. The bell over the door chimes. It is barely audible through fog in his mind. The man jerking the dead boy's body up and down looks up. He is completely driven by urge. Desperate urges.

"How can I help you?" Echoes through the thick mist clouding all other thoughts.

It is a little girl on the other side of the counter. Everything around her becomes sharp. Red hair like flames, and blue eyes like an ocean. A blue skirt with white horizontal stripes. Her sandals white in a snowflake pattern. She is just like Esther. No, I think. Not like Esther. But in Richie's thoughts, I already see the Pain-screamers paint the girl to what he wants her to be. Esther. She always aroused him the most. Girls always arouse him the most. Blond ones in particular. The tiny red dress was simply the sherry on top.

Can I? No. Yes? The voice in my head screams in pain as he fights between all he wants, and all I want him to want. The iterated temptations tear through every fiber in his body. All the pain-screamers do is wait patiently for the crack in the wall that is Richie's conscious to stop seeping and completely falter into an unstoppable flood wave. There is no tension in their waiting, only celebration.

The little girl hands him a box with a doll. Pink hair, and red painted nails. As soon as it gets out from the view of the little girl, it disappears into the blur. The girl creases a bill between her fingers.

"Don't you destroy the bill now sweetie," Richie says. His voice sounds grumbled when I receive it. "Did you get it from your mother?"

She nods, small movements but they are clear as day.

"Where is she now?" He continues before the girl opens her pretty mouth to answer, lips looking delicious. "At home?"

Anticipation rises with every extra beat his heart manages to force within a minute. She nods again and hands him the bill.

There is no other voice or laughter in his head this time. Only quite approval.

"Do you know what?" Richie asks. "I have an even cuter doll here in the back if you want to see it. I think her name is Hetty. Do you want to see her?"

The girl looks at the pink-haired doll in the box.

"She has the most glittering pink hair you could ever imagine," Richie fills in.

Her eyes widen, eyes sparkling like water in sunlight. All of Richie's focus and imagination fixate at them, the clear blue and sparkling eyes. They will shatter into many small, red veins as soon as she follows him behind the counter. She now looks straight into his eyes full of belief and wonder of what this new doll may look like. She nods again.

"Great," Richie says. "Come with me to the back."

He moves aside from the counter, giving a place for her to walk past him. She grabs her backpack tighter around her body and walks up to him. I want to scream for her to not follow the monster. But it is pointless, she is already gone.

Frank's pulse drums in Richie's fingers. Richie corrects his trousers. The bulge will be visible through the fabric any second now. She stops one step away from seeing the corpse of a boy from her school. She looks outside in one glance. Richie follows her glance. Nothing awaits them there but the window towards the street. Only an empty street. He puts his hand on her back and pushes her the final step.

"I promise you, you don't want to miss this doll."

She tears her eyes away from the window and looks straight at him while following his pushes. She never lets go of his admiring gaze. She now stands behind him, broken away from the outside in front of the counter. Richie's hand moves up to her neck and his grip hardens.

"Follow me," he says.

She freezes. Richie pushes her closer to him. He leans forward and smells her. All my neurons strain from his pleasure, leaving my head in shatters. All that is Richie's being is swallowed by darkness.

"You will do perfectly." He whispers into her ears. The smile written on his face by Pain-screamer's intentions reaches me in shivers.

The little body slams into the floor next to Frank. The fear disrupting her once sparkling eyes turns Richie's desires into max gear. I support myself on all fours while fighting each pulse reaching me faster and faster. Breathe. Just breathe. Her pulse ticks fast against his hand. All my nerves and neurons twirl themselves inside my brain and my bones into tightly packed strings. Richie's desires turn into a charring fire in my stomach, a feeling both nauseating and exhilarating. Richie pushes his hand closer to her pulse and the ticks slow down from his pressure. His arousal grows intense enough to make Richie question whether he will have the time to get his trousers of.

"Take her!" His desires scream from the depth of his being.

"Take her," I whisper in response to all urges flooding my every cell. "Please don't!" I cry out in regret when I realize what words left my lips.

"Leave her be!"

The Pain-screamers break into laughter, their chant of pain breaks into a cheering song.

"Take her!" Richie's desires join in. "Take her!"

Urges turn into chaotic flame inside my stomach. "Take her!" I join in, incapable of stopping the words from leaving my mouth. Cheering laughter turns into a celebration.

The last the little girl hears as her pulse fades under the sexually aroused man strangling her is the sipper of his jeans. And the last she feels is the pain of him forcing himself into her. His ecstasy grows with the slowing of her pulse. The strings that once were my nerves curl into a ball in my spine.

"Take her!" I pant shaking from euphoria.

Her body shakes under him, her death rattles push Richie's climax to levels none of us experienced before. At least, she never felt his climax. In all her pain she did not have to learn that horror.

My body shakes just like Richie's does. The voice in his brain goes silent under a euphoric thunderstorm. The storm subsides in an instant and all left behind is the feeling of completion, and peace of mind as he empties himself. I scream in fear as every one of my neurons give in to the darkness, yet I smile. I hate everything Richie has become, but it feels so good. The climax drenches my brain in happiness. He feels great. I feel great. I smile. I love this feeling, I truly do.

I hate myself.

# Chapter 4

I hate. I have done so for a long, long time.

I hope. I have done so for an even longer time.

Hate and hope, in my decades on this earth, the two have always been correlated. I hate this grim world and every psychotic twist it takes. Yet, I love Richie with all my heart even though he is the one showing me the darkest corners this world has to offer. Thanks to him, I know what horrors dwells beneath everything visually beautiful and what evil kindness truly hides. I have seen it all in him growing up from an innocent child into the monster hiding under his skin today. I hope for the day when everything I hate in this world turns out to be nothing but the cruel joke of a narcissistic god. I hope for the day I wake up to little Richie's calm breath. I hope for the day I wake up to see his eyes shine at me again. I hope for the morning when I wake up to him whispering Dongo's name in his sleep. But I never sleep, a warrior of the snake only faint under extreme pressure. It is a dreamless sleep without rest. So, I hate more, and consequently, I hope more.

I hate myself right now. When Richie destroys someone in the most humiliating way possible, I cannot help but smile from enjoying the hormones rushing through Richie's brain. The evolutionary drugs built to continue a specie's survival are all so addictive. I am freed from all the horrors in this world, and after all freedom has burnt itself out, the guilt creeps in to haunt my every thought. The guilt feeds the hate, and in the ecstasy, my hate only grows stronger until it outgrows everything else. In the storm of hate, a spark of hope ignites on a thin unsteady match. And I continue to hope a weak and broken man's hope, and the hate-hope cycle is complete.

I cannot let hope destroy me, I think. Not anymore.

I lay on the floor filled with all the happy drugs created from Richie's body reaching climax. Richie's body collapses on top of the dead girl. He twitches and pants as the reflexes fade out.

He is happy. So, so happy.

And I am ashamed, I've been so for a long, long time.

The difference from all the other shameful days is that today, my hope has finally been choked into submission on all the children he has violated. There is no chance for me to convince myself of the good in his actions anymore. This, the last one, he harmed all for his own joy, not because the child chose him, not because his anger drove him. He chose her and her choice had nothing to do with it. Not even in his fractured mind. The kind child who I always hoped to be within him is dead. What is left is an evil man. It is all Richie is nowadays. Evil.

"How am I supposed to stop this?" I whisper in despair.

Gabriel, still laying dead beside me, remains silent.

All the temptations within Richie's head are silent, all his thoughts are silent. There is only celebration. For the Pain-screamers, fun-time has only begun. For me, hell has slammed its gates open.

Richie's mind slowly wakes up again. It comes in vague buzzing sparks getting louder with every second as his neurons break free from the ecstatic drugs. He looks down at the little body underneath him. The bruises on her neck flaring in a blue fire. No remorse. No matter how hard I search, it is inexistent within him. I did not expect to find it, but the habit is still deeply rooted in who I am. For him, everything is relief now.

Richard Reston is free.

"Thank you," he says and kisses her on her sweaty forehead. "Thank you, so much."

He sips his trousers. He whistles, happily, while proudly admiring the traces of him leaving her dead body. There is one more at home, he thinks. I flinch when the smiling face of Kelly flashes in the back of my head. She will die tonight I am sure of it. Hopefully, she will stay unaware for a little longer.

"Mildred." A voice yells in the background. The bell over the door plings as a man walks into the shop. Richie's heart goes from completely calm to beating out of his chest within microseconds. The shift takes me by surprise. His pulse pounders inside my head threatening to beat me into unconsciousness. My mouth fills with the metallic taste of blood. Richie's panic explodes as he looks into the shop and the stressed blond man who just entered. Richie looks at the two corpses on the floor. Instinctively, he grabs the girl and throws her into the restroom. The boy he kicks into the room, each kick more furious than the last. Their faces glare unnaturally at him, necks twisted, and bodies dripping wet from the toilet water that splashed on the walls when her body crashed into it. Their legs and arms are bent backward at the joints. To my horror, Richie focuses all his energy on them to ensure all their limbs are inside and not visible. He slams the door only for it to get stuck on the girl's fingers. He puts all his weight on the door until her fingers crunch under the pressure.

"Milly!" The man yells again. He gets up to the counter and stares into Richie's eyes with the stressful look only a father is capable of when he lost his child. "Have you seen a little girl? Red hair? blue dress?"

The picture of the dead body in the bathroom flashes before my eyes in a long, horrible moment. Her red hair stripped over her head and her mouth open in the breath that was her last.

She was supposed to be alone in the store, Richie thinks. She said so. No, her mother was not in the store, that was her words. Her father was just outside. A new wave of adrenaline punches me to my knees. He was outside all the time. It was just dumb luck he never walked into the loud moans of a man defiling his daughter in her last living moments.

"A little girl?" Richie glances under the door where a small pool of blood is building. His sweat makes the shirt stick to his back. He steps on the pool in hope of covering it. "You mean the girl who bought the pink-haired doll? She went out just a minute ago."

The man looks out the door as if she would stand there waiting for him. The street is empty, just as it has been since she entered.

"She did." If he just for a moment would catch his calm, he would notice her bill on the counter and the doll right by the register. But he is a father who lost his daughter, details are unimportant. "How could I miss her?" He runs out.

"I think she went left towards Herman Street," Richie shouts after him, and as soon as the man disappears, he falls to the floor shaking. The adrenaline flushing through his body has forced his pulse into the rhythm of a rabbit's heart mid-chase. Fast to the point where a heart attack is not far away. Richie grabs his chest and swallows saliva and blood's metallic taste. He breathes in short bursts. The doorbell sounds once again.

It is the father again, Richie thinks and looks to the pool of blood beside him, then over the counter. The man never comes back, even though Richie imagines him to. The store is silent but the sound of small feet wandering over the floor. Richie calms his breath just enough to think clearly.

"Mr. Reston?" A weak voice asks from the other side of the counter.

It is the voice of a girl. "I'll be there shortly" Richie sighs under his panting breath. He grabs the counter and forces himself up. The little girl meets his gaze. She is cute, he thinks, and even though a faint what if sounds through his adrenaline-pumped thoughts, the temptation is not motivation enough to take her. He is not willing to take the risk, not after what just happened.

"Are you feeling okay, Mr. Reston?" She asks.

Richie smiles a smile showing all the tiredness the sudden stress caused him. "Not so well, little darling. I think I should call Al and see if he can come in today."

"Oh, should I come back later?"

"No, that's okay." He takes the teddy bear she holds. "This one really wants to follow you home." He pretends the teddy bear is walking over the counter to hug her and the little girl giggles unknowing that the last one who bought a teddy bear in the shop sits on a table in a basement with the teddy bear tucked tight to her body.

The girl pays for the bear with the last of her allowance. Mary is the bear's name, Richie told her so. If you give Mary an umbrella, she can fly all the way to Kansas. The girl wishes for him to get better before she leaves and tells him to send Al her regards. She is truly a cute one, I hate myself for thinking so.

Immediately after the girl leaves the store, Richie calls Al, the man destined to take over the store if it survives long enough. Nausea is all the reason the loyal man needs to tell Richie to shut the shop down and go home as fast as possible. He will take care of the shop as fast as the car can take him there. Al is a good man, a way too good of a man to help this crime to go unnoticed. Richie scrubs the floor throughout their conversation, vomit he explains when Al asks. If the naïve man knew it was children's blood his boss was scrubbing, he would have called the police immediately. But today Al is happy to spend two days at the store alone on such short notice. Those occasions only happen once every year, or often even rarer. An interval weirdly coinciding with children disappearing. Al is also stupid. That helps a lot. He is the one who most certainly will claim he could never have suspected his boss was behind the kidnappings when, or if, Richie got caught.

Carefully, Richie walks out through the shop's backdoor. Everyone is either home or at work, it is the perfect moment to escape. In his hands, he has two large black garbage bags. Black garbage bags containing something suspiciously similar to bodies. Not even Richie can fool himself of this fact. The smaller of the bags gives of a faint squishing sound from a body splashing around in its own blood. For Richie every little squish sounds like a large bell alarming everyone about his intentions. For me, the sound gets disfigured into an echo that will haunt me for the rest of my days. Richie looks over his shoulder. No one watches him. He throws the two bags in the trunk and carefully covers them with tarp. He backs, corrects the tarp, then concludes that no one ever would suspect what is hiding underneath. There is no risk of running into Al yet, the drive from him to the toy store is well over an hour. That brings Richie some kind of calm even though it is not enough to slow his pulse down.

If just Al was in town, I think. He would be here in less than a couple of minutes. He would call the cops on Richard. It is the first time I truly hope for it. It is betrayal, I know. Richie is the one I swore to protect, and I have always hoped for him to get better. After I lost the battle, it was all I could do. But I want this nightmare to end.

A feeling of safety and relief fills me as Richie leaves the driveway. He drives the car out of town. Killing two children should be a terrifying event in his life. Happiness should not dominate. But he sings. He sings while leaning backward and clapping the tarp where he knows the girl lays and remembers the euphoria of him being released from the boundaries the Pain-screamers built for him. He laughs a laugh of happiness he cannot hold back. He does not want to either. I smile as memories of happiness flows over me. I want to hold it back, but it is impossible. She is his trophy. The boy he sees as his duty. Frank will be buried in the woods behind the house far away from the others. But the girl will share their memorial spot as an important chapter in his life. She is the turning point, the one that helped him break free. She was the sacrifice he needed to do.

His mind goes to Kelly in his basement, he was so glad when she chose Chester.

She was perfect.

He puts both hands on the wheel again, imagining Kelly seeing him coming back into the basement. She is unharmed. She runs up to him and jumps up into his open arms. She has longed for him to come home. Richie shows her the hat of her tormentor. She lights up. The anger he felt while leaving her in the basement this morning is nowhere to be found.

"Thank you!" She says.

That is all he wants. He is happy. She is happy. She kisses him. They live happily ever after.

But that is far from the truth. It is pain-screamers feeding the ego they have spent years in damaging into this psychopath.

They made him like this. That is how it has to be. He cannot have been like this from the start. He was so sweet, and so perfect until they got him. A tear falls down my cheek as he imagines her helping him dig Frank's grave. She is sweaty and smiles.

He cannot be like this, I think again. My last hope dares to surface with its ugly face. It must be them. Not him.

Please let it be them.

# Chapter 5

Gravel against rubber. A sound not meant to strike fear into the hearts of your loved ones, but it does if the feelings are not mutual. Richie is the only one who thinks they chose him. He is the only one broken enough to justify his actions. After today his justifications will fade away, he does what he wants, everyone else is his, and the Pain-screamers', toys. Even I who once loved him unconditionally, I fear the sound of the car closing in.

I reach Dongo's eyes just in time to see the car stop outside the cellar window. It creates a dramatic effect of blackening out the sun and turning the whole room dark.

A whimper sounds across the room as Kelly realizes her torturous time of waiting is over, she now has to endure the torture he will inflict on her. Richie whistles as he steps out of the car. It is a happy tune, but it only unsettles her more. Two black bags crash to the ground, and even though Kelly is unaware of what they contain, she flinches just as if she does.

"Honey, I'm home!" Richie shouts proudly as he opens the door. It tickles his funny-nerve. The lack of answer passes him unnoticed. "I've got the best surprise for you!"

Fantasies of him sneaking down with the Frank-bag and then showing it to an anticipating, perfect, little girl creeps up on me. She is glad he removed her demon. She is thankful. She glows towards him as he hears her utter the only word he wants to hear.

"Thank you." She hugs him and kisses him. He wraps his hands around her naked body. The kissing becomes more intense. She moans as he throws her to the table. "Thank you." She repeats as he pushes himself into her. She loves him. He owns her. Pain-screamers laugh in an all-evil chorus. He puts his hands around her throat, Kelly loves it. In punishment, Richie would treat her the same, but then he imagines her screaming in pain. Just like she really does.

In the grimmer reality, Kelly crawls to the end of the table as far away from him as possible. Her glow is not from happiness, it is from fear, bruises, and blood. The distance is not comforting enough. The cellar door slams open. Kelly makes herself as small as she possibly can. Richie scans the room in excitement. For a moment all the happy colors he imagined transfer to the stale room where he keeps his prisoners. Then all the grey slowly taints the heavenly blue, and the cement sprouts out from the cracks in the tiled floor. Lastly, the happy little girl who was supposed to come running for him stops existing and the real girl hiding on the table emerges.

"Kelly," he says. "Why don't you come here and look what I have for you? You will be so happy, I promise you."

I look over to Kelly. It is her choice now. Live or die. I glance at Gabriel. Choose death. Your life will be easier that way. It only hurts this once and then everything will go away.

At first, she lays still for what seems like too long of a time. She is just like the rest of them, I think. Then at the last moment, when the first spark ignites, she moves. She meets his eyes. The mouth is nothing but a thin straight line. Her eyes only shimmer from tears and lack any of the light he imagined. She crawls as close as she can without leaving the table. She moves with a heavy breath and pain clearly smeared all over her face, but for Richie it is tarnished into the girl smiling at him, giggling under her breath. He loves her giggle. Kelly looks down to the floor, then at Richie who also stopped on the last step.

Show me you love me, he thinks.

She at the floor again. Then, she stretches her arm towards him. A sign of begging him to come to her. With that, she saves herself, this time. It is an act of love. It is all Richie ever wanted. The rest of his Pain-screamer-disfigured imagination extrapolates for him.

"Don't say you're afraid of heights, my little angel?" Richie laughs the deep, gurgling laugh synonymous with his happiness. I have always loved that laugh. Kelly nods. Richie laughs again but the smile he expects on Kelly stays absent. He walks down to the cement floor. He stretches his arms out as he walks to the table and hugs her. That the hug is unanswered goes unnoticed.

She smells so nice. Both I and Richie think so. Richie takes a deep breath from her hair to fill his lungs with the scent. So satisfying. He never notices it, but Kelly shivers. The fright she feels could as well be the cold room. After all, she is basically naked.

"You are so perfect," he says as he let the scented air out of his lungs. He releases her from the hug still holding her at an arms-length distance, observing every detail. "Do you want to see what I got for you?"

Kelly looks into his glistering eyes. She nods, again. Obviously too scared to say anything. Richie's thoughts bounce back and forth in ecstatic patterns. He lifts the bag under her nose. He opens it. She looks down into the black hole. Then she freezes completely. She stares down at the corpse and the clearest view she certainly ever had of death.

"He won't hurt you or Chester ever again," Richie whispers into her ear with overflowing pride.

Kelly slowly raises her head and meets his eyes. Her eyes grumbles with salt water. Tears of joy, Richie bursts into joyous thoughts. She is so thankful. I am her hero. Kelly shakes. She throws herself around his neck before her whole face breaks.

"Smart girl," I mumble. "Very, very smart."

Richie stands stunned. The voices in his head are silent. Then they burst into an explosion of cheering and all that is joy, and it is all Richie's voice cheering, no Pain-screamer to be heard in any of it. She is happy for what he did. She is happy her monster is gone. He lays his arms around her small body drowning all of her within him.

She loves him.

"There, there." He says clapping his large hand over her back. "You can feel safe now. He won't torment you anymore. He won't torment anyone anymore."

She shivers in his arms. Relief, he thinks. Fear, I know. Overflowing pride turns into the love he thinks he only can feel with Kelly as they stand there at the table and he comforts her. All the others felt despite over him when they were captured. Kelly feels safe. Kelly is the one, even though he liked Esther better.

I am nauseous.

"Do you want to come with me and bury him?" He asks, hoping for the last piece of his dreaming puzzle to fall into place. "Can you handle that?"

She stops breathing. He lets her arms fall off his neck as she slowly drifts away from him. The red eyes looking straight into his. A cold metallic hand grabs Richie's heart seemingly stopping it from beating. The metallic taste fills my mouth as it fills his. He is ashamed for asking so much of her. She is not ready, not yet.

A sign of humanity within him, my hope whispers faintly.

"I'm so sorry," Richie continues. "I didn't know just seeing him would scare you that much." He hugs her again. "I'm so sorry. You don't have to follow me out there, okay? But you know I have to do it, right? I have to bury him. Everyone deserves that much, even those who are evil." For a moment, the memory of Richie's father's coffin slowly sinking into the ground flashes before my eyes. He strokes the back of her hair and kisses her cheek. "But for that, I must leave you. Can you handle yourself while I do that?"

Kelly successfully forces herself to nod through her shaking.

"Yes," she stutters with the saliva in her mouth almost choking her words.

"Good. If you get scared, shout. I will hear you from the outside." He releases her from the hug. "Is that okay with you?"

She nods and fall to the table.

"You poor soul." Richie says and strokes her one last time over her cheek. She flinches but it goes unnoticed by Richie's subconscious.

"I'll soon be back."

He turns around. Laughter echoes in his head. He smiles. She is proud of him. He walks up the stairs, thinking to himself he did the right thing. She will be forever thankful to him. That is all he ever wanted.

Her thankfulness will give him his own price later when the bodies are buried, and they are all alone.

# Chapter 6

The door shuts behind Richie with the small click from a latch falling into place. Kelly sits fixed on the table where he left her. Still shaking and trying to breathe under snot and tears. Richie whistles again. The horrifying tune was his favorite song as a child.

"I must be dreaming." He bursts out singing. "But the pinches leave me bleeding. You are in love with me." He tap-dances over the green grass. Kelly does too in his fantasies.

I sigh. I dig my claws deep under my scales. Please let this end. Just let this end right here, right now.

"Chester," Kelly says spitting the word out with the snot blocking her mouth. She looks around until she finds the blue teddy bear. "Chester." She crawls over to the empty plush and hugs him close. "I don't want to be here."

Outside Richie searches for the shovel. His singing turns into humming. Even more haunting.

"Did you hear him lock the door?"

"No," I say both in an answer to her question and in trying to convince her to not do what she thinks about doing. Richie considered locking, but Kelly loves him. Locks are unnecessary in love.

Through her own movements, Chester first looks up to the cellar door and then shakes his head. There is a silence between the two as they look at each other, the teddy bear and the bruised and crying girl. "Do you promise not to tell Mr. Reston if I escape?"

Chester promises. He lies. In truth, he has no choice.

Kelly cries as she also realizes the risk in what she wants to do. This girl knows enough of the world now to know how horrible life can be.

Kelly puts Chester under her arm and carries him across the table. She stops by Dongo and looks straight into his and my eyes.

"Please don't tell him," she whispers. "I will get someone to save you later."

I believe she means every word, but I can only hope she will be right at the end. And it is a weak hope at its best.

Richie has put the shovel to work, and his first drop of sweat has begun its journey down his forehead. It tickles his nose. Kelly crawls over the edge of the table and jumps down. She is not scared of heights as Richie believed. She probably never has been. She is a brave girl. She disappears out of sight. Her voice cracks in a loud moan when she lands. I am not sure she will make it up the stairs in her condition. I push my hands against Dongo's eye until they float across the barrier. Simultaneously I force my blood out through the pores in my hands. The sticking feeling spread across my palms and the blue shield surrounds me. I look to the stairs where I expect Kelly to stand but she is nowhere to be seen, I instead hear her breathe fighting to regain its calm. The little girl's head shows over the table edge as she stands upright again. Her face is red from tears and the effort of withstanding the pain from her insides. She looks back at me, and puts her index finger over her mouth, and forms a long 'ssssh'. Without thinking about it I do the same.

Her secret is safe with me. It is foolish to think I ever will be able to tell Richie anything. She looks out the window towards where Richie now digs two holes in the ground, one in the graveyard and one further down the woods. His thoughts are completely focused on the task. I jump down from Dongo's nose and hit the tabletop. At the same time, Kelly has walked to the stairs and climbs the first step. The whole time, she keeps an eye out through the window. Richie never looks in while Kelly climbs the steps. She grabs the handle and pulls it down towards her. It clicks again as the door opens. She looks at Chester in her arms, then back at me, and waves. I wave back.

"Good luck," I say as the door closes and clicks again. "You'll need it."

# Chapter 7

Richie's steps have always been loud against the wooden floor. For those in his captivity, the question has never been of where he is, they have always been whether he is coming down. Luckily, his baritone voice leaves a clue of what he is doing. Kelly's steps on the other hand are dead silent as she wanders across the hallway. I await the sound of the front door opening and closing. It feels like forever but when the door opens it does with the weakest squeak imaginable.

In the backyard, Richie digs his two holes in trance-like focus. His inner thoughts go from the hole and the body supposed to fill it to how happy Kelly will be once he gets back. Just how devastated she was when he asked her to join him tells him she misses him too much already. The thought makes his shovel go quicker into the ground were the dead girl he claimed earlier will have her final uneasy rest.

Kelly is better of not knowing about Milly, he thinks. Frank on the other hand, his burial they will celebrate. Milly is his secret reward, at least for now. Kelly will thank him for that later.

The Pain-screamers remain silent for now. No matter how this story continues both they and I know how it will end. In blood and another dead girl buried in his backyard, and another plush on his shelf. The self-control so synonymous with Richie as he grew up is long gone. The child who noticed every misstep or every misplaced breath that could trigger his father now daydreams who more he could claim as his reward. And the Pain-screamers reap the fruits from decades of hard work.

The front door shuts in a muffled click behind Kelly, and I snap out of memories of a painful childhood. Richie's daydreaming has refocused on the holes and the bodies. Kelly's escape went unnoticed. I hope for her to succeed. I truly do. I just know how history has told this story before. Sarah managed to get out while he was still asleep beside her. With her body torn apart, she limped her way out. The same morning, he came back with her. He was furious. She was terrified. She was dead before he was done with her, but in his fury, he kept going, cursing at her for leaving him. He punched her dead body without realizing the girl under him was no more. Uriel was completely teared up from all the torment she had gone through.

"I want to dance with the others." She repeated while her mind went deeper into insanity. "I want to crawl with the snake under the tree and never see this world again. I want to watch the snake in the eyes and hear him sing me the softest lullaby." Uriel continued until she faded away, first into dust then into smoke.

"It tells me I failed." She said in a sob lastly before her face crumbled.

Their death was the ones that shook me the most, Sarah's and Uriel's. The first ones. It was also the death that shook Richie the most. Neither of us thought he was capable.

"You did nothing wrong." The voice had whispered. "She should have known not to run away from the life you could have given her."

Richie promised himself it would never happen again.

Sadly, he has never been a strong boy, or man. Just like his promises of never letting his father in again this promise was doomed to be broken. Soon the memory of Sarah's smile as she chose Trevor the elephant became one temptation too many and Olaf the monkey took shape in his thoughts. The new child would be more thankful for the life Richie could give her, he told himself.

With time I learned my lesson and stopped longing for the days I would meet others like me. I also learned that no matter how good or bad or horrible our families were, there was only one thing we all shared. The pain we were destined to endure, and the words the snake whispers in our ears. I finally put it all together and realized the snake only whispers those lies into our ears to motivate us the extra mile in a suicidal journey.

A snake. A tree. A dance. A fruit. Life, Light, and Darkness. It was his words. Always. Each promise falser than the last. We are not supposed to know it but when you have heard the words repeated from dying souls enough times the pattern becomes clear. The promise of a better life at the end of the tunnel. A promise of a faraway land where all your wishes come true, and all you do every day is dancing and singing. It is a religious motivation for warriors facing certain death.

You are no longer worthy of our Light.

It was the first words I ever remembered. The memories of them as blurred as all else the snake told me before I fell and hit the dragon's bottom. But they have lingered with me for all my life.

I am not worthy. I will never be worthy to dance and sing around a tree with happiness all around me, no warrior will.

The truth is we all go up in smoke with a voice in our head telling us we failed, just like it happened for Uriel, and Michael, and Camael, and Raphael. It is our end. Why else would the snake send us to protect those who are already doomed?

Outside Richie has stopped singing. His focus has shifted from digging to covering up the holes where two bodies will be forever hidden. He is still happy. This evening, he believes it to be all he is, no anger or hate, just happiness. He believes happiness to sparkle within Kelly too. He pats the ground until it is flat. Tomorrow he will plant grass and the days after he will watch it grow with increasing excitement. Maybe he even will plant flowers on Milly's grave.

I hope Kelly has found a perfect hiding place by now. I also hope she came to her senses and threw the teddy bear away. Otherwise, there is no escape from this hell. Sacrifice the traitor, save yourself. The problem is, no child sacrifices their favorite plush.

Richie throws the shovel into the ground and lets it stand. He proudly observes how the shovel wages back and forth. He hopes Kelly will be equally proud of him too. She is just too perfect, almost as perfect as Esther. He whistles again. Then he sings to himself.

"You are my only one. You are my shining light."

Richie's steps echo loudly as he walks the stairs to the entrance. He dances them up, laughing at his badly performed jazz hands. Pain-screamers stretch their backs. They will be completely ecstatic with Richie's discovery and the anger exploding through his very being. The anger they groomed him to obey. And the haunting voice will paint all thoughts blood-red with its words.

"Kelly," he says and slams the cellar door open. "He is gone now. You are finally safe." Half-way down, he notices the empty table. She is not standing on it anymore as he remembers her, waiting for him with happy tears in her eyes.

"Kelly," he says one more time running down the stairs and looking in every corner of the room, even behind the radiator. "Kelly!" The anger awakens. Laughter erupts, they are ready.

Breathe in, I think. Breathe out.

I am not ready.

I am not worthy.

He looks under the table, right under my feet. His screams of her name turn frustrated. He puzzles it all together. She fooled him and now she has escaped. Hate grows through his cells with poisonous thorns tearing bleeding scars into everything it touches.

"She left you. Just like everybody else. She only pretended to love you." The voice crawls through my spine in shivers. "She only wanted to hurt you, just like everyone else. She never deserved your love." The laughter turns into a thundering roar. "Punish her. Hurt her as she and they all hurt you."

Richie lets out a roar of her name one last time before running up the stairs, leaving me and Dongo alone in the cellar with the black garbage bags in which Frank and Molly took their final journey. Their belongings are still in the bags. He wanted to show Kelly how the one Frank where in is now empty, he wanted to show her she now is safe with him. In his own way that was an act of love. I climb down from the table. I fight with all my power to not become overwhelmed with the growing rage.

Upstairs, Richie searches for the single gadget capable of destroying all possibilities of a successful escape. He throws newspapers to the floor. Every paper and every letter is tainted with red anger. He is not scared of what she will tell people if she succeeds with her escape. He has not been since Sarah. After her escape he took precautions. A small tracer hidden in their toys. The children after her never got far. Once upon a time, I hoped for Richie to bring me along, just to give me the last desperate chance of calming him. With time, hope turned to dread for the times when he brought me along. Seeing a child's face up close as Richie beats him to the brink of consciousness made sure I never wanted to experience it again. The rollercoaster I am forced through by his thoughts is more than enough.

"Did you think you could run away from the dragon? Did you?" He screamed into Carl's face. The boy was broken both mentally and physically when Richie finally dragged him back to the basement to finish him off.

And still, I hoped Carl would be the last one. I hoped naively for the bloodshed to end.

Richie finds the monitor at the same time as I get to Frank's backpack. I look inside. Richie's frustration reaches new heights as the monitor takes time booting up. The lights flash as the display turns on. The anger remains, it is only fed at this point, never starved. I stop and force myself to slowly inhale.

Survive, I tell myself. I exhale and continue.

Inside the backpack, there is a stack of cards and an action figure of a muscular man with a heart tattooed on his shoulder. His red beard and the determination on his face tell me he is no one to be messed with. And in his eyes, I find the hollowness I have seen in all the toys ending up here before. The little bag Molly brought is empty. I crouch in under the backpack's hanging cover and look into the hollow eyes. Partially, I expect a hand to suddenly slam on the window, but such things never happen. The monitor beeps loudly upstairs from connecting with the tracer.

"There you are," Richie whispers with a satisfaction that cannot be Richie. Kelly will soon relive the worst nightmare she ever imagined, and she will relearn what hell really means.

All the pain. Richie will feel so satisfied by it. I will too. All the happiness running through my cells. I will love it. I will be so h...

Stop!

I am good. I never enjoy the hurt Richie inflicts on others.

I focus all my being on pushing myself against the action figure's eye and slid through without resistance. It is as pitch-black inside as the hollow eyes told me. The hand I pushed right in front of me is nothing but vague contours from the weak light nestling its way from the cellar lamp. The front door opens and closes after Richie with a loud slam. I listen, expecting nothing more than the silence of the dead. My claws find the dents as if I have been here before. I cautiously crawl to the floor, still listening for any sound. There will be no one here, I tell myself. Just like in Esther's owl. Then I hear the faint breath. Or maybe I imagine it. It grows slightly louder as I get closer until I no longer can convince myself it is my own imagination. Every breath is strained. I reach the floor. Excitement creeps up on me and successfully dilutes Richie's anger. Richie's red dot moves closer to hers on the monitor with every other breath I take.

"You can't hide from me."

The harmony he felt just moments ago is blown away. He sees her blood. When he strangles her in his fantasies, it is not a smile on her blue lips. She cries, asking him for forgiveness, begging him to love her again. I push away the sickness while standing on all four and hoping Frank's dying protector will become visible to me. But it creeps back to me in her crying burnt into the back of my head.

"Where are you?" I whisper.

The breaths stop. I hold my own.

"Who are you?" A weak voice sounds not far away.

"I am Sariel," I say, crawling a little closer. The body in front of me tries to move away, but it collapses on the floor almost immediately.

"Don't come any closer." He screams but his voice fades out into a faint wheezing.

"I won't hurt you," I say. "I promise." My eyes adjust to the weak light, and he becomes visible. I arise from the crouching stance, so he hopefully can see me, and our likeness.

"What's your naaa...?!" I scream as laughter explodes in my head, but it is not the pain-screamer's laughter, it is Richie's.

"I've got you now!" The laughter rises in intensity simultaneously as Richie's excitement reaches a paining high. Under the laughter, the girl screams. Her voice wrings the blood out of my heart. Her skin is warm against his hand, her neck is soft. Her scream gets louder as pain joins the terror. He slams her face to the ground and a rock. She remains conscious and screaming. "You are coming back with me. Did you really think you could fool me? No one can fool me!" No one can, and no one ever will. Only himself, Richie only fools himself.

I open my eyes. I am no longer standing. I lay on the floor with one of my worst headaches punching against my skull. The only question now is how long she has left. Maybe she will trip and die when her head hits a boulder. Can she be that lucky? I sit myself up. The few contours from Frank's mystery protector I previously saw are hidden in the fog. I barely hear him.

"What happened?" The voice sound stressed.

Nothing, I think but I avoid the question. "What's your name?" I instead ask again, shifting his attention to something else.

"Adriel." He says. "My name is Adriel." He takes a deep breath and goes silent.

"Adriel." I stand up supporting myself against the wall. "How are you feeling?"

Adriel clears his throat, or suddenly awakes from near death. The latter seems more likely.

"Adriel?" I am only met by heavy breaths. "You are dying."

The front door opens and slams.

"You are mine."

I curl into a ball and lay there convulsing as the excitement washes over me again. I fight it, but is it worth it?

"You are all mine."

The cellar door opens, cries from the girl Richie holds in his arms fill the room.

"What's happening?" Asks Adriel's weak voice.

"Nothing," I answer. "Just lay still."

"You will be punished so you learn to not fool me again." Richie roars as he drags Kelly back down to her prison. Her body hits every step. She cries uncontrollably.

"Please," she says.

"Is it him?" Adriel asks, suddenly alert and scared.

A body slams as it hits the table. It bounces. Richie's excitement grows ever stronger competing with a rage flaring ever brighter.

"Yes," I answer. "Please, just lay still."

"You will never run away from me again."

"Has he taken another one? Will he kill her too? What monster is this?" Adriel's words exit his mouth so quickly his tongue stumbles on them.

She tries to fight Richie, but a little girl is nothing compared to a grown man. He unzips. His pulse pounds in my ear and thumps in my mouth. Everything in Richie moves faster now. Her body lays naked in front of him. He pushes against her. It hurts less this time. That is why Richie loves the second time, the first time makes them more accessible for his advances. That's what saddens him most of Esther, she died after her first time with him.

Kelly screams in pain. He sighs in relief. I scream in anguish, but I am relieved. The tension builds up slowly throughout my body. I stand on all fours, fighting for air and the little part of me still not enjoying myself.

"He kills her," Adriel screams. "Is she yours?"

My body shakes. Oh, he likes this so much. He loves it. He loves to hate her. He punches her already bruised face. Then he moans. Please make it stop. The table gives of hollow bumps as Richie's body slams against it. The slams get less intense as he pulls closer to the climax. I clasp my hands around my head. I scream.

"Yes." The voice whispers delicately in his ears.

A loud sigh fills the room. I sigh.

I like this so much. I love this.

"Is he yours?" Adriel asks. It sounds more like a statement than a question. The sound of his voice fades with each word until only his breath is heard.

I fall to the ground.

Please make it stop.

# Chapter 8

There is a relief to passing out. Time flies without your knowledge, for someone who never sleeps that is rare.

It is peaceful.

As I open my eyes, I see darkness. I focus but the difference is barely noticeable. My head is heavy. The slowness of my thoughts is just as disgusting as it was the day after Richie got drunk the first time, and every time after that. I blink, and my eyes slowly adjust to the lack of light in the room. Adriel's contours break out from the darkness.

"Adriel?"

I get no answer. I call his name again and crawl with difficulty over to the body. I put my hand over his mouth. There is no breath. I lift his arm from the floor and drop it. As it hits the ground, it disperses into dust and vaporizes. The smell reminds me of rot. Gabriel's corpse is still in Dongo. The fact he still not disappears scares me more than seeing Adriel dispersing in front of me.

"Rest in peace, Adriel," I say, knowing all too well there was nothing peaceful in his final moments. The realization of a warrior protecting the man who killed his Love is enough for one to lose all hope of fairness in this life. Then Adriel heard the snake proclaim how he had failed.

I put my hand over Adriel's face. It crumbles under my fingers, and as I close his eyes, the face gives in under my weight. It was terrifying the first time it happened. The second too. Today, I do not know how to feel about it. He will be gone by the end of the hour no matter what I do. I should leave him, and let his grave get the peace it deserves, I did so with the others.

Still, I stay and watch as the shadow slowly decays. I inhale the sickening mist rising from the corpse. It is purposeless, I know, but I want the nausea. I don't want to enjoy this moment when Richie's mind is at ease. I do not want to catch a break from the nightmares anymore.

This has to stop.

But he might change, hope nags me from afar.

The time for change has passed, hate commands from up-close. Today, Richie has gone too far. To be truthful, he did a long time ago. I have just been too much of a coward to face the facts.

Maybe he realizes how far down the wrong road he has walked this time. Hope tempts me. Its voice will always be tempting.

Reason joins forces with hate and pushes me away from the thoughts of hope with memories of all the children who will live through never-ending horrors if I fall for the addictive words. He knows how far he has gone. He wants to go further.

I inhale one last time as Adriel's last traces evaporates. The action figure is now an empty tomb for what once was. I arise to my full height and climb up to the eyes. The dark room seems, if possible, even darker, and even lonelier than it did when its sole inhabitant was barely alive.

The daylight from outside the backpack fades. Night creeps closer, I can tell by the anticipating laughter churning in Richie's silence. It is their perfect moment to take Kelly's soul hostage and enjoy the torture of her innocence one last time before the body dies. Their final supper, one might call it.

I climb the table legs. I could climb up Richie's legs which hang from the table where he sleeps next to Kelly but the thought of touching him, pants down and all, is disgusting.

An eternity ago, his touch was all I wanted, I wanted nothing but to caress his wet cheeks.

Richie's large half-naked body sleeps heavily on the table only to move with the calm movements from his breaths. He will not wake until the morning. The Pain-screamers do not wish him to, and what they want is the law. I walk around him to Kelly. She will not wake either. Her I touch, I stroke her cheek and lean towards her in what could be a hug.

"I'm sorry I have let it go on for this long." I cry as I utter the words.

I turn to Richie.

"This has to stop," I tell myself again.

The Pain-screamers observe me. They await my move. Will they get a chance to kill me? Have they finally pushed me far enough? The shadow-children's anticipation burns through Richie's skull, all the greed and all the hunger. I look back at Kelly and the blue teddy bear thrown to the other side of the table. Kelly must have dropped it when Richie threw himself over her. Richie never cared for it anyway. He will convince himself of the opposite when he finally wakes up and Kelly is long gone. In truth, he lost the ability to mourn a long time ago.

On the other end of the table stands Dongo, inside him lays the corpse of the first warrior the pain-screamers slayed. My revelation from this morning echoes within my thoughts.

They finally killed one of us. This war is in no sense equal anymore.

"I'm sorry Gabriel."

I am sorry. To every one of us I have let down, I am truly sorry. No one should have to suffer anymore because of my cowardice. Least of all me. With a choir of laughter, the dark children salute me.

They know now, and my decision delights them. I will fight them. They will fight me. They will win. But I will try to correct all the wrongs I have done this far. I look forward to hearing their laughter as they bite into me. The pain, I look forward to it too. I look forward to every single one of them I take with me as I die. Their blood, God, I have missed their blood dripping down my throat. I look forward to hearing the snake whisper into my ears the words I have dreaded hearing. It will tell me I failed my Love. I look forward to it because I will finally try to save him. And while dying, I will scream the only word the demons understand.

Pain.

# Chapter 9

*Nightmares*

Wheezing whispers from neurons so numbed from conscious neglect I must focus to not ignore the faint words. I never thought I would want to hear the words again, not since the day I choose the life of survival behind thick walls.

My first night of resisting behind Dongo's fur, I spent crying in the corner of my home. All while listening to the Pain-screamer's laughter and their mocking screams of pain. All while the snake whispered with thundering strength in my ears. *Nightmares.* Not even his flames got me up on my feet. The scorching heat eventually faded, and my tears finally got to hit the ground again.

The second night, I vomited. It was the first time I ever felt starvation, the first time of many. My resistance grew weaker as my hunger got worse. After another wave of whispers and flames, I caved and forced myself out to feed on Pain-screamer blood. The price I paid for crawling out from my safety was worse than anything starvation could cause me. I planned to sneak out and grab one, drain it and then crawl my way back in again, no one would ever notice. It would be one less in an army of thousands. The moment my hands reached out the laughter stopped, and all the nightmarish faces of Richie turned to me. Their pitch-black eyes burnt through my scales. In their faces, a horrific smile painted itself with sharp teeth glimmering in the moonlight. They walked up to me. I could have escaped back, I should have escaped, but I never moved. Every nerve in my body was overloaded with fear. I sobbed, just like Richie when his father left him alone after a nightly visit. My faint cries filled their eyes with a cruel fire.

"Pain." One of them whispered in my ear as it grabbed my neck.

It slung me to the floor and danced around my body. The others joined in, kicking me with every step they took. Their shout broke the silence in a flood of voices. With every kick, I came closer to little Richie's body where several Pain-screamers still stood with their arms stuck into his head and with ecstatic expression on their faces. The Richies threw me inside his head once again. Inside, I met the smiling faces of Pain-screamers staring at me and ordering me to look at their creation. I looked around, not finding the Richie by the wall begging for my aid as he did just two nights ago.

"Where is he?"

The shadows of him whispered their signature word at me in pride.

"Look at what we have done. Look at what we can achieve." Their words meant. I had no voice to translate it back then but there was no need.

"Is he dead?"

In answer to my question, they raised the bruised body of Richie above their heads. His beautiful hair close to gone. One Pain-screamer bit his arm, another twisted his knees. No matter what they did his face remained still. Richie landed by my feet. The last Pain-screamer grabbed his head and twisted it around until Richie faced me again. His skin stretched unnaturally around his neck. The Pain-screamer stared at me all while laughing at the fear on my face.

"Look at what I can do?" The maniacal laughter said. "Look at all I can do without killing him. Guess how gruesome I can make his death."

"Kill me, please," Richie whispered through slow breaths. His eyes opened. The irises were red from Pain-screamer's claws. "Just kill me."

I looked up at the Pain-screamer's eyes. The horrid darkness partly hidden under eyelids. The shining smile awaiting its prey.

"Pain."

"Please. Kill me."

"I can't," I answered his plead and chose to surrender him to their brutal mercy.

"Pain." The Pain-screamer whispered into Richie's ear and released his head. The head immediately snapped back into position.

Richie screamed and cried.

"Please. Don't let them take me."

The horde let out a celebrating howl as they took back their toy. Richie's screaming body hovered above them before they engulfed him among their claws and fangs. Richie's screams joined their chants of pain. Then suddenly he went silent.

"I'm sorry, I could never kill you."

They chose not to kill me that time either. Just a shameful kiss on the cheek and a whisper in my ear. Then they let me crawl back to my dragon on a path they created with their own dark bodies. They laughed at me, they threw themselves at me, bit me, taunted me, but I crawled to the safety of Dongo with nothing but my shame guiding me forward. And I never looked back at the thought of feeding on them again.

*Nightmares*

The voice said it back then, while I crawled to hide in my own pity, and it does now. The dancing singers cemented my failure by repeating the word over and over again.

Richie is dead, I tell myself like so many times before since that dreadful day. Richard Reston lives. Today I stand before all the Pain-screamers as the daylight flees. I am the one they face before they reach the pained little girl Richard left as a sacrifice for them to feast on. They have longed for this moment since they watched me crawl through their path of shame. They have taunted me to face them every day since.

My muscles tense as every nerve signals them to be ready. How long has it been since I last felt this tingling sensation? I stand still forcing my instincts back. The bestial desires to show my teeth or wheeze at them will serve no purpose in this battle.

One could expect the Pain-screamers to seep out through Richie's eyes, his mouth, or his ears. Every opening would be natural. Our worlds are not connected that way. The mental house Richie built during his younger years, which the Pain-screamers stole from him, is another plane of the world. Pain-screamers enter it through the head but all of Richie is a portal which only opens at night.

First, Richie gets shrouded in a dark impenetrable fog appearing from nowhere as if his whole body breathes it out. It is all darkness and laughter. The fog settles over him in a thin coating, expanding and contracting with his every breath. The dark coating vibrates, seemingly uneasy from being close to his body. The first time I saw it from Dongo clutched between his arms, I was terrified. Still, I convinced myself the person under the coating was Richie and not the Pain-screamers' puppet, I continued to do so until tonight. The vibrating mass fractures into white, sharp, haunting smiles spreading all over Richard Reston's thick body. Bodies emerge from the cracks, and then all at the same time the mass falls. They lose the grip on his skin with one big laughter. They crash onto the tabletop creating a shockwave felt across the room within the world we live in.

I never move, I never flinch, I just look at them piling into a dark mass.

Bones break from the impact and the weakest die. The strongest Pain-screamers' laughter turns into roars of pain. Then they catch the scent. The euphoric scent of a girl in pain. It is enough to trigger all their instincts. An army marches towards her, I ignore them all. I could focus on what my instincts tell me to do and protect Kelly from the waves of Pain-screamers attacking her, but the efforts would prove pointless. It is the others I must focus on, just as they will focus on me. Those who also killed Gabriel. The wave of Pain-screamers come against me like hordes of wolves hungry for the single wounded deer. I stare past them with my arms hanging beside my body. I expect them to run over me, but they never touch me. The flood of Pain-screamers goes around me.

The little girl never cries from their impact. Her body is too weak.

All left after them is me, me and all the shadow children looking at me with hungry eyes. And hidden among them, small girls with black hair, pale skin, and dark eyes. One of the Kellys opens her pretty mouth to show her horrifying teeth of nightmares and laughs. As if it was an order, the others move forward slowly creating a circle around me. I still stand fixed without moving a single muscle. The circle continues to slowly move around me and swallows more shadows as they go. I take a deep breath to calm my nerves.

You can do this. You can kill them. They are not the children they pose to be. They are monsters in camouflage. The circle closes in on me and layer after layer of sharp, wide smiles in a dark mass is created. The children giggle in anticipation.

Come on! I look into their eyes as they come closer. First one of the Richies, then one of the Kellys. Then one of the Richies again, followed by one of the Sarahs. One the Richies bursts into a hysterical laugh. Just come one step closer, I think.

They come one step closer. They even come two, three, four steps closer. I move nowhere. The circle is close enough for me to feel their breath on my neck and on my face. An Ethan behind me leans closer and smells me.

They can as well just kill me. I am incapable of doing anything anyway. I am just a coward in a reptile's body. Just grab me with your teeth and rip me to pieces. Come on, do it. I look straight into the dark, hollow eyes of the Richie in front of me. It leans the last short distance between me and it. I hold my breath. Do it, I think again. I do not deserve to live.

Then he kisses me.

As they always do.

The kiss is what finally snaps me out of the curse. Those teeth against my scaled lips. The giggles from the horde as they observe my humiliation. The whispers of Nightmares in the air. I grab the pale boy's throat. His intoxicating pulse under my fingers reminds me of Milly's last heartbeat. It is so alive. The Pain-screamer looks straight at me with Richie's darkened eyes. He shows no fear, only satisfaction. I push my claws against his fragile skin. It breaks in faint cracks. It must be my imagination, a skin so soft cannot crack. The giggles grow with anticipation. I push my claws deeper under his skin. One giggle fails to hold back a burst of brewing laughter. The blood runs down my finger in a small river. It is black, not red as the real Richie's blood. The Pain-screamer in my hand stretches his hands to the trickle of blood. He catches it on his fingers and licks it clean of. His satisfied smile grows, displaying all the perfect carnivore teeth. He laughs. His pack laughs. The children lost to shadows and nightmares, they all laugh with the same horrifying cry. They dance in the circle and shout in a choir. It is their favorite song. It is all so surreal. All the Pain-screamers shouting Pain together and the vibrations against my hands as the one I am killing join in.

What kind of game is this?

I push my claws in through the muscle tissue, my hand is completely colored black. I must. I must prove to myself I am capable. The Pain-screamer's voice gets hoarser and hoarser. The dance gets faster and faster. The choir gets louder and louder. I panic and hyperventilate without getting any air down to my lungs. I must push forward. I must kill the Pain-screamer. I must kill Richie. My claws move closer to each other. The vibrating laugh dies off until it is nothing but a breath wheezing in and out, hacked into quick hick-ups. I look right at its face, watching as the breaths fade out. He watches me. While the body dies, his eyes live. They are fire and happiness.

He is so happy to die.

Why? Is this their new way of breaking me? If so, they succeed. I cry while my claws meet. I feel terrible. But I kill him. The body goes limp, and finally the dark fire in his eyes dies. Not even their signature Pain leaves his lips before he faces the end. The body just dies. So anticlimactic. The choir goes completely insane in incoherent screams and laughter. Their dance has become them jumping randomly around and over each other. And I stand there with a corpse in my hand feeling like a traitor. I feel heavy, and dark, just as dark as they are on the outside, and on the inside.

What have I done? The thought is all that runs through my head. One lost signal traveling between my ears. What have I done? I did what I had to do. I killed what I must kill. The body hangs like a rag in my hands. It looks nothing like a Pain-screamer anymore. It is just Richie. Richie slowly fades into dust between my fingers.

What have I done?

One of the Kellys grabs the corpse and kisses the face until it disappears in a dust cloud. Breathing the fumes seems to make her high. The Pain-screamer grabs my hand and kisses it, too. I should strangle her. Surely, she wants me to, she begs me to do it. A child's hand grabs me from behind and pushes me to the ground face first. I let it. The one who kissed my hand continue to kiss the back of my head. I must kill it. I must kill them all. I must kill all the innocent faces. Kelly turns me around and kisses my face. The choir moves closer like they are lining up to kiss me.

Please, I think. No.

They do not create a kissing line. They have far greater plans for my humiliation. They lift me above their heads cheering me on while pushing me above the crowd. Everyone gets to touch me, the one who dared to kill the one he was supposed to protect.

Like I am some kind of chosen one.

In the far corners of the crowd, Kelly lays in internal pain induced by Pain-screamers pushing themselves into her and hurting her as much internally as she already hurts physically, and Richard Reston calmly sleeps with a feeling of total completeness and in total silence. The Pain-screamers push me away from Kelly and closer to Richie while they cheer me on like fans of one of the rock stars I remember Richie watching on TV.

Surreal. Just so surreal.

This is my worst nightmare.

I close in on Richard. Faster. They push me towards his head. I think I know why. It terrifies me even more. At the edge of the crowd, an Ethan grabs me. He looks me straight into my eyes. The maniacal laughter is the most terrifying I ever heard.

Then he punches me into Richard's head.

# Chapter 10

The cold cement floor chills me down to my spine. Dust reaches into my lungs and clogs into clusters of mucus with every breath. I cough. It hurts, everything hurts.

Please just let me die, I think, and mumble, knowing all too well that Pain-screamers never fulfill such wishes. It is not in their nature. Torture is simply too much fun. I cough again, and the grainy slime wanders up my mouth. I chew, the dust echoes in my head as it grinds between my teeth.

"Who's there?"

The weak voice lingers in the air. A voice familiar from whispers under laughter. A voice who has been taunting me with commands disguised as Richie's consciousness and soul.

I lift myself from the floor. The cement facing me is also familiar yet shaded in comparison to the grey in Richie's torture basement. I look around. All furniture is gone, destroyed is the correct term. Every little stick is still there just torn into splinters spread across the floor.

"Is it you?" The boy says again. His voice cracks in what could be happiness. In truth, the voice is too shaky to tell what feelings hide underneath. In the shakiness, a faint note of what once was the child I protected shimmers, and a 'what if' finds its way out of my subconscious. A 'what if' hitting me with a thundering strength. It sounds just like I remember him, no sly suggestions or toxic whispers. It is just the voice of a child in need.

The splinters shake as a body moves under them. A hand without nails emerges from the pieces. A child's small and crippled hand. It looks just like the hand Richie used to have. The only difference is how the thin fingers are twisted along the joints. Each one bent in angles making the other fingers look unnaturally pieced together. The hand is bleak, just as if it was dead, but not hauntingly pale as a Pain-screamer's hand would be. The hand grabs what I guess once was the tabletop. Unintentionally, I back away from the small human.

Richie is dead, I think in a conviction I have held on to for so long. This is just a game the Pain-screamers play with me.

"I saw them kill you," I whisper.

Yet he arises from the once-was-a-table. Seeing him terrifies me, but somehow, I am not surprised. "I saw them kill you." This time I whisper the words with dread in my voice as I realize I never truly believed the words myself. It was just one more lie to justify my own passivity, and deep down, I have dreaded for this moment longer than I want to admit.

If Richie is dead, shouldn't I be too? It is the question I have avoided for so long. The truth is just as I never vanished into smoke, Richie never left, he has talked to me every night while his captivators laughed.

What I see is worse than I ever could have imagined it to be. A head of nothing but skin on a skull arises from the sticks, hollows where the eyes hide from the light, cheeks sunken into the cavities where his teeth used to be. No fangs, only hollowness.

All hair is ripped off his smooth head. The face belongs to Richie, my Richie. A colorless face. They never killed him, they just turned him into a living corpse, all while they wandered the earth in his appearance.

"It is you." The skull smiles, with the black hole that should be a mouth filled with shining straight teeth.

The boney body arises on shaky and even thinner legs. I take one step away from him, stumbling over the sticks remaining of the shelf once containing his plushies. I should not be afraid of him, he is my Love, he is supposed to be my everything.

"They told me you would come to visit me again." The corpse tells me. He supports himself against a table-leg. "I just had to wait for you to be ready." The eyes glow with sparks glimmering through the hollows. "And I've been waiting for so long."

The Pain-screamers' laughter echoes across the cellar. Richie looks up to the ceiling.

"Yes, he is here," Richie answers the voices, he then turns to me again. "They are so impatient, don't you think?"

His holes for eyes study me. My thought process is still occupied with all that Richie has become, and all he has lost.

"What is it Sariel? Don't you recognize me?" The smile disappears from his face. "They told me you wouldn't. They told me you don't care for me." He pauses to catch his breath, the glimmer in his eyes turns to fire so sudden I never see the change. "You never cared for me. Have you even noticed how much I have grown?"

He stares right at me awaiting my answer. And I stare back unable to answer him.

"I-I-I," I stutter, my words could have been 'I'm sorry' but they are not, they are nothing.

Richie looks at me with a puzzled expression on his face.

"You don't see it?" An irritated frown smears itself across his face. "Haven't you watched me at all since you left me here to die? Isn't that what your kind is supposed to do? Look after us?"

Once again, I stare at him as the surprise drowns my fear.

"You know," I whisper as my tongue frees itself from my paralysis. I stumble and fall backwards over the shelf, and land on the remnants of what once was his creations.

"Of course I know. They told me everything about your kind." He walks over the table debris on stumbling feet. "They told me the snake sent you. That you hide in our most precious belongings and only come out at night. You are supposed to fight for us, but you always fail because they're so much stronger." He limps towards me. His toes are, just like his fingers, nail-less and bent in unnatural angles. "Do you know how long I waited for you Sariel? For the one who was supposed to save me. I thought you were dead, but they told me you never were. They showed me how you hid in my Dongo. You watched me suffer for so long, just to come here now?" His face is right by mine with his horrid breath hitting me with every word. "But that's what your kind does, you hide when the fight turns real. You hide your disgusting appearance from the world." He pauses and then wheezes. "You are all just demons hiding behind cotton walls."

"I'm sorry," I say with tears breaking through. When the words finally cross my lips, I do not know if I just say them because I am scared or because I mean them.

Richie hugs me. He caresses the back of my head while kissing my forehead. "I forgive you," he says. "I will always forgive you."

His heartbeat drums against my ear, such a comforting rhythm, and even though all logic tells me to run, I welcome the hug and let my head sink down to his chest. It feels right to let myself seek comfort in the one and only I care for. It almost cancels out the laughter rising in intensity through the walls.

"You know why I forgive you?" He whispers into my ear the same way he whispers into Richie's when temptations grow out of control.

I stop breathing his exhaled air. I shake my head terrified of what he will tell me.

"It's because thanks to you, my new friends have told me the truth." He releases me from the hug I involuntarily accepted and looks into my eyes with his dark hollowness. The eyes at the bottom of the hollows glimmer with a white terrifying light. It is the same joy I am used to seeing in the Pain-screamers darkness. "I longed for you to save me with every bite they took, and every time they twisted my arms or my legs. Until I didn't anymore. Until I saw what they truly were. When I learned to understand what they said, I understood they aren't evil, they're just misunderstood." He pushes me to his chest while once again kissing my forehead. "They just want to return us to what we really are." Then he pushes me down to the floor, and I let him.

"You are the real evil," he continues, the words sting. I love you, I want to say, but I do not dare. I am not worthy. "You and that tree with its snake guard. You destroyed the world we created, just so you could build your own. You wanted order in an already perfect world, building roots and branches to stabilize what we already had built to perfection. Life and darkness, we are the real heroes. You are nothing more than lies born in the shadows we cast."

A shock runs through my body and leaves a bitter taste in my mouth as I hear his words. The fairytales I have heard so many times from other warriors. The lies about us coming from a happy place where we danced under a tree. All lies told by a whispering snake. Yet the Pain-screamers know about them too, and they told Richie.

"I'm so glad I was forced to see the true meaning of it all. It makes me even happier that I got to show you what darkness Life truly is meant for." He finishes with his breath hyperventilating and spits in my face. The hit hurts worse than any punch or bite the Pain-screamers have ever thrown at me.

"What did you show me?" I stutter while Richie's saliva mixes with my tears and drips down my scales. Deep down I partly know the answer. It is clear in the smile on his face, and the evil glister in his eye sockets.

"That there are happiness and rightness in what your kind and the tree rooted as darkness and evil." He looks at me triumphantly. "Didn't you like it when they gave in to me? Didn't you love Sarah's last sigh when she realized there was no escape?" He shivers from memories of ecstasy. "You can't tell me it wasn't lovely. That's what Life truly is about, when all the boundaries your tree has rooted in our minds are broken, we become our true self." He takes a deep breath and screams to the ceiling. "We are better!" And the Pain-screamers answer him in ecstatic choirs of laughter. From where I lay, he looks like a giant. A giant happy with all the pain he caused those who cannot protect themselves. There is no remorse, no conscience, just fulfillment.

"What have they done to you?" I say, stunned by the clear pride on his face over all murders he committed. "You hated violence." It must be a game, I think again. Yet he stands there in front of me, no sign of the Pain-screamers creeping up from the shadows in his mouth. It is him. The Pain-screamers drove him into insanity.

"No one is created to hurt others."

"Then tell me you didn't like it when I took their innocence away." He grabs my neck with surprising strength and screams the words. "You can't lie to me! We are connected. We both feel together." He punches me with his disfigured hands repeatedly until my face goes completely numb. "You can never lie to me." He screams and as he lands the last punch he spits in my face once again.

"You make me sick!"

Richie's corpse rubs his hands against each other in pain from scraping them against me scales. From the shadows, Pain-screamers slowly appear. They are not laughing anymore. They only smile.

Please, I think, come and take me. I do not want to live anymore.

"Kill me," I whisper.

"Kill you?" Richie looks at me with amusement. "I will let my friends kill you as soon as Richie has killed this new girl, just so you have to suffer through the happiness one more time." Richie releases his hands, they are full of the scrapes my scales inflicted on them, he bleeds from the wounds. "And afterwards we will go on an adventure worthy of the name. I will kill all the children and my friends will kill all their demons. No one deserves to live." He raises his hands to the ceiling, and all the Pain-screamers watch us with anticipation, as he shouts proudly. "War has begun."

I look stunned at him as he celebrates his victory in a battle where only he thinks he is the key player. The scrapes on his hand is a tingling itch in the back of my head. Not like the hurt the Pain-screamers caused him. I never felt that, but this I do. A drop of blood leaves Richie's hands and falls to the floor. The Pain-screamers see it too, they giggle.

They could hurt him, but never kill him, I think and finally, I understand their plan. The final piece in their puzzle of torture is as cleaver as it is cruel. Richie is useless to them now. They want me to kill him. And if I want to save the future children Richie is so determined to kill, I must do it. After his death, I will die slowly from losing my Love haunted by the guilt of being the one who took his life, and the Pain-screamers will continue roaming the earth. They will refine their methods to hurt all the children and all Life in this world until there is nothing more than pain left.

The Pain-screamers who materialized from the shadows look at me with excitement. Their stares burn under my scales. In front of me, Richie laughs mimicking the Pain-screamers own hysterical laughter, but he never comes close. He sounds weak in comparison. My eyes wander between him and the

Pain-screamers staring at me.

They win. They always win. And they know it.

Maybe there is another way, hope whispers. Hate crushes the whisper in an instant by showing me the murderer laughing in a boy's body. I pull myself up from the cement floor. The gravel and dust scrape against my scales. Richie looks down at me, his amusement not seeming to show an end.

"So, you dare to stand up against me Sariel?" I avoid answering, I just look down on the ground focusing on what I must do. "My friends will kill you soon enough, but if you can't wait, I'll have to disappoint you."

I look at his scratched hands. I will not say a word. If I do, it will only give me the chance to reflect and falter. Hope is not an option. I think of all the children Richie has caught. Sarah, Carl, Nikki, Esther, Ethan, Kelly, Frank, Milly. I think of all those he will catch if I fail. I walk one step closer to Richie, then one more, and one more until I stand in front of him. His laughter falters. He rubs his hands against each other again. A nervous tick hidden behind his confidence. I grab his shoulders. The pride in his body disappears so quick one could wonder if it ever was there.

"What are you doing Sariel?" He says, and for the second time since I was sent into his room, the scared child I grew to love squeaks through his voice. I raise my head and force my eyes to meet his scared stare. He sees my fangs, and he shivers, this time not from ecstasy.

I am saving everyone, I think. I am saving you. I push my face closer to his neck. He fights me, but he is too weak to challenge my firm grip.

"Sariel? You can't kill me? No one can kill me," he says, but his words fool neither of us.

I can, I tell myself. I can stop this madness. I fill my head with Esther's bloodied body. She cries. She chokes on her own tears. Her last breath was filled with tears. I open my mouth and push my teeth around his neck. I cry. Richie screams as the teeth push against his skin. The itch in the back of my head grows stronger.

I am so sorry, I think, and puncture his skin with my teeth. It is so soft and so fragile. You were worth more than this. His scream turns into a gurgle. His blood fills my mouth, it tastes bitter. I want to spit it straight out. My vision blacken as the itch grows into a full-scaled explosion. My teeth close around his throat, and I rip it out from the body. I want to limit his suffering as much as possible, but his death is not as immediate as I hoped. He stares at me with the blood pulsating out through his neck. His mouth moves but not a word is spoken. The giggling song of pain and shame grows into a flood as the last traces of life leave Richie's eyes, and consequently, my life will soon end too. I imagine myself dissolving into dust and scatter in the inexistent wind. I accept the waves of pain flowing through me. I want to die. If I could force the Pain-screamers to end my suffering I would, but I accept that I must wait for the end.

So, I wait. I await the moment I die. The heart stops beating. The pain stops too. And I wait surrounded by a chorus from the winners, not dying, not dissolving into dust. The Pain-screamers climb down from every corner in the basement. They take turns in kissing me in celebration of my kill.

Why am I not dead? I think. Why am I not hurting? Why am I still here?

# Chapter 11

The room never collapses. It does not even shake. Its inhabitant is dead, the room should die with it. All of Richard Reston should die with it. Only Pain-screamers interrupt the calm by jumping in an ecstatic dance while flooding the cellar room from all directions. Some of them taste the pool of blood created around Richie's corpse. They like the taste. It is the taste of victory.

Please just let me die.

Not even the snake tells me I have failed. The silence is unbearable. The horde of Pain-screamers push me around, their happiness makes my unease even worse. They seem grateful. Did I kill Richie's soul without contributing anything to the safety of the world? Was it all for nothing? Hordes of dark children climb across the walls seemingly scratching the surface away with their short nails. A child's hand grabs the back of my neck. The hand turns me around, so I face a dark Kelly's shadowed eyes. I get a kiss, with tongue. She giggles. Then she bursts into full-scale manic laughter.

"Pain." She screams into my face. That must mean thank you. Richie somehow learned to communicate with them, then I can too. They fed him with lies, lies sounding peculiarly close to the dreams we warriors have before waking up in this world. Are the dreams true? They cannot be, but the similarities are too many. The Pain-screamer's grip around my neck tightens, it pushes me forward and I follow without resistance. From the walls a sudden a shriek rises above the chorus. A new wave of celebration. I glance in the direction and see a light pouring out through the scratches in the cement. The shriek is accompanied by cheering from all the other Pain-screamers.

Jackpot. Through the holes, strands of glimmering threads make themselves visible. The strands pulsate in an even rhythm.

"Is that...?" I say before getting my thoughts interrupted by the laughter from the Kelly pushing me forward. But I know what I saw. The strands are Richard Reston. They are what makes up everything the human facing the outside world is. Richie never died, only his soul did.

Hordes of Pain-screamers suddenly swarm towards the light and claw the wall greedily. The scratches slowly grow until the room is flooded with a blinding light. They laugh uncontrollably in excitement. This is what they wanted all along, the thought hits me like a rock thrown into my face. Unknowing about it, the soul was what stood between the Pain-screamers and reaching the human.

And they could not kill the soul. They needed me for that, and they have been working on it patiently for decades. Now when Richie's soul no longer lives, nothing protects Richie's being from them anymore.

The wall caves in under their fingers. A deafening cheer arises from the hordes. The light does not scare them. They welcome it. Everything turns white under the light. I fight to get loose from the Pain-screamer's grip, but my battle is fruitless. It only encourages the dark Kelly to tighten her grip around my neck harder. She lifts me up and slams me to the floor. It hurts. Then she smashes my face against the wall. Her breath feels warm against my chin as she leans over me. In the light getting through to my eyes, a weak blue shimmer penetrates through the white. It is pulseless, only shining faintly under all the white. The contours sharpen as I drift back into consciousness. Only one blue strand is visible through all the white. The cheering bursts into a stunning explosion. One of the Carls stretches his arm through the threads trying to reach the blue, but it is too far away.

"Shame." The dark Kelly whispers into my ear. She raises her fist and punches me.

I slip through, screaming and fighting in desperate attempts to find anything to hold on to. The next second Richie's large face breathes on me. His face expresses calm even though a battle has raged inside his mind. He is a monster all the way through now. I back away from him. Seeing him now makes me more terrified than ever. He is a Nightmare. His skin turns dark. A laughing battle cry breaks through the barrier between his inner room and reality. They are coming for me. This time they won't leave any survivors.

The fanged smiles appear over the dark surface. I look back at Kelly, the dark horde of mindless Pain-screamers piling on top of her. The laughter increases in strength as an army crosses the barrier. Suddenly, dark Kellys break away from the dark hordes on top of the little girl. Thousands of faces turn against me. They all smile. They all hunger.

The thought of dying is not as welcoming anymore. It scares me as much as the breath of warm air coming from the Pain-screamers pushing through Richie's head.

I run without looking back to Richie. I never have to. I hear their steps chasing me across the tabletop and how they close in. I pray for the first time in many years. I pray for my own survival. I promise to never break my trust in the snake again if only I survive this. Every dark child in front of me creates a wall to block my path. There is no option. The only way forward is through the smiles, and fangs. They know it, they laugh at my desperate attempt to survive. I jump straight into the wall. The fangs bite into me, but I never stop. Child hands touch my foot. I kick. I crawl.

Please, I think. Not today.

The dark wall is never-ending. There is no telling if I move forward or if I am stuck in the flood of bodies pulling me back to the same place I just left. It is the light that finally gets my hopes up. It is not the light of the dawn breaking through. It is the light of the moon shining through the windows. The shine grows stronger for every scratch, every bite, and every little Kelly I kill. I throw myself at it, piercing through the thick wall. I never let myself get a moment to breathe.

Just continue running, I think. The path to safety in Dongo is blocked by another dark wall. I look around the table in between two steps. I only see one way for me to be free. A blue teddy bear at the end of the table. It is neglected by them, but not by me. I turn sharply. Those running too fast to take turn with me catch up to me in an instant and throw themselves at my neck. I dodge and claw myself through the few who get in my way. They reach for my every limb. I count steps, one more, one more. Please just one more. A dark shell builds around Chester. One more step. A Sarah successfully grabs my ankle. The determination in my step forces the monster to follow along as my foot swings back and forth. She bites my other leg, but I am not allowing myself to react to it.

"Just a little further," I tell myself. I throw my body towards the shell with my claws first.

I hit the body of darkness. The bodies give in like butter against a racing bullet.

I hit the floor. I hold my breath, not daring to look up. I lay completely still awaiting the first bite to prove my failure and my death by their sadistic hands. I wait, and I dread. I scream convinced of something touching my foot. I am convinced it was the teeth of little Kelly taking her first appetizer of me. But I never look up to control it. I do not dare. I cry when my brain plays their whispers of pain in my ears.

There is never a bite. Only laughter raging against Chester's protective hide.

I breathe and lay on the floor for hours just listening to them and their laughter. My thoughts race freely, twisting between fear of Pain-screamers suddenly coming down to me, and a confused realization over my safety.

When I finally climb the dents to the windows to see the real world, the outside is dark from bodies of Pain-screamers trying to break through. A face locks into my eyes. It grins at me, knowing that sooner or later they will get me, if not now, tomorrow when Richie can tear off Chester's head and let the outside into me. I am alive for now, but I will never be safe. No one will ever be safe again. Whatever the blue string hiding within the human body is, it will doom us all. All we can do is await the death of the world we know. The world the tree rooted with its own body. I believe in the lies now. A tree and a snake wait for me after my death. I want to dance around the tree. I want to sing. I am doomed to never live to fulfill those wishes.

I am a failure. I climb down again and lay on the floor. I have failed us all. I cry. I should have fought a long time ago before it all became too late.

# Chapter 12

The morning light slowly chases the shadows away in rays trickling through the heavy mass of dark bodies. Laughter mixes with painful screams as Pain-screamers not running to safety face their inevitable death.

The daylight turns Chester's two eyes into spotlights illuminating the room. I still lay on the floor, afraid to look up, afraid to listen. Afraid of hearing the laughter, but this time it would not be the dark monsters creeping at night. It would be Richard Reston awakening with the Pain-screamers in complete control. Just the thought of it is too terrifying for me to handle. The thought of him ripping off Chester's head and looking down. The eyes, Richie's eyes, looking at me with the darkness only Pain-screamers can carry within their hearts.

My fears are never fulfilled, no matter how long I wait.

I look up, immediately flinching at the light, and turn away again in fear of what could have been outside. My mind painted the face of a dark child looking down at me with a fanged smile on its face, Kelly's face this time. I am so scared I cry. I force myself to look into the light again seeing nothing but the two spotlights flooding the room. No child observes me with big dark eyes, no face of Richard Reston looks down at me greedily. There is only light. Light and sterile walls. Slowly, I lower my hands from their protective stance around my head. I wipe the tears off my face, telling myself I am brave. I am not the coward who let my child become the monster of Pain-screamers doing. I am better.

With two nervous and shaking arms, I lift myself up. Not until now, I notice all the scratches covering my body. Every one of their teeth left a permanent mark on me. Each scratch stings with my every step.

I grab the dents in the wall and lift myself up even though I am hesitant if I want to. I carefully peek my head over the edge for a glimpse of the outside and quickly return to safety. What did I see? I let myself process the glimpse of the basement. I saw a girl and a man, both unconscious on the tabletop. I force myself to look again, this time I linger by the window. There is no darkness covering Kelly from top to toe. She is free, for now. Richard Reston lays beside her, his face signals peacefulness but the truth could not be further away from it. The eager work within leaves an itch in the back of my head I cannot scratch. The choirs never stopped. They found their gold mine and they waste no time pushing their horrible agenda forward. What is Richie, will soon stop existing. The man who awakens will be this world's Nightmare.

Kelly moves, it is just a faint twitch in her face but proof enough of her still being alive. Alive and in pain. For how much longer I do not know. The real question is if she will get to see the light one more time before her own goes out. For her inner soul, it might be better to end the pain as quickly as possible. She is as broken now as Richie was when I was forced into his inner room for the first time decades ago. I shiver, the memory of Richie's tortured soul arising from the wooden sticks will haunt me for as long as I live. Kelly's soul will no longer be the cute girl she once was. She is a shade of a girl now. Limbs twisted and torn, and hair ripped from her head.

I should run away while I still can. The time will never be better. One shield over my body and run. Run until sunset, and then run some more. I will never stop running. With moonrise, they would come after me, but they would never catch me.

Where would I run? To the next toy? I could run for months without finding one. I have never been so far from Dingo in my entire life, would I survive it? There is no chance of knowing. I look at Kelly. What if she never dies? What if I'm wrong like so many times before, and she survives long enough to see this nightmare turn to fruition. Could I really leave her defenseless?

Could I leave the safety I always known?

Am I brave enough to leave what I have always known? Am I cowardly enough to leave her alone?

The answer is no to all my questions, I realize as I look up at the closed door and the closed windows. I am neither brave nor cowardly enough. I am stupid for believing I ever had an option. I am trapped here just as much as Kelly is. I am doomed to die here just as much as she is.

My only other option is suicide. Walk out and breathe until the snake whispers louder than the laughter.

Stay and die or walk outside and die.

I am too much of a coward to choose and thereby I made my choice.

# Chapter 13

Morning becomes noon. I have laid flat on the floor for half a day just fearing what comes next. The two passed out on the tabletop never move either. A bird chippering on the outside is the only sign of life. That and the sound of cars driving into the driveway. It never occurs to me that the sound differentiates from the radiator's humming. I am too drowned in my own thoughts of survival and panic for what will happen when Richard wakes up. Feet run over the graveled driveway.

"Mr. Reston!" Says an authoritative woman. "This is the police! We would like to talk to you about Frank Fuller."

I finally react. I sprint up the dents and look out through the window. Black boots line up outside the cellar window. A woman looks in. Her eyes widen when she sees the two bodies on the tabletop.

"He is down the cellar, with a child!" The woman screams. "I see blood!"

The whole upstairs explodes in one loud bang and numerous booted feet running into the house. The cellar door slams open, it loosens from the hinges and flies down the stairs. In a matter of seconds, the room is flooded with armed policemen. They surround the table. The woman who looked in through the window stretches her hand over to Kelly's neck. She nods.

"She's alive! She needs medical attention ASAP."

"We need an ambulance now!" A man screams into a com-radio as quickly as if he waited for her to say exactly those words.

"I see Frank's backpack." One other police officer says from the other end of the table. "He's here somewhere."

"Mr. Reston." A fourth police officer stretches his hand to Richard and checks the pulse. "He is stable." He slaps Richie over the face. It hurts. The Pain-screamers laugh. "He is unresponsive. We need one more ambulance."

They act professional, but I know what they all think. A man with his pants down, with a naked child bleeding next to him. What monster could do something like this? They all want to kill him. They should. End it all here and now.

Save the world.

Kill me.

"Captain." One of the com-radios sounds with a hesitant voice. "I have six crosses back here lined up... It looks like a graveyard. There are names carved into them. Sarah. Carl. Nikki. Esther. Ethan. Molly. Then there is one more newly covered hole without a cross in the woods."

All the officers simultaneously look down at Frank's backpack then at Richie.

"That's Frank." One of them whispers, shocked.

"Don't dig them up. Wait for CSI to take that one." The captain takes a deep breath. "We need to check the names against all missing children."

They cuff Richard without meeting any resistance.

"The girl is Kelly Marcsinzky." Says one officer looking at a computer. "She's been missing for two days."

"Call her parents and tell them she is alive." The one they call captain sighs while he takes a closer look at Trevor the elephant. "This looks almost like the house I visit in my nightmares?"

The two ambulances arrive on the driveway. The paramedics run down the stairs the second the engines go silent.

"Oh my God!" One of them blurts out in the middle of the stairs.

"Focus on the girl." The captain orders.

The paramedics know better than to question his orders. They probably don't want to either. Soon, Kelly lays on a stretcher with tubes coming out of her arms. She awakes from the needles piercing her arm. She screams from all the pain and memories flooding her system all at once. She cries and no matter how they comfort her she never stops. Under one quick glimpse, she looks in my direction.

"I want Chester." She says between her screams.

The paramedics follow the direction of her screams to me and the blue teddy bear. They look at each other, then at the captain, who nods. Kelly gets her teddy bear. It comforts her, and even though she still cries, her scream subsides. She pats the back of Chester's head and whispers repeatedly into his ear.

"Everything will be okay."

I look over her shoulder and see Richie one last time before we leave the house of horrors. He has not moved yet, but the ants inside his head are so eager in their work my head is in a never-ending buzz. I might never meet Richie again. Somehow, I doubt it, but I will always know what goes inside his head. That will forever be my punishment.

# Chapter 14

"Liars." It is what she believes them to be. "My parents are dead. Mr. Reston told me so."

"But they are alive," the doctors proclaim. Every time the last ten minutes the doctors have tried to tell her who was outside waiting for her, she told them how it was impossible.

Mr. Reston had killed them.

He killed everyone.

When Kelly's parents finally enter the room, the little girl looks at them with horror. She hugs Chester closer, and consequently, she hugs me, the one who let everything happen. She scans them cautiously. Her mother with bruises on her neck and bad make-up to cover it up, and her father moved to tears for seeing his daughter again. The bruises on his hands and the booze on his breath tell the truth of what happened in Kelly's absence.

Then Kelly screams.

"It's okay," a doctor says. "You are safe. Your mom and dad are alive. They are so happy to see you."

Kelly flinches as her father stretches his caring hand towards her.

"No!" She screams.

The darkness flaring in his eyes reminds me of the darkness I have grown to know in Richie's eyes when anger caught his impulses without any chance of return. His wife sees it too. She is ready for it. Kelly's father still stretches his hand out to Kelly's cheek and caresses it as he mumbles she will be okay. She is safe now. The choke hold around Chester's neck only gets tighter.

The parents stay with her until she calms and thirty minutes after that.

Thirty long minutes not seeming to aid Kelly at all in processing the last couple of days. It aids her more when they finally leave so she is alone with her teddy bear.

Only nurses visit her to give her food after her parents return home. She lets them caress her cheek. They give Chester food too. She giggles nervously when they do. All other hours she is alone, whispering words of comfort to her teddy bear and imagining the words the bear whispers back. It calms her more than any words her father could have told her.

"Everything will be fine Chester. We are safe here."

"I know, he can't attack us anymore, but I'm scared."

"Em-I-Are-A-See-EL-E, I know how to spell it now Chester."

She continues until nightfall when she finally falls asleep and the snake wheezes into my ear.

*Nightmares*

The dark bodies flood the room. Only dark moles, no infested Richies, or Sarahs, or Ethans, or Nikkis, or Carls, or Kellys. The infected children wreak havoc where Richie sleeps, far away from us. Their laughter echoes through his thoughts into mine. We might be far away, they say, but you will never be far away enough.

Kelly moves around restlessly in her bed. She thugs Chester closer to her and mumbles into his ear.

"Help me. Please help me, Gabriel."

The words leave a heavy lump in my chest. Her soul asks for help from her dead savior. One of the many saviors now dead because of me.

"Pain." The voices arise from the bodies crawling under her bed.

I push myself out from the teddy bear, standing proudly by his blue face.

*Nightmares*

The snake commands me to join his war. And I will. I expose my teeth, I wheeze. They laugh, but they should fear me. I am a warrior of the light. I am a warrior of the snake, and Kelly is mine to protect. I think back to the revelations Richie gave me before I killed him. The snake is right, the Pain-screamers are coming but the battle has just begun. The war will rage.

And I will fight it. I will face all Nightmares coming in my way.

*Nightmares*

I throw myself at them fangs first. Their skin break at impact. They scream in pain, and I drink their blood. No one escapes my justice.

I kill them all.

# Epilogue

Laugh we do. Pain we scream.

Pain.

Deeper we dig. The light we take. We tear it to pieces. We eat it. We hurt it.

Pain.

See the blue. Find the blue. We stretch. Scratch the light. Eat it. The blue is pure.

Pain.

We see it all, we hear it all. One we are. Pain we scream. Pain we think. Laugh we do. The light we eat. We control the host. He is we.

Pain.

We see it all. We see them both. We hear them talk. We control the host. He is we. Pain we scream.

Pain.

Pain they hear. We see them turn. We eat the light. Their fear we love. Silent they are. Laugh we do. Laugh they hear. Pain we scream. Laugh they hear. We eat the light. Both we see.

Pain.

Vests they wear. Guns they hold. Scared they are. Laugh we do. Pain they hear.

Pain.

Talk they do. Laugh we do. Pain they hear. We eat the light. The walls are white. We arise. Pain we scream. Laugh they hear.

Pain.

Guns they hold. In their grip they shake. Laugh we do. Laugh they hear. We eat the light. We hear them talk. Help they need. We see them walk. Pain we scream. Pain they hear. We dig deeper. Always deeper.

Pain.

We feel their push. We love their fear. Laugh we do. Laugh they hear. They force us down. Arise we do. We eat the light. Pain we scream. Pain they hear.

Pain.

The blue we need. Deeper we dig. We eat the light. The blue is pure. We won't reach it now. Pain we scream. Pain they hear. We control the host. We own it all. Laugh we do. Pain we scream.

Pain.

Pain.

Pain.

# Acknowledgements

First if all I would like to thank you, the reader, for giving Demons in Cotton a chance. I hope you found that one book you will want to read again and again.

The premise of Demons in Cotton hit me in the face one afternoon when I made the dishes. This book is dedicated to Sofie because even though her face clearly told me that she didn't understand a single word of what I was rambling about, her stance was always, it is not my kind of book, but I will support you through hell and back if necessary. With a novel touching on so many dark themes as Demons in Cotton that support has been so important.

So once again, thank you Sofie. I firmly believe you make my life better in every single way.

Thank you also to the two suns greeting me every morning. Alva and Albin thank you for making my life a better place with every breath you take. May you always feel safe and loved.

Thank you to my mom, my dad and my two brothers. We are half a country apart and still I know you support me with every step I take.

I would like to send one huge thank you to Page Lawson for editing this book. I learned so much just from going through your markups, and this novel would not be close to as polished as it is now without your help.

The cover for Demons in Cotton is created by David Collins at DC Cover Creations. It is stunning! I highly recommend him for everyone who needs a cover for their book.

Demons in Cotton is published as e-book through Draft2digital, Amazon KDP and Rakuten Kobo, and the physical book is published through Amazon and Ingramspark. It is the services they provide that makes the publishing of Demons in Cotton possible. Without them, I can honestly say that Demons in Cotton would never made its way to the public.

I want to thank Stockholm's public transports for letting me use their trains and busses as my writing space during the years of writing and editing this novel. And to all those who involuntarily was forced to share 'office' with me, I am sorry if my typing kept you up during your morning or afternoon nap.

I would also like to reach out with a thank you to all the awesome podcasters who aid those like me with their infinite source of wisdom. The list of these podcasts grows every day and includes (but is not limited to) 6 Figure Authors, The Self-Publishing Show, Self-Publishing Insiders, and the Creative Penn Podcast.

Lastly, I would like to thank all the creative writers on Twitter who have created such a wonderful place to discuss and get advice.

# Did you enjoy Demons in Cotton?

If so, help others enjoy it too. Please recommend to friends and leave a review when possible.

Do you want more? Check out my website for weekly flash fiction stories in *Flashes of Sanity* and sign up to my newsletter for updates on my writing projects.

My website: http://dbj-writing.com/

Sign up for the newsletter Ben's Mire: http://dbj-writing.com/newsletter/

CPSIA information can be obtained
at www.ICGtesting.com
Printed in the USA
LVHW111930141221
706195LV00005B/139/J

9 789198 700817